WINTER'S WRATH

THE PALATINE JOURNEY: PART ONE

KAY ELLEN GILMOUR, MD

Dedicated with love to my mother

Mildred Florence Seckner
1910-1999

1931 Crouse Irving Hospital
School of Nursing
Syracuse, New York

Registered with United States Copyright Office
January 21, 2011
TXu 1-737-189

Prologue

The family farm passes from father to son
'Til pitiless fate intervenes.

As when death steals the farmer and wife
Leaving no child behind to take up the plow.

Or nature attacks with no quarter given
Bringing weather too hot or too cold,
Too dry or too wet.

Or pestilence attacks the fields and the barns
Sickening spring crops in the ground
Slaughtering livestock in their stalls.

And when wars wreak havoc with weapons and fire
Stealing boys lives and girls innocence
Scorching all hope, home, and hearth.

• And so it was on the farms of the Palatines in the SE corner of Germany in the winter of 1708-09 - the coldest in five hundred years.
• The wars with the French King Louis XIV had raged for decades spilling blood and devastation across the Rhine.
• The cruel German rulers pressed extortionate taxes on their farmers to pay for their battles and the lavish lifestyles they coveted to rival that of the French Sun King.
• Queen Anne of England sent out a call for colonists to till the soil of her new American settlements.
• The war-weary, cold-starving Palatines rushed to her by the thousands to make the journey from German farms to the shores of Manhattan.
This book was written to acknowledge the courage, forbearance, and at times, just plain good luck of these, my Palatine forebears. What about yours?

The characters mentioned in this first book of my Palatine series are fictitious. My true ancestors will be introduced when these archetypal characters reach London. The **capitalized** names are the main characters of the series who will be your guides throughout these Palatines' historic migration.

I. Main Characters
- Peter and **ANNA** Margaretha Baam Seiler
- **JACOB** Seiler   (Peter and Anna's nephew)
- **EVA** and **MAGGIE** Seiler   (Jacob's daughters)
- **HANS** Schall   (Anna's ward)
- **HENDRICK** and **CHRISTINA** Schäfer

II. On The Rhine
- Severin Hraban (Rhine boat captain)
- Aksel & Beate Koerber with son Baldewin
- Paulus & Diskretion Kramer (Merchant)
- Mr. Portier (Farm Manager)

III. In Amsterdam
- Agatha Arents (Beguine)
- Aharon & Esther Hraban
- Cornelis & Josina Jansen
- Beatrice Presler (Beguine)
- Reus (Body guard and Guide)
- Karel & Antje Van Brearley

IV. In Brielle
- The Meyer brothers (Johann, Georg, and Peter)
- Matthias & Apolonia Yung (Merchant)

April 1, 1709 to May 12, 1709

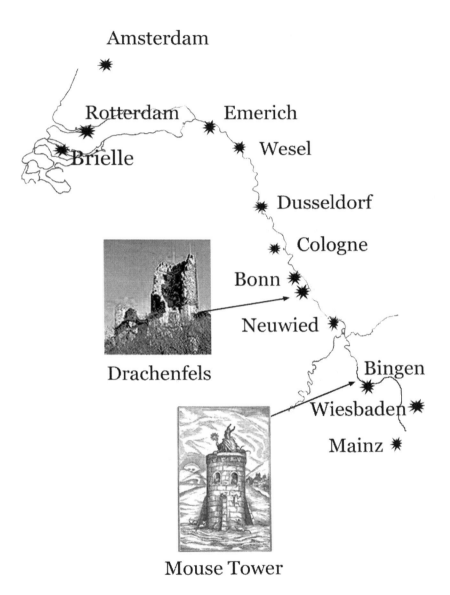

Amsterdam

Rotterdam · Emerich

Brielle · Wesel

Dusseldorf

Cologne

Bonn

Drachenfels

Neuwied

Bingen

Wiesbaden

Mainz

Mouse Tower

Chapter 1

He ran.

His mother's whispered command rang in his ears, "Run boy! Bring the white woman to me. Run!"

He ran shivering from the bitter cold and stunning fear. For the first time in his young life, he was running towards the white woman, not away from her.

Morning light was glowing behind him; his shadow leapt before him on the icy ground. He fell and laid on the ice-coated cobbles until he could catch his breath and beat off the terror holding him pinned to the ground. It hurt to fall as it was too cold for snowfall to soften the ground or the scene. The cold had not lifted for weeks.

"Run boy. Bring the white woman to me. Run!"

He got up once again and ran. He was breathing too hard and too fast to warm the air through his nose. Instead, his gaping mouth gulped the searing cold air, un-warmed and unimpeded, directly into his bursting lungs.

At least, the local dogs were not at his heels. Those that had been kept outdoors were either still huddled in some windbreak or had already died of exposure. The dogs still alive had learned not to bark at people passing their home's windows for fear of being put out. They huddled with children near the fireplace if the family still had wood to burn. Most did not; their windows remained dark.

He no longer had to fear Mr. Walrath's mastiff. The old dog had died of the cold early in this harsh winter's grasp. But in the massive dog's absence, a chorus of howling told him the local wolves had become fearless and were more closely approaching the town in search of cold-weakened prey. Today he could wish for the company of that dog.

He ran even faster.

It was not like the winters of earlier years when men and boys would have been on the streets at this hour going to shops or herding the hogs and cows out to the fields for the day. The women would have already started the morning's breakfast fires, warm cooking aromas would be rising from the chimneys. Flickering lights would have shown on window panes. This morning, nothing stirred and no lights shone.

When he reached the edge of town, he turned onto a dirt road and saw the white woman's house not far ahead. The dirt and gravel offered better footing than that of the icy cobblestones. So when he reached her gate he was running at full speed.

The sun was just above the horizon and had not yet warmed the frozen hinges. With arm fully extended, he slammed his palm against the gate latch but the gate held fast. A lightning bolt of pain exploded in his hand. He fell to his knees - bent over and stunned. A few moments later, he managed to straighten up, but still on his knees, he paused while his stomach wretched and emptied from exhaustion and pain. Tears of frustration and fear froze on his cheeks.

Through sheer will, and his mother's voice still ringing in his ears, he got to his feet and climbed over the frozen gate. He made his way to the front stoop, lowered himself onto the large field-stone step and, with a soft moan, fell against the door.

Anna rose with the sun. There was no reason to do so other than to maintain a semblance of normalcy in her life. She missed Peter the most at this time of day when they curled together one last moment before beginning the day.

She hung the kettle in the fireplace and added a small piece of wood to the night's dying embers. Peter had walked miles into the mountains during the waning light of summer evenings to gather the wood that now sustained her during this forever cold.

The soft thud at the door brought her to instant alert. It was not a knock. A woman neighbor would knock and announce her intentions and there was no reason for a man to be at her door. An animal searching for food or warmth? Over the sound of her heart and the crackling of the fire came that of soft crying. That was not an animal; it was a child!

Three quick steps covered the distance across the small living area to the latch. As she pulled the door open, a small figure slumped onto her feet uttering a high squeal. Startled, she jumped back and echoed the small creature's cry with a louder one of her own.

The boy worked himself into the smallest ball possible while shielding his eyes with folded arms. If he couldn't see her, could she see him? But the moaning would give him away.

"Stop! Be quiet!" he repeated to himself.

But of course she could see him. Her momentary confusion gave way to the task of pulling him through the open door and out of the painful cold. Her size and strength made this an easy undertaking. She easily snatched him off the floor by the back of his coat and the seat of his pants. She placed him softly on her bed where he resumed the fetal position.

"Are you hurt, boy?"

He remained silent and motionless.

She reached for him and took his left hand. He screamed in pain; she withdrew her hand and stumbled backwards. She stood for an instant, took a deep breath and declared to herself, "It is time to be calm and help this injured child."

She began by softly singing a child's bedtime song. By the second verse, he visibly relaxed. Next she took the chance to touch him again. This time she stroked his hair and avoided his hand.

On the third verse, he allowed her to clean his face of the various fluids that had emitted from eyes, nose and stomach which now had thawed in the warmth of the room.

The fourth verse led to removal of his inadequate boots. His feet were white and hard but warmed quickly when she wrapped them in the thick sweater she was wearing over two other layers of wool clothing.

He continued to cover his eyes with his right arm.

"I *will* not look at her eyes!" he repeated to himself.

The older school boys had told him what would happen if he saw her eyes. He and all the youngest children never walked by her house; if forced to pass that way, they ran as fast as they could go.

But now, here he was, not running past the house of fear, but horrifyingly within it. Every part of his body exposed to the cold was now thawing. This was a familiar, always painful, wintertime process but this time it was agonizing. It felt as though his face was being attacked by a thousand stinging bees and his hands and feet were throbbing and burning.
She rubbed his right hand and face with her warm hands and continued to hold his feet close to her soft midriff. His pain became tolerable; he sat up and swung round to sit on the side of the bed.

Anna wore a cross on her ample bosom dangling from a heavy blue ribbon. He riveted his eyes on the cross. It was a safe place to look.

"I will not look at her eyes!" he repeated to himself.

"Is your hand hurt?" she asked.

"Yes" he whispered to the cross.

"I won't touch it. Just let me see what is the matter. Use your other hand to take off the glove."

She spoke softly with the same voice his mother used whenever he was to follow her directions. The familiar tone signified there would be no debate. He would do as she asked as it gave him an excuse to lower his eyes without appearing disrespectful.

Very slowly, he removed the glove.

The problem was quickly made obvious. The long finger was out of joint and pointing to the side. She knew how to put it back in place but also knew that her new-found trust was about to fly away in a burst of pain.

Again she hummed her soft song and gently took hold of his wrist above the sidewise pointing finger. His eyes stayed riveted on the cross. With one quick move she grasped the end of the injured finger and pulled out and downward. There followed a hoped-for popping noise and the anticipated scream.

The boy retreated to the opposite side of the bed and she to her fireside chair. When he realized he could once again close his hand without pain and that she was producing enticing cooking aromas over the fireplace grate, he resumed his original seated position on the side of the bed. Moments later, he gathered his courage and gave into his hunger. He took the six short steps to the small stool close to the comfort of the fire, to a cup of hot apple cider and a warm breakfast bread. A feeling of composure returned to the house.

"What is your name, boy?"

"Hans"

"What is your family name - your full name?"

"My name is Hans Schall," he informed the cross.

"Are you the son of Adolph and Maria?"

"Yes. But my father is dead. The soldiers killed him. My mother is sick and sent me to get you to come to her."

"I am very sorry to hear of your father's death, Hans. When you finish your drink and we will go to your mother."

Anticipating the condition of the boy's mother and home from the boy's spare clothing and hungry stature, she gathered

6

kindling and soft firewood, a loaf of bread, a jug of juice, a pot of apple butter, and her collection of home medicines.

She helped Hans back into his boots that were now better insulated by a pair of wool socks she had knitted for her husband. She gave him a cap large enough to swallow his ears and a pair of man's mittens to fit over his thin gloves. He was warm; his sweat of fear and running had dried. Warmly dressed, he was ready to lead the way to his home.

The sun was fully up but still gave off no warmth. The sky remained steel blue and clear. There had been no clouds seen in weeks. Never before had the people heard their pastor pray for clouds. But they needed those clouds to serve as a blanket to warm the earth. A blanket to melt the river, to free the ice-shackled mill wheel, to grind the wheat, to make the bread, to feed the flock.

The oldest grandmothers of the congregation could not remember a winter of this misery, nor had they any memories of their mothers or grandmothers telling of such a time.

Anna and Hans made their way through town. She walked close behind him and used his shoulder when needed to steady herself on the slick icy surface. Boys on the street showed open astonishment at seeing him leading her down the street and allowing her touch. He saw their looks. They were looks he would not soon forget.

He would remember this walk for the rest of his days as the time that he came to know that the appearance of courage made others look upon him with respect. And if they believed he was brave, why shouldn't he believe the same of himself.

His posture straightened, his chin rose, his eyes left the ground and focused on a new world laying in front of him. He would never again lower his eyes from fear.

Men tipped their hats to her as she walked by. As schoolmates in years past, these same men had avoided her at best and mocked her at worst. Then years ago, they had come to accept her when she became the wife of the most highly respected man in their town's commerce and politics. In time, they even came to respect her for her own unique talents. The women of the town remained indoors. Most would have greeted her warmly. Most - but not all.

Hans opened the front door and stood aside to let Anna enter his home. As she stepped into the home's interior from the brilliant outside light, the darkness surrounding her was complete. There was no sight or sound.

But there was a smell - not yet of death - but of disease mixed with the odors of a person too ill and exhausted to contend with the exertions of hygiene. A sick mother would not ask her eleven year old son to tend to such matters. But she could ask him to outrun his fears and bring the woman who had the knowledge and courage to help her. And he had done just that!

A thin shaft of light stabbed through a crack in the single window shutter. When Anna's eyes adjusted to the dark, she was astonished to see that the room was empty except for a small table and single stool beside the lifeless fireplace.

A strangled cough sprang at her from a mound of rags in the far corner of the room. As Anna moved closer, the rags developed a death-mask. The shock of this sight was intensified by another smothered gasp and a rattling cough coming from that mask.

"Mrs.. Schall?" Anna asked softly.

"Yes, Missus. Is my boy with you?"

"Yes. Your very brave boy is right here with me. I'm going to ask him help me start a fire and then I'll be back to you with something warm to drink."

"God bless you, Missus"

"It's Anna, Missus."

A weak smile followed and then "God bless you, Anna."

Anna unwrapped her bundle and gathered together the kindling and light wood. Skillfully arranging the kindling, and using the embers she had brought in a pail from her home, she quickly started a fire. A charred bedpost spindle in the dead ashes told her what she already suspected; the bed and other furniture had been used for firewood. The remaining small table and stool were certainly scheduled to meet the same fate.

She put Hans in charge of maintaining the fire as she warmed a cup of cider. On the table, she set out food and drink for him and then turned her attention back to his mother.

As the temperature rose in the room, so did the odor coming from the rag pile. It was time to begin peeling off the layers of cloth covering the ailing woman. But as she did, the miasma intensified.

A keening "Ohhhh" became sobbing joined with a plea, "Forgive me, Anna. I am so ashamed."

"There is no need for shame, dear woman." Anna assured her.

9

Anna stroked the woman's filthy hair as she finished uncovering the pitiful body. The smell now made her gag. Her eyes filled with tears of nausea, pity, and horror.

Surrounded by her own excrement lay a form that had once been a full-bodied woman. In its place lay a skeleton covered with tight skin colored a sickly yellow. What had once been a full round breast, a source of nourishment for her infant son, had become a rock-hard monstrosity clawing at her chest.

She knew and feared this woman's disease. Anna knew that the yellow eyes and skin proclaimed imminent death. But while this poor soul lived, Anna would protect her dignity.

"Boy! Get up! Go to the blacksmith and ask him to send someone with a cart to take your mother to my house."

"Another duty for a man," Hans thought as he rushed from his home to fulfill this new assignment.

The blacksmith's wife, Dorothea, arrived with Hans and her pony-drawn cart. She was surprised to see Anna but was stunned on seeing Mrs. Schall. She quickly disguised her shock and set to work helping to clean and comfort the dying woman.

Anna had no trouble lifting the tiny woman in her arms. She placed her softly in the cart and in short order, they had delivered her safely to Anna's home.

Anna's medicine had eased some of the throbbing in the frightful breast. A pallet was placed near the fireplace for the mother with a smaller one next to her for the son. Together, exhausted, they slept.

Anna watched them from her fireside chair. "Milk," she thought, "would be good for the boy. I wish I still had the cow."

Peter had loved that cow. They had never really needed the milk but he had not been able to resist the little animal. He had come home one summer evening with the calf in tow and a huge smile on his sweet face.

"She's all white, like you," he said. "I'm going to name her Cloud."

Yes, it was quite true. They were quite similar. The calf's hide was cloud-white; Anna's skin was milky white. The calf's mane was silky white; Anna's long flowing hair was glossy white.

But there was one major difference between Cloud and Anna that Peter could not deny; the calf's eyes were a deep rich brown; Anna's eyes were the bright pink-red of an albino.

*****

Every evening, on returning from the fields, Peter sang to Cloud, milked her and settled her down with fresh straw. Her milk was stored overnight in the cool spring water behind the house. Each morning, after spending the night in her corral, Cloud gave up a full pail of butter-rich milk to Anna's warm hands. At Peter's insistence, the milk was sold to local families for whatever they could afford and given free to those with children who found themselves in need.

Peter's little dog, Midget, never left Peter's side unless she was told to stay at home by her master. Each morning, she and Peter walked Cloud from the corral to the far woods and swampy area where she could stay cool in the summer heat. Every evening, Midget would go to retrieve her but only if *Peter* asked her to do so. She would never obey Anna's request to do this chore.

11

Occasionally, Midget could not get Cloud to come with her. She would return to the house, gather Peter up and together they would go to round-up the stubborn beast. It was on such a beautiful summer night that Peter shook his head, heeded Midget's pleadings and laughed as they headed off to the swamp to bring his beloved Cloud home.

Although hours had passed, the summer sun lingered high in the evening sky. He had not taken this long before. Anna was somewhat annoyed as she had a hot supper on the table. She threw off her apron and headed down the road to urge the two animals and the man to quicken their pace home.

The woods were quiet and there was no answer to her calling. She followed the well-worn path of Cloud's daily march into the tall wet grass to the edge of a small pond. There she found them. Peter lay face down in the mud and the lifeless body of Midget lay silently over his legs. Peter's feet and back were bare. Blood caked his hair over his left ear. In his right hand he grasped Cloud's leather collar with her bell still attached. Anna thrashed in the mud and managed to roll him over. His lifeless eyes stared into the clear blue heavens.

*****

The old man startled and stopped his field work to listen. From the distant swamp came a demonic wailing. His heart raced in his throat and the hair raised on his thick bronzed forearms. Frightened, he waited and listened; the sound began to change to that of an animal rather than an apparition. He raised his sickle and moved as quickly as he could towards the sound determined to put the poor wounded animal out of its misery. Instead, he found a demented, wailing, mud-covered woman lying over the body of Peter Seiler.

The funeral for Anna's much-loved and respected husband was attended by families from miles around. The pastor decried his death and the deaths of other men who had fallen protecting their homes and families from the employed battle-hardened French soldiers during wartime and the unemployed scavenging French soldiers during peacetime. Bands of them had crossed the Rhine with impunity and taken or burned whatever fell before them on these lands for the last 30 years.

Although no women visited her home after Peter's death, the men continued to come. They came with injuries all too familiar to farmers. She sewed up their wounds and applied poultices that hurried the healing and helped to draw out pus. She set bones and popped fingers, elbows, and shoulders back in place.

Other men came almost too drunk to walk, holding his jaw with one hand and pointing frantically at his mouth with the other. She used the special instrument the blacksmith had fashioned to pull the rotten tooth and applied another of her poultices to dull the pain.

*****

Dorothea sat next to Anna on the bed and watched over the sleeping Maria and Hans.

"I knew Maria's husband, Adolph," she whispered to Anna. "He was killed in June right in front of our smithy."

Dorothea remembered, "It was early on a market day and Maria was walking unsteadily down the street leaning on Han's shoulder. I believe she was already sick by then. A small group of French soldiers were marching through the town past our shop. One of their officers was riding his horse recklessly down the street; he didn't even slow as he came upon them and knocked both Hans and Maria to the ground. Maria screamed out in terror - not for herself but for her boy.

"Adolph was in our smithy doing business with my husband. I was standing at the door of the shop watching the people coming and going on the street and enjoying the sunshine. I saw Maria fall and cried out. Adolph heard Maria's scream and my cries and nearly knocked me over as he rushed to get outside.

"He saw his wife on the ground and the Frenchman circling his horse around her. He rushed at the horse screaming curses in German; the rider screamed back in French."

The horse knew neither language but did understand the wrath of the man charging at his head.

"The horse reared and struck out with both front hooves. But it took only one to poor Adolph's head to strike him dead. The officer hesitated and starred down at Adolph. But then out of the corner of his eye, he saw my dear husband rushing towards him with his heaviest hammer in hand. He whirled his horse and whipped him down the street and out of sight. He and his men were not seen again."

Anna had listened to the narrative silently and at the speaking of death, reached over and took her companion's hand. That hand stiffened but did not withdraw.

Anna looked up, their eyes met, held and smiled.

Dorothea felt ashamed. She had never been in this home before nor had Anna ever been invited into hers. In truth, no women of the town had ever accepted an invitation and crossed this threshold.

In the days to follow, she would tell her husband of the pink-eyed woman's sweet nature and compassionate care of the dying mother and convince him and herself that she had never believed any of the hateful gossips.

She pronounced, "The children may remain afraid of her appearance but it's up to us God-fearing adults to set an example; we must accept this wonderful woman as one of the Good Lord's creations."

But then, she thought that it might be best to wait for "just the right time" to share her new insights and resolves with other women in the community. She might listen to future gossip but she determined not to add to it. At "just the right time" she would counter their accusations and set the record straight. The woman of the bright pink eyes was not to be feared or shunned. She was just like each of them.

But then again - at "just the right time".

Chapter 2

Wednesday, March 16, 1709

Mrs. Schall died two days later - dignified, clean, pain free and with her new friend, "my white angel", and her emotionally exhausted son at her side. She had been well aware of her impending death. One day beforehand, she summoned the strength to formulate a life plan; it was not for herself but rather for her son and her white angel.

"I have seen you at the back of the church during the summer. I know you have listened to the pastor preaching against the Golden Book of the English Queen and those who, believing in her promises, are planning to leave for America. Are you one of those people?" she asked.

"I have listened," was Anna's guarded answer. "My husband's nephew, Jacob, is considering the move. His crops failed again this year and the cold has left all his chickens and ducks dead in their coops. His wife died last year leaving him with two young daughters. He has asked for my help with the children during such a journey."

Mrs. Schall grabbed Anna's hand with an unexpected strength and managed to raise her voice above a whisper.

"Please! Take my boy with you! He has shown you that he is an obedient boy and he can show bravery beyond his years. He is small now but he will grow into a large man like his father. If you protect him now as a child, he will protect you for the remainder of your years. I beg you to watch after him."

Anna squeezed her hand but did not speak. But Maria saw her face, saw her eyes, and knew she could trust her Hans to this beautiful woman. At the funeral, Hans stood straight and strong at his mother's graveside holding fast to Anna's hand. Neither could remember the exact moment that Hans had met her eyes, but all hesitation had passed and would never return.

They walked together through the cemetery to another graveside. The stone read, "Petrus Heinrich Seiler: 29 July 1670 to 16 July 1708: Beloved husband of Anna Margaretha Baam Seiler.

"Goodbye, Peter. I have decided to leave this land but I will never leave you. Where my heart goes, you will always be with me. Goodbye, my love."

*****

There was not much to sell. The house and its furniture were quickly bought by an elderly widower. He said he would be proud to live in the home of the esteemed Mr. Peter Seiler. His decision was made easier for him by the absence of any woman fearing the home of *Mrs.* Peter Seiler.

The blacksmith bought the Schall hovel and made it into a stable. Anna helped Hans pack up his few belongings. She found a bull's horn his father had used to carry gun powder to the hunt and a carved skimming paddle his mother had used in making their butter. These, his memories, and his mother's cross were all he would have of his family life in the Palatine.

Anna had not been able to part with Peter's clothes. Now she got out her scissors and thread and fashioned them to fit Hans with a little room left over in which to grow. Their clothes, a few personal effects, her medicines, and some food were carefully packed   into the small handcart they could haul together.

She made a visit to bid farewell to the minister as a sign of respect but he was angry at her leaving and would not receive her at the parsonage. She was certain there were no others who might want to wish her goodbye and farewell; no one appeared on her stoop to prove her wrong.

Their journey would begin the day after Easter, a day their minister still celebrated by the Old Calendar. Jacob had picked that day to allow the girls to celebrate the Holy Day at their mother's church one last time. The sermon was unusually brief; the pastor was as weakened as the members of his flock by the winter's grinding and unremitting cold with its attendant hunger. Almost in a whisper, he spoke of God's will and his spiritual conviction of better times to come in this life or the next.

"It will be *this* life for my girls," Jacob swore as he glanced at the two beautiful girls seated next to him. His baby, four year old Eva, pressed against him and slept. His twelve year old, Maggie, held his hand and cried softly for the loss of her mother. Later, in the churchyard, she cried loudly over the upcoming loss of her schoolmates and all other things familiar and comforting.

Chapter 3

Monday, April 1, 1709

As planned, they began their trek towards their new life at dawn on Monday, 1 April 1709. Although it was still very cold in the mornings, the sun had recently remembered its duty to warm the midday air. A stiff wind blew from the north adding physical misery to the emotional discomfort of leaving home. Ice and snow filled all shadowed areas; mud took its place in the scattered islands of brilliant sunshine.

The continued cold was a mixed blessing for Anna as she was able to wear comfortably the clothes needed to protect her albino skin: a long skirt sweeping the ground, a long-sleeved blouse and a large-brimmed hat held to her head against the wind by a wide ribbon.

Each morning she would start the walk wearing her long wool coat but the exertion of pulling the handcart would soon make that layer unnecessary.

Her sensitive pink eyes had to be shielded from the sun's direct rays and its glaring reflection off the snow. Draped over her head and held in place by her secure hat was a thin black veil. It covered her shock of white hair worn braided and piled high on her head. It also gave protection to her eyes and face, and covered the nape of her neck. To a passersby, she gave the appearance of a substantial woman in deep mourning.

So, in truth, her garments served two essential purposes; they acted not only as protection from the sun but as a shield against the astonished and sometimes hostile stares of strangers.

19

In her home town, her appearance had no longer shocked her neighbors. However, in the recent months, among some of the older women, a rumor, a suspicion, and then a recipe of gnawing fear was prepared and slowly brewed that her presence in their midst might well be the cause of the winter's wrath. When the word, "witch" was whispered about, the pastor took immediate action to quell this hint of Satanism.

He began the following Sunday's sermon with glowing words of praise for the elders of the community. He waxed poetic over the positive influence their steady God-fearing leadership held on one and all, old and young alike.

The prominent elders in the sanctuary's front boxes radiated sanctimonious self-congratulation and certitude in their vaulted place over the lives of those seated behind them. The upturned face that glowed the brightest with spiritual confidence was that of she who had first whispered the soon to be forbidden word.

All smiles vanished as the sound of thunder rained down on their heads from above. Impossibly louder than the first, a second boom of thunder crashed down on them as the pastor's fist hammered down again on his vibrating pulpit. The faces of the congregation registered stunned astonishment. Hearts pounded and vision narrowed to include nothing but the stormy face of their clergyman.

"It has come to my attention that the name of Satan has been raised among us! To call his name or to speak the name of any of his minions invites him to come among us, thus to poison our hearts and lead us from the righteous path to Paradise towards the frightful path to damnation!"

An eternity passed in total silence. Not even the sound of breathing could be heard.

He lowered his voice to a near whisper. Even against their will, the awestruck assemblage leaned closer to his wrathful visage to hear his following words.

"This has been a winter of hardship and weeping. Now turn your hearts to Isaiah 55:8-9 and hear these words,

> 'For my thoughts are not your thoughts, neither are your ways my ways, saith the Lord.
> For as the heavens are higher than the earth, so are my ways higher than your ways, and my thoughts than your thoughts.'

"We have suffered and been tried by this winter's wrath. But we will be patient and listen to the words of the Lord whose ways are beyond our understanding. We will never be tempted into blasphemy nor call up Satan.

"We will not name our neighbors as servants of the Prince of Darkness nor will we call up such words as witch or warlock. Our town will be safe in the arms of the Lord and protected by the faith and goodwill of all who live among us; *every* member of my fold is blessed by the Lord and will not be vilified."

They all knew where she was, but no one turned to look to the back of the church where Anna sat stunned. She gulped for air as she swam safely to the surface of the pool of suspicion that had threatened to drown her.

On the front steps, after the prescribed handshake and benediction of the parishioners, each of the guilty slipped quickly away to sit in personal contemplation at a silent dinner table.

Before bedtime that very night, the pastor's words of rebuke had been thoroughly willed away; only his praise for the personal qualities of maturity, humility, and religious fervor remained in the memories of those certain he had aimed *those* words directly to their hearts.

"Witch", the word forbidden at that Sunday service, was not heard abroad for years to come. Anna hoped that with her functional disguise she would neither hear the word nor see it flash in the eyes of strangers she would meet on her way to the New World.

*****

The little caravan was led out of town by Jacob pulling his large handcart. It was quite heavy but had tall wheels giving it good clearance in the rutted roads. It carried his family's meager belongings during the day and when emptied and overturned served as a shelter throughout the night. Jacob, a tall straight man, had lost all excess body weight during the harsh winter but had maintained his wide shoulders and bull-like strength. At times, the cart seemed to rush to keep up with him.

Little Eva, too young to keep up her father's pace, rode either on his shoulders or in the cart. Maggie walked safely at the back of the cart; Jacob forbade her to walk to the side or in front. The cart might manage to tip over on its side, or rush him downhill, but he would never allow it to pull out of his powerful hands to roll backwards to do her harm.

Anna's cart was the smaller of the two. Though lighter in weight, it had small wheels making it difficult to maneuver. It was hard to get moving from a complete standstill, particularly from thick mud. But her labors were made manageable by Hans' willing work. He was living up to his mother's expectations, gaining in strength and confidence with each passing day.

His original fear of Anna had been replaced with a growing love and a fierce manly determination to protect this strong woman. To get the cart in motion, Hans had to push from the back as Anna hauled at the front. Once moving, Hans rushed forward to help pull. Maggie walked just ahead of Hans.

On the first morning's march, Maggie appeared to be unaware of his existence and passed her time in silence. At midday, she casually dropped back to walk next to Anna and spoke a few words. By evening, she had shifted sides and walked beside Hans. Distance had been conquered, but conversation still lagged even as they stopped to make camp for the night.

Jacob was in no hurry to push each day's pace. As a boy, he had accompanied his father as he transported his crops, wine and wife's woolen handicrafts to the Rhine's wharfs. From there they were transported downriver to customers as far away as Amsterdam. He had accompanied his father on this route many times and knew it would take a fit man two nights and three days. But with the children and Anna's unwieldy cart, they would need at least an additional day and night.

They had practiced at home to make a rapid transition from trekking to camping in case there was a sudden storm. So now that they were ready to bed down for their first night, everyone knew his assigned tasks and went quickly to work. Jacob unloaded the carts and stacked everything perishable under a heavy woolen blanket. Maggie gathered wind-fall for their cooking fire. Hans brought back bowers of evergreens to line their bedding area and add protection over the perishables.

Jacob started a fire, Anna fed her flock, Hans and Maggie cleaned up after the meal, the evening's entertainment was supplied by Eva's giggling antics and Jacob's tunes on his old recorder. The carts were overturned and the ground covered with spruce boughs. Exhausted from the unusual exertion of the day, they wrapped themselves in wool blankets and fell deeply into sleep.

Chapter 4

Tuesday, April 2

Anna was the first to awaken; it was not yet dawn but she was miserable from a combination of the cold and an insistent call to nature. There could be no hurrying to get out from under the cart as every muscle in her arms, legs and back was stiff and painful from the previous day's hauling. Moaning and groaning, she managed to wriggle out into the open without hitting her head or waking the girls huddled together in a back corner.

She was surprised to see that there were still live coals in the cooking fire and even more so that the evergreens that last night had draped their pile of supplies had somehow made their way to the other side of the fire-pit. Curiosity would have to wait; she made a dash for the tree line. While there, she gathered new wood for the morning fire.

It would be pleasant to have a warm reception for the children when they finally awoke.

On returning to the fire-pit, she dumped her heavy armful of wood onto the wandering pile of evergreens. A startled male shout was echoed by a screech from Anna. She tripped and fell backwards landing on her backside with her feet facing the mounded greenery - her dignity preserved by the long skirt around her ankles. Her night cap had fallen down over her eyes. adding further to her stunned confusion.

From under the brush, a woman's shouting had joined the man's. Pandemonium accelerated as Anna's men-folk scrambled out from under their night-cart demanding explanations for the mayhem around the fire.

25

Anna pushed her nightcap out of her eyes and saw a vision she would always remember - a mound of freshly cut evergreen boughs framing a pair of wild-eyed faces. There was sudden silence as all involved took in the scene.

Then the evergreen pile spoke, "Dear woman, may I present my wife, Mrs. Hendrick Schäfer."

"Please call me Christina," Mrs. Schäfer quickly added.

They all let out a breath of relief; there was no danger here.

The look of astonishment dropped from Anna's face as she saw the scene for what it was; a pile of foliage offering her a formal introduction. Her brightening smile brought relief to Mr. Schäfer who ventured a muted chuckle. His heavy bass was joined first by Anna's contralto and then Jacob's hearty tenor. When Christina added her piercing coloratura to the chorus, the little valley rang with laughter.

Hendrick and Christina brushed themselves off and gathered around the breakfast fire. Anna crouched down to coax the fire into life. When she looked up to her visitors, her eyes burned as bright red as the coals she stirred.

A short intake of breath and a politely abbreviated stare was the couple's brief reaction to her appearance; it was a response never again to be repeated. Anna's love for this couple took life in these moments; it would grow in the months to come.

Hendrick busied himself helping Jacob and Hans ready the carts for the day's march while Anna and Christina heated water for the morning meal. Porridge was the primary fuel for a day's start. Liquids provided additional food value; Jacob had brought the remains of last year's beer and wine and Anna had with her the dregs of her summer's cider. The adults enjoyed the spirits, and the children, the cider.

Even in normal winters, whole families could show the results of poor nutrition. The afflicted became weakened and complained of aching joints and sore muscles. The most common sign of this slow seasonal starvation was the telltale thickening and bleeding of the gums. If untreated by an early summer harvest, the tortured gums spit out painful rotted teeth.

Those who had cider to drink throughout the year seemed to stay healthy. But this winter had been so long that the healthful drink had become scarce. In its place, Anna made a daily tea of dried dandelion roots and leaves.

The old women of the town had always rejected out of hand Anna's knowledge of folk medicine. But their daughters saw the results of Anna's ministrations on her family during times of want and had their husbands seek her knowledge through her husband, Peter.

They were reluctant to let their mothers know they had even indirect communications with Anna but they were not reluctant to use her knowledge to keep their families in good health. Thus did dandelion tea become a staple of the winter breakfast table and was now the morning potion of outdoor camping.

At breakfast, Hendrick explained that he and Christina were also walking to the river to join those making their way to America. They were newlyweds who were setting out to seek the promised land, a safe home and a decent livelihood for themselves and their hoped-for children.

Christina came from a large family with many needy mouths to feed. Her parents grieved and feared their daughter's departure;

for in her eyes, they saw both youthful anticipation of starting a new life and a childlike fear of leaving her old one.

But go she must and her elders must permit it. They would trust her safety and happiness to her new husband, a suitable stable man they held in high regard.

Hendrick continued, "Over the past year, the newspaper, Augsburger Zeitung, occasionally reached our village. We read about the hundreds of our fellow citizens who had made their way to London. Then the Englishman with the Golden Book came to our village. The book had a picture of the English Queen on the front and the first page had letters written in gold.

"He told us the book said the English Queen promised transport to America and free land for all who would come to London and ask for her assistance. We are young and strong and know that with God's help and guidance we can make this journey and reap the rewards of our faith in each other and the future.

"Our village is a full day's walk further from the river than yours so we had been walking for two long days when we came upon your camp," Hendrick explained. "We came up quietly so as not to cause concern and found all of you sleeping soundly. We were very tired and cold so we gathered wood to keep up the fire and bedded down under the evergreen boughs that have this morning given you so much cause for mirth!"

Christina added, "We hope that you will allow us to accompany you the rest of the way to the river. We have money to help buy supplies as we travel. We would appreciate your good company and the safety that increased numbers would afford."

Jacob replied, "You are most welcome to stay with us as long as you wish. We have not had as good a laugh this whole year as you have provided in one short morning. Please join us."

A responsorial, "Amen" sealed the compact and the preparations for the day were completed.

The terrain had become easier to negotiate. The day before, the way had led them down from the highlands. They had spent hours negotiating steep grades and long switchbacks with inclines made even more treacherous by the icy paving in the rutted paths.

There was not a lot of forward progress made that day but they had now reached the lower, smoother valley country. But here the snow and rain did not run off as easily and mud became the challenge for their second day of hauling. Modesty was abandoned as the ladies hiked up their skirts and Eva was banished to the cart so as not to get sucked down into the mire.

Hendrick took Anna's place at the head of the small-wheeled cart. Hans was quite annoyed at the loss of Anna's attention but welcomed the strength of Hendrick in the thickest mud.

Maggie rode in her father's cart, legs dangling and swinging behind. This backward view put her attention on the second cart in general and on Hans in particular. Each time Hans saw her glance, he stood taller and transformed his face from that of wretched physical toil to one of philosophical contemplation.

Hendrick noted the boy's reaction and smiled the smile of youthful memories.

Anna and Christina walked and talked together behind Anna's cart. They would not run out of words that day nor any day in the future. They were as old friends picking up where they had left off after just hours apart in spite of the fact that they had never laid eyes on one another before this morning.

They finally came upon smooth dry ground. Jacob was setting a much faster pace than the day before in response to better footing and Hendrick's muscular pulling power of Anna's cart. At times, Hans could not keep up with the long strides of the much taller man.

"Jacob, can we stop a moment?" yelled Hendrick. "I'm a bit worried about Maggie."

"What's the matter?" asked Jacob worriedly.

Hendrick answered, "Oh don't worry, it's nothing dangerous. It's just that she's getting a terrible ride on the back of your wagon with all the bumping along.

"I believe it would be best if she walked for awhile but I wouldn't want her walking between our carts. I would feel more comfortable if she walked behind this cart."

Hans shot Hendrick an angry look. He was removing Maggie from his sight and away from her watchful appreciation of his strength and cart-pulling prowess.

"But I would like to ask Hans if he would be willing to take a break from pulling to make sure Maggie and the ladies are well looked after by one of us men," Hendrick added conspiratorially while raising his eyebrows and nodding his head in Hans' direction.

Jacob looked first at Hendrick, then at the weary Hans and then back at Hendrick. He understood Hendrick's assessment of Hans' condition.

Knowingly, Jacob answered, "Thank you, Hendrick. I have also been a bit worried about the ladies walking unattended at the back. Hans, would you please accompany Maggie to the back and make the walk as pleasant as possible for the ladies. Please get them water to drink whenever you are asked."

Hans stood momentarily opened-mouthed and mute but recovered quickly enough to casually raise a hand to feign resignation at this change in assignments. Hendrick would have to do without him for awhile as he was needed for a higher calling than manual labor. He must assume his place as protector of the women-folk.

Anna saw the method in Hendrick's plan. She nudged Christina who signaled her understanding and complicity with a quick smile. The ladies would play their parts to perfection in this theater of youthful discovery.

The morning passed quickly. The pulling was now easy for the men and conversation was even easier for the women.

As for Maggie and Hans, they had overcome distance and shyness and now chattered on about their past lives and friends. They knew nothing of the possibilities of their lives to come so there was nothing there to discuss. All was well in their world.

At the noon hour, they stopped for their midday meal on the outskirts of an old hamlet. There were six poorly thatched homes clustered around a dilapidated gristmill. Though the building appeared in jeopardy of collapse, the mill-wheel itself was trim and turning smoothly. Its power-stream flowed vigorously, freed from winter's ice. These hungry peasants were once again able to mill their wheat into flour. And that flour would be baked into their staff of life, warm nourishing bread.

Anna donned her "mourning" garments of long black coat, with black veil and hat and accompanied by Christina went to investigate the possibility of buying a fresh loaf. Their own traveling supply had been baked at least a month before and although the deep freeze cold of the food storage locker had kept the   maggots out, it had made the loaves rock-hard and stale. They could only be sliced with an axe when first brought into the house.

New-baked bread would be a miracle.

As they approached the mill, they could see the form of the man working the grinding stone. He was square as a tree trunk and broad of shoulders. His wide face was topped by a shock of fox-red hair and weighted down by a full beard.

"Good day to you," Anna called out to the miller. There was no response. He did not look up, but rather, turned to face away from them.

Approaching closer, Anna called out loudly, "Good day to you sir!" Still the noise of the grinding stones covered her greeting.

She walked into the mill and tapped the miller on the shoulder.

He jumped as though shot and whirled around to see Anna towering over him in her black raiment.

Quickly regaining his composure, he shouted, "Grosser Gott im Himmel, woman, you near frightened me to death!" Further calming himself, and noting Anna's attire, he added, "And may I add my condolences for your loss."

Anna caught his meaning, apologized for his fright, and thanked him for his kind thoughts.

Anna explained, "We were traveling through your area and saw your spinning mill-wheel. It is wonderful to see a mill at work again; many of the streams in our area are still frozen hard with the wheels still imprisoned in the ice's harsh grasp.

"We have come to ask if we might buy bread from your family," she added hopefully. "Our own supply is old and stale."

"I fear that will not be possible, Missus. We have barely enough to feed ourselves. We had a good spring wheat crop this past season and were able to harvest it before the first frost. But then the cold came and froze the wheel. I am just now beginning to grind the little wheat we have left.

"We managed to get the winter wheat planted at the proper time but I fear it is now frozen in the ground; we have little hope for a normal harvest this spring. There will be many more days of hunger to come. I am very sorry that we cannot help you."

"The regret is mine, sir, that your people are burdened by this suffering." Anna answered. "Our party will pray fervently for the return of abundant fields and good health to your family and neighbors. We will detain you no more; we leave you to your labors."

The women returned to their companions and explained the miller's plight. They ate their stale bread with thanks and sent up their promised prayers.

The rest of the day flew by without incident. During the first day, they had been passed by a few solitary travelers. But with Jacob and Hendrick pulling the carts, they managed to overtake several small groups, although most were slowed by small children in tow.

There was no schedule to keep, so every new meeting produced a short respite from toil as the parties introduced themselves, their place of origin, and the depth of hardships that had led them to strike out for America. No one was sure of how the journey was to unfold; they only knew there were certain destinations to be reached.

First, they should reach the Rhine - then by boat to Amsterdam or Rotterdam. There were some differences of opinion concerning from where they must embark for London, but they were uniformly certain that somehow they must reach England. Queen Anne awaited their arrival.

Night and darkness came quickly. The moon was in its new phase; the stars shown brilliantly in the clear black sky. The wind was down but it remained uncomfortably cold if one was not active or close to the fire.

Evening chores went smoothly. After eating, the adults sat talking near the fire's warmth; Eva was sent to bed early and without fuss; Maggie and Hans were sent to their gender-based carts at an hour they considered too childish; they put up a modicum of fuss. In time, however, all were bedded down and sleeping soundly.

Chapter 5

Wednesday, April 3

Once again, Anna was the first to stir. Her head was cold; her nightcap had come off. She was aware of a gentle pulling on her hair. Still in light sleep, she smiled demurely and reached out to touch Peter's chest. He softly woke her each morning by stroking her face and hair.

But the hair pulling became more insistent.

"Ouch, Peter, not so hard," she complained. But Peter didn't stop. And waking further, she remembered, "Peter's dead!"

Her eyes shot open and she found herself staring up the pink, bristle-haired nostrils of a cow! Its long tongue reached out and wrapped around another strand of hair, giving it a severe tug.

Once again, Anna woke her fellow pilgrims with a loud screech.

As she sat bolt upright, she smashed her head against the lip of the cart. Stunned she fell on her back and moaned. She was jarred out of her momentary concussion by the evermore insistent pulling on her hair. This time the tugging was accompanied by a blast of bad breath and stentorian mooing.

The men had reached her and were pulling the caressing cow away from Anna's head. She regained her senses and crawled out into the open.

On her hands and knees, she was eye-to-eye with the bovine's beautiful large brown eyes.

The cow gave a low grunt and nudged Anna's face. Anna bolted to her feet, pushed Jacob to the side, threw her arms around the cow's neck and screamed,

"Cloud!"

There they stood, Cloud contentedly chewing her cud and Anna, with head buried in the cow's neck, crying loudly. Her shoulders shook in time with her sobbing. She called out the names of Cloud and Peter when breath was possible. The onlookers again stood transfixed by this new morning's dramatic one-act play starring a cast of two, an albino woman and a pure white cow!

Anna was unaware of her companions nor anything else in the universe other than Cloud. She backed away, rubbed Cloud's neck, scratched behind her ears, and moving to the front, looked long and deep into those two huge pools of brown. She held Cloud's head in both hands and rested her cheek against it.

No one would know how long this greeting might have persisted, because the reunion was cut short by the appearance of tall, gangly young man. He was agitated and demanding Anna's attention.

"Madam! Madam! What are you doing to my cow?"

Anna reluctantly turned away from her beloved bovine towards the voice behind her.

Could the nerves of the group stand another shock? They were tested when Anna let out with a shriek the volume of which put all previous screams to shame.

"Murderer! Murderer!"

The second oath was drawn out and took the crescendo quality of a wounded wild animal - a bear-sized female animal charging to protect her young. She crossed the short distance between the young man and herself in the blink of an eye and threw herself full-bodied onto his astonished frame. They fell to the ground in a heap, Anna beating him around the head and face. The boy-man could not bring himself to strike this woman so only tried his best not to do her harm while attempting to protect himself from her unremitting fury.

"Murderer! Murderer!

The men watched this battle with confusion and secret admiration. It soon dawned on them that they should take some form of action. But whose side to take - their friend who was crazy with rage or the youngster who was getting a thorough beating?

They opted to remove Anna from the fray and restrain the young man to keep him from leaving the field of battle. The situation was suddenly increased in complexity by the appearance of another man wheezing over the embankment to their left. His voice joined the others with a complementary tone of anger and amazement.

"What are you people doing to my son?" he yelled between his tortured breaths of running.

"Murderer! Murderer!" rang Anna's refrain.

Jacob drew a deep breath and shouted, "Stop," in a voice heard half a mile away. "STOP!"

He managed to draw all attention to himself and everyone stood in their tracks as though turned to stone. He was holding Anna's back against him with a bear-hug around her waist. She stopped kicking at his shins and relaxed in his grasp.

Careful not to loosen his grip enough for her to break loose and resume her attack, he gently turned her around to face him. She was quite tall for a woman, actually slightly taller than he, so he was looking up into her eyes - bright red-pink enraged eyes.

With the calmest, quietest, most reassuring tone he could conjure, he asked, "Anna, what has happened? What is the matter? Who is this man and what harm has he done you?"

Anna's eyes were still wild and she could not hear nor understand human words. She knew only animal madness and had no language yet to express the intensity of her rage.

"Anna, what has happened here?" he repeated. "Anna? Anna?"

He saw her eyes begin to see again. They softened and filled with tears. She began to tremble and cry, but this time in grief, rather than joy.

"He murdered Peter," she whispered to Jacob.

"What!? How do you know such a thing?" he whispered back.

"He is wearing Peter's boots and Peter's favorite shirt. They were stolen from his body when he was murdered at the swamp. That man killed my husband to steal his cow, the cow you see beside you that Peter named Cloud."

Jacob looked over Anna's shoulder at the two men standing side by side awaiting their expected explanation and apology. The father held firmly onto his angry face; his son retained his look of total confusion as a bright bruise blossomed on his forehead.

The boy had assumed a stance that would allow rapid retreat should the mad woman resume her attack. But as the moments passed, his self-control returned and his carriage took on the attitude of his father. His expression morphed from that of pain, to utter confusion, to simple relief. In the end, he managed to harden his face and eyes to mirror his father's anger.

"Anna, will you promise not to attack him if I turn you loose?" Jacob asked.

Her eyes turned angry again, but after some considered hesitation, she answered, "Yes."

He first tested her resolve by only loosening his grip from around her waist.

When she didn't tense or bolt from his grasp, he softly asked once more, "Promise?"

She nodded her head in assent. She was drained of all energy including the power to speak. She walked back to Cloud and, blocking out the humanity around her, once again lost herself in those deep brown eyes with remembrances of Peter and home.

Jacob could now turn his attention to the boy who had caused his aunt to go mad. Where should he begin? He decided for the most direct line of questioning, "Where did you get those boots?"

"Off a dead man," he answered confidently.

There was a crescendo moan from behind him. Jacob turned quickly and saw terror once again rising in Anna's face; she stared at the boy as she would a rabid dog.

"Anna, No! Stay with Cloud. Please stay!"

She looked to Jacob for the strength to do so and was able to turn away from the boy and back to the cow.

"Tell me about the dead man," Jacob asked in a forced voice of calm and casual curiosity.

"If it's any of your business, you can speak to me, not to my boy," spat the father.

"I apologize, sir," said Jacob, willing up a tone of respect. "You are absolutely right. Will you do us the kindness of telling us the story of the dead man and his clothes?"

The father, mollified at the change in tone, visibly relaxed and settled in to tell his story.

There was some milling about as everyone found a place to sit. Anna took a place on the edge of her cart, her back to the target of her near insanity. Eva, who had been horribly frightened by all the screaming, was huddled in Cristina's full bosom.

Maggie was afraid to be near Anna, and wasn't invited to sit with the men, so she retreated to sit on the larger cart. The men gathered to the side of the road, Jacob's entourage sitting across from a story-teller father and a boy wearing a dead man's clothes.

Everyone grew silent and attentive as the father began his story.

"We had record crops last summer. By July, the wheat stood dense and tall. The women's kitchen gardens were heavy with ripening vegetables and apples were ripening on the trees. Our harvest was bountiful, Praise the Lord!"

"Amen," answered the gathering.

"It was towards the end of the harvest season that the two men came to my farmhouse door. They asked if I and the other farmers in the valley had any work for them to do. They said they would work for a small wage and a hot midday meal. I spoke with my neighbors and we decided to give them two weeks work.

"They were both mid-aged with dark skin and coal-black hair. I asked where they were from but all I learned was they were from, 'far to the east'. They came to be called, 'the foreigners'.

The older man was called Masiv. His companion, Boxe, told me their names; Masiv never once spoke a word to me. Masiv was just that - a massive man - at least a head taller than my son."

The story was paused, and at his father's insistence, the boy stood up for all to gauge the height of Masiv. They were in awe at the possibility of such a man.

Satisfied with the effect his theatrical pause had made on his listeners, he resumed his narrative.

"His hands were half-again the size of mine. He was strong as an ox and possibly just as dumb. I know he could talk because I saw him many times having angry conversations with his companion. They seemed to fight all the time.

"Boxe was the younger and smaller of the two. He was of normal size and strength but also a hard worker. He did talk to the men but never said anything to the women-folk. This was made easier by the fact that the women were all afraid of them and kept their distance. The girls were told to stay indoors whenever the two were out and about. When the wives brought

41

the midday meal out to the workers in the fields, they would not go near 'the foreigners' and made their husbands distribute the food.

"Masiv was never without his rifle. Every night, after the field work was done, he would hunt rabbits that had been disturbed by the wheat cutting and quail in the grasses along the tree line. It was something else the women did not like about him - the sound of gunfire during the evening meal.

"Boxe had but a small pistol that he wore tucked in at his waist. He occasionally fired at a bird but never hit anything.

"We men-folk never begrudged them hunting for food. But what did trouble me was Masiv's smile. The only time I ever saw him smile was when he held up a small-animal kill. His smile was evil. I uttered a prayer each time I witnessed it.

"The day came when the two did not come to work. We had heard the sound of gunfire the night before so thought they must be staying in their camp to enjoy some larger game food.

There was no gunfire that night and they failed to come to work the second day. We considered going to look for them, but there were no volunteers to go deep in the woods for the search. We all decided it was safer to just assume they had left our area.

"Later that second day, my boy was down at the edge of the east woods and heard a moaning sound. He fetched me to the spot and I also heard the sounds I thought sounded like a cow mooing. I decided to investigate but took the time to gather three neighbors with pitchforks to accompany me.

"We followed the sound and came upon a horrible sight. Both men were dead, each with a gun at his side. Boxe must have gotten off the first shot with his pistol. I say that because Masiv had died of a shot to his throat and could have lived long enough to fire the second shot. Boxe could not have lived for more than one more heartbeat after Masiv's shotgun tore off half his face. The flies were everywhere and the stench was strangling."

He lowered his voice to spare the ladies' sensitivities; then for the men, he embellished the description of Boxe's mangled head and face with graphic clarity. His conspiratorial tone had the desired effect on the men and acted as a magnet for all the women but Anna. They drew close and inserted themselves into the semicircle of listeners.

Anna continued to bury herself in conversation with Cloud.

Jacob stopped the proceedings for a time to fetch a cup of beer. The father took it with thanks; he took his good time wetting his tongue and watched with satisfaction as his audience grew restless awaiting his next installment. He smacked his lips and began again.

"The mooing began anew. Hidden behind tall brush, we found her hobbled and tied to a tree. She was in misery for want of milking. My boy saw her distress and milked her there on the spot. The poor thing was thin and filthy. Those miserable men had not taken proper care of her.

"As you have only taken the opportunity to beat up my son but not to talk with him, you would not yet know that he has not been successful in his schooling. He doesn't learn bookish things easily. He finds it hard to do numbers or to read. But he is kind to his mother and obedient to me. He loves animals of all kinds and they return his love in whatever way their kind can manage. He is a special boy.

43

"When my boy finished milking, he led the cow to the stream to drink. He took off his shirt and washed her from head to tail. He pulled up fresh sweet grass and fed her by hand. All the while, he paid no attention to the dead men, he only attended to the needs of his new friend.

"The boy named her Edelweiss. They have been inseparable ever since. The cow follows him wherever he goes. They walk to the fields together after milking each morning and he watches her as she grazes. In the afternoon, they return home side by side. He has brought her back to good health.

"She now gives a full bucket of milk each day - rich with fat. We share her generous gift with all our neighbors.

"And you asked about his boots and shirt. They were worn by Boxe. The men with me that day saw the kindness my son gave the cow and elected to reward him by giving him Boxe's boots and shirt. He washed his new shirt in the creek and shined the boots when he got them home. They are the finest coverings he has ever had. His mother worries him nightly to get him to remove the boots for bed.

"He wears that same shirt every day. My wife must wash it every other day as he won't wear anything else. She does so with little complaint as she will not have him seen dirty by her friends. Masiv's clothes were too big to fit any man in the valley. The women cut his things up for rags.

"And that is the story of the dead man's boots and shirt. And may I now ask why you were so eager to know the story?"

Jacob was the only one present, other than Anna, who knew the account of Peter's murder. He told the details briefly and quietly so not to further disturb his distraught aunt. When he had

44

finished, the adults understood and shed away their fears for Anna's sanity. Her past rage would not be forgotten, but rather stored in the safe place of story-telling, not held in ongoing uncertainty. She would come back to them in mind and spirit given time and love.

Maggie and Hans heard of Peter's death but lacked the deep compassion that is forged by such a loss. They would harbor some fear of Anna for awhile. But time would erase their anxieties. As children do, they would live their lives in the present moment.

"Jacob, bring the boy to me," Anna called.

Jacob took the boy by the elbow and tried to move him in her direction. In panic, the boy yanked his arm away. His father stepped forward and gave him a sharp slap to the back of the head.

"You do as the lady asks! Act like a man and go sit by her side," he commanded. And in a quieter voice, "It's alright now, boy. She will not hurt you again."

The boy took a seat on the cart right next to Anna and awaited his fate. As he did so, the cow shuffled her bulk to the side and pushed her head between the seated figures. In this formation, Anna spoke into Cloud's right ear and the boy listened in Edelweiss's left one.

"Boy, I have wrongly accused you of a monstrous crime. I am very sorry and ask your forgiveness."

"You can't take her away, you can't, she's mine, it's not . . ."

"Shh. Hush. Hush and listen. In her old life, her name was Cloud and she was my husband's friend. But now, you have given her a new name, Edelweiss, and she has become your friend. It is a beautiful name, a perfect name for her new life, in this new place with you. So she must remain with you. She is young and will be your friend for many years to come. My husband and I thank you for her past care and are certain of her safety with you in the future.

"Now take her home. It's milking time"

Perhaps Anna heard a muted, "Yes. Madam," but for certain she heard the universal, "Cumbossy, cumbossy," that calls a cow to home.

Cloud turned away from Anna and Edelweiss took her place at the side of the boy and moved away.

Under her breath, she commanded, "Oh! I must stop this weeping!" For in what seemed to her an eternity, but had spanned but one short hour, she had shed the sudden tears of physical pain, the copious tears of utter joy, the glazed-eyed tears of rage, and finally the soft, slow tears of release and relief.

There would be many more tears to come in the years ahead, but never again would there be a single event capable of bringing together so many causes and kinds as this.

Chapter 6

Thursday, April 4

Anna and Christina had all day to talk and did so. This was not true for the men-folk. The pathways were never wide enough for the two carts to travel side by side so there was no conversation between Jacob and Hendrick during the pulling hours.

Though it stayed cold throughout the day, the two men produced a heavy sweat with their labors. At night, the temperature dropped suddenly as soon as the sun went below the horizon. The damp clothes next to their skin rapidly stole their body heat forcing them to strip off their wet shirts, put on a dry nightshirt, and wrap up in their wool blankets. They crawled under cover of the man-cart's canopy and sought the warmth of common body heat.

In the smaller women's cart, Maggie and Eva were squeezed between Anna and Christina for added warmth. Hendrick and Jacob suggested the same arrangement to Hans who at first refused the offer. But within an hour, the howl of a distant wolf pack and the penetrating cold had changed his mind; he crawled in between the two men.

He was comforted by their warmth but bore the burden of their raucous snoring on each side. He could not remember that either of his parents snored. The volume of noise that these two men could produce was painful. Hans had a terrible time getting to sleep and for the next few weeks was annoyed throughout the night by their noise.

However, in the months beyond, as dangers grew around him, he found restful sleep only in the cocoon of safety signaled by the cacophony of a grown man's snoring.

Hendrick's first night in camp had been particularly harsh. The gusting winds had intensified his misery. Luckily, the night's ground cover had been collected and supper finished just before a wall of sleet and snow came at them from the north. The best place to be was under the cover of the carts wrapped in warm blankets. The open ends of the overturned carts were covered with a canvas tarpaulin which kept out the wind and kept in the comfort of body heat.

Jacob and Hendrick had had no enthusiasm for man-talk that frigid first night together but during this second night the sky was clear and the air dead still. The two men wrapped themselves in their blankets and sat by the fire after the others had gone to sleep.

They were already very easy with one another; they were the right temperament and the right age to be brothers. Jacob was thirty and Hendrick had just turned twenty-three. They were both above average in height and winter-hungry thin. But there the similarity ended; Jacob was dark of complexion, hair and eyes. Hendrick was fair with blond hair and blue eyes.

Jacob was easier with conversation than Hendrick and began the telling of his history first.

"I had a small farm on a series of south facing hills. For three generations my family had a vineyard and an apple orchard on those slopes. We made wine for ourselves and had volumes left to sell in the market. My father, Christian, and I even had some years when we had such a volume of spirits that we made this trip to the Rhine wharfs to sell our wine for export.

"My grandfather, Andreas Seiler, was a master of stone construction. He built a small apple house against a hill with field stones. It was ventilated well and kept dry. We had fresh apples from the autumn picking and the stored apples were made into puddings. The fruit kept us all well during the usual winter months.

"I had 15 hives in my apiary; my bees produced the sweetest honey in the region. My wife raised chickens and ducks. We had fresh eggs every day and meat from the fowls on special occasions. A hog was raised and slaughtered every year and a goat gave milk for the girls.

"Anna's husband, Peter, was my father's brother. Peter had flat land for growing grains. I helped him with his wheat harvesting and he helped me with my apple picking. We shared the abundance of our fields between our two families. Anna and my wife, Margaret, went about making the wine and preparing the apples for storage. Each had a kitchen garden bursting with vegetables.

"Margaret and I felt blessed by the Almighty Lord and free from all wants and cares. Our joy was only increased when she told me she was once again with child. Anna attended at the birth and there seemed to be no more than the usual pain and tension. But the baby boy tried to come out feet first.

"Margaret and Anna worked through the night to get him to come out into this world. I know he fought as hard as he could but he could not be turned. In the end, after two days of unimaginable suffering, both my beautiful wife and my cherished son died. My paradise was lost.

"Margaret died in April last year and Peter was murdered in July. Anna and I together worked the fields and orchard but used the grapes only for cider. There was no time left in our days to make wine.

"And then the cold came, the bitter never-ending cold."

Jacob grew silent and busied himself rearranging his blanket around his shoulders.

Hendrick rustled about in his coverings as well and then took the lead. "Jacob, I am of sore heavy heart to hear of your terrible loss. Christina and I will keep your wife and son in our prayers," promised Hendrick. He felt the need to relieve Jacob of the burden of memory so he began his own account.

"I believe I have told you that Christina and I are from Rosbach?" asked Hendrick.

"Yes. I know the place," answered Jacob. "You are but a day's travel north of my village."

Hendrick continued, "Yes, that's true. My family has lived in that area for over one hundred years. We began as farmers but from the time of my father's grandfather, the Schäfer men have made their living as coopers and carpenters. I worked as an apprentice to my father from the time I was big enough to pick up a hammer.

"Our family home is on the edge of town; there's land enough for a few fruit trees and some egg-laying fowl. Mother has always had space for a kitchen garden, two bee hives, and a chicken coop. Most years we raised a hog for meat. We never had the land area to grow our own wheat; we have always had to buy our mother's baking flour from the mill.

50

"Since our families live so close together, I am sure we suffered the same fate. The cold struck us the night before Christmas with a hard freeze - a freeze that is still on us. The ground remains frozen even today. There soon followed violent snow storms with howling winds that sliced the cold right to the bone," Hendrick remembered.

"Yes, that is how it began for us as well," agreed Jacob. Most of the congregation came to church on Christmas Day - but did so in air almost too cold to breathe."

"Yes, Jacob. That is so true. Taking in that air was pure misery. As the youngest son, it was my morning duty to walk to the cooperage to start a heating fire for the day's work. The wind, snow and cold joined together to create a frightful pain in my nose, on my face and down into my chest. There were not more than a handful of mornings since Christmas Day that I did not dread that walk from home to work.

"In the past two months, all of our fruit trees were killed to the ground; the cobs of our chickens froze and the birds finally died in their coops. Mother's winter garden perished.

"In the wilds, birds fell frozen out the trees. The deer died in their tracks in the woods. The sound of thunder on some nights was in truth the explosion of tortured trees. Men took their lives in their hands to go into the woods fearful that even the largest and strongest of limbs, burdened heavy with ice, might come crashing down upon their heads. We feared to let the little children search for firewood under the fragile tree canopies.

"All our neighbor's sheep froze and several cattle perished in their stalls. All the grape vines died down. The streams froze to solid ice and the mills no longer ground our grains. Mother would not bake every day for fear of running out of flour.

"The earth froze as deep as a mare's tail. We could not bury our dead or plant our winter seed. What seeds and seedlings that had been planted in the late autumn are now locked in an icy grave.

"We saw the hardships heaped upon our neighbors and heard stories of the starvation in surrounding farmlands and came to realize that there would be no monies to buy my father's services for months to come. We had some funds saved and some food stored. But when would both be depleted?

"And then another blow was struck. In spite of our people's desperate circumstances, our Elector Palatine, Johann Wilhelm, sent his emissaries into the province to demand further tribute we did not have. We had paid his tax at the new year, but now he demanded further monies to continue his war with the French come the spring. I don't know how our soldiers will be able to find a French army to fight; we have heard their people are suffering the same torments as we from this winter's wrath and that starvation is stalking their countryside.

"My older brother began talking to me about this journey a month before my wedding. He first made it clear that he would miss me terribly. But then he spoke to me of certain truths; there was not enough work for both of us at the shop; our parents were in poor health and the Lord might take them at any time; he was unmarried with no family to feed other than our aging parents; my marriage would add the responsibility of a growing family to our meager stores; the wars would start again in the spring and soldiers would raid the land once more; and there was no foreseeable help for any of us to once again enjoy a peaceful and bountiful life.

"In trying to make me feel better, he held out the possibility of joining me in America; but we both knew he didn't mean it. We talked about it, we fought about it and finally we agreed to it. It was my place to leave this starving land and make a new life for myself and my new family. We waited to tell our parents until after the marriage. In my parent's eyes, for me to leave was for me to die; we would not see each other again in this lifetime. Mother held out hope for reunion in the life to come; Father's eyes said goodbye forever and wished me God's speed.

"I was able to sell a few personal belongings too bulky to carry. Christina has the money sewed into her garments and I have some hidden among my carpentry tools. All else is in our cloth bundles in Anna's cart; it is now all we have in this world except for each other, Praise God."

"Amen," they both intoned.

"It's getting late," noted Jacob. "We still have a full day's walk to the piers at Wiesbaden. There we should be able to find a suitable boat to go downriver. If the mud holds us back today, we may have to stay out another night. I don't think it would be wise to arrive at the wharfs after dark; we might be badgered by hungry desperate men eager for food and escape from this forsaken land. If we arrive early enough in the day, we will have time to stop to seek advice from an old friend of my father. We will see. Only time will tell."

The next morning began in unusual peace. It was Jacob's time to be the first to rise and start the fire. Anna slept deeply beyond the first morning light. Physical and emotional exhaustion had taken their toll.

It was still bone-chilling cold in the mornings before sunrise. The evening dew had turned to frost and their belongings were hidden under a blanket of snow.

Would this cold never end?

Jacob set two stumps up on either side of the fire-pit. He cut a small notch in the top of each and laid a limb between them as a crossbar. From that he hung a pot to heat the water for Anna's dandelion tea. Once that was heated, he put his own family's pot over the coals and prepared the breakfast porridge. The cooking smells awoke the camp.

Christina took the bright red rag from off the crossbar yoke of Anna's cart. The bright strip of material was the "no men allowed" flag. When a woman went into the bushes for necessities, she took the banner with her and put it in clear sight of the camp. This informed the men to avoid the area and seek their own relief on the other side of the camp. Eva used either side with whomever had the time to attend to her sudden urges.

Chapter 7

Friday, April 5

The remainder of that morning's travel was unremarkable. They had come out of the forested hills onto a more gentle slope with open views. Each time they approached the intersections of wagon paths, Jacob chose the wider alternative.

He was taking the route he had used so many times before; it would lead to the home of the wealthy merchant, Mr. Paulus Kramer, with whom his father had done business in the past.

The widened paths became carriage roadways with the deeply cut ruts of heavy-laden horse-drawn wagons and coaches.

Knowing they were ever gaining on their intended destination, the men tried to hurry their progress. But their carts' wheels were too close together to ride in the frozen wagon ruts and too far apart to hold to the sloping middle ground between the ruts.

Over and over again, one wheel or the other fell into a rut. A major effort was each time required of the men to regain the middle ground. This intense physical effort was matched only by their efforts to suppress the hearty swearing they deemed appropriate for the task. The presence of women and children within hearing kept the men's tongues in check.

At midday, after hours of this struggle, Jacob had them pull the carts to the side of the road at the base of a small rise. He gathered everyone to him and asked that Hendrick lead them in prayer to thank God for a safe deliverance to their destination.

"What destination, Jacob?" asked Anna. "I see nothing."

"Patience, my good Aunt. We will see it together after we have made our thanks to God," he answered.

They knelt in the grass and Hendrick led them in fervent prayer. At the chorus of "Amen," Jacob bid them rise and follow him.

"Leave the carts where they are and come with me."

The little party began the climb to the top of the hill. Jacob led, Hendrick followed with Hans at his side, Christina held the hand of Maggie and carried Eva on her hip and Anna anchored the group with a strong stride, a determined tilt of her chin, and a look of great anticipation in her eyes.

Suddenly the forward progress of the front rank was halted. Anna bumped into Catherine and almost dislodged Eva.

"What's the matter?" she asked with a bit of an edge to her voice. "Let me pass."

No one answered her, so she pushed her way forward to stand with Jacob. There she stood, dumbstruck with mouth agape, at what she beheld in the valley far below - the storied capital city of Wiesbaden - home to over 700 souls. Just beyond she could see the shimmering waters of the massive River Rhine.

She had thought she would be prepared for the sight. She was wrong. Village men had been going to the river to trade their wares for years and had come back with stories of city life that she had discounted as tales only for the children to enjoy. But even had she believed their chronicles, they could not have equipped her for this moment of unforgettable awe.

The tomb-like quiet passed and was replaced by laughter and excited conversation. There were hugs all around. The children caught the joyous temperament of the adults and jumped for joy. Almost as if to the sound of a bell, the celebration stopped and all stood mute. Their eyes, which had but a moment before been riveted on the beautiful cityscape below, slowly turned inward; the weight of a new reality bore down upon them; this wondrous city would not only be a place of excitement and discovery, it would also be the portal through which they would leave their past lives, friends, and families behind - forever.

A sober group resumed its pilgrimage.

Jacob brought them out of their reverie by announcing that they were within an hour's walk of the merchant's home and added "He has a wonderful mansion on a hill. It has been named Schönes Haus. From his front glass windows you can see into the city below. There is a hot spring nearby where we can take a bath and clean our clothes. He has a clear-running stream fed by a cold spring that keeps meat, milk, beer, and wine cool even on the hottest summer days."

The women's mood changed instantly with those two magical words, "bath" and "clean". They looked at each other with utter glee and laughed aloud. There was no more foreshadowing of things to come or gloom over things past, only the vision of warm bathwater and clean clothes now held their rapt attention. They harried the men to pick up the pace and lent their hands to the effort by pushing the carts with strong backs.

"Cristina! Imagine it! We will be clean again!" shouted Anna.

"Thanks be to God," echoed Christina.

They left the road and trekked across a ridge towards a stand of trees. This brought them to the north side of the house sheltered by a stand of evergreens. The full wall of vegetation provided the house with a windbreak and, for the time, hid it from the view of the oncoming travelers. It was therefore with a shock of surprise that Anna got her first glimpse of the mansion when they were nearly atop it.

It was a two story structure of massive gray-black field-stones carefully and skillfully quarried and chiseled into rectangular blocks of stunning regularity. There were eight windows at the front, two on either side of the entrance and four more looking out on them from the second floor. An archway of smaller cut stones framed the entrance with its massive oak double-door. Two tall chimneys standing erect at either end of the high pitched roof bespoke the wealth of the inhabitants.

On the top front step were two life-sized stone lions - one on either side of the entrance - set to guard the family's fortune.

The men marveled at the statues - the women at the curtains framing each window.

A large, broad-shouldered man rounded the south side of the house, smiled broadly and greeted them.

"Mr. Seiler, it is so good to see you again," he said as he approached Jacob.

"Hello Mr. Portier. It has been too long. You are looking quite well and strong. I hope your family is well also?" Jacob inquired.

"Yes indeed," Mr. Portier replied. "The wife and all the children have made it through this terrible time of cold. Mr.

Kramer has made it his duty to make certain that we all have had food on the table. God bless his soul! And how does your father fare?"

Jacob answered quietly, "I am sorry to have to tell you that my father died this past year during the summer. He was struck with a weakness on his right side and died two nights after. His illness was short and he seemed not to suffer any pain. The whole family was with him when he passed."

"I grieve for your loss and the loss for your whole community. Your father was a strong man of noble character. He had such a wonderful sense of humor. Oh! The jokes he could tell! Praise God that he did not suffer."

"Amen," from one and all.

There followed a brief round of introductions during which Anna learned that Mr. Portier worked for the master of the house, Mr. Paulus Kramer, and had done so for over 20 years.

Though a servant and a man of little schooling, Mr. Portier was trusted with some business negotiations at the docks and, more importantly, with the safety of Mrs. Diskretion Kramer and her three daughters, Pietat, Karitas, and Umsicht. Mr. Portier exercised all his obligations with pride, diligence and good will.

Pietat, having heard the conversation in the courtyard, came to the door to welcome the new arrivals.

"Please come in, dear guests. Mama will be so happy to hear that we have company."

"Please do not take offense at our refusal to cross the threshold but we have traveled for several days in mud and snow and we are filthy in person and clothing. We must not enter such a fine home in our present state. Please send your mother our best wishes and thank her for her family's offer of hospitality," answered Anna.

Suddenly the door flew full open and Mrs. Kramer made her appearance. She was a large-framed woman of middle years with a round pleasant face of even features. She was quite handsome for her age; she had undoubtedly been a beauty in her youth.

She set her blue eyes on Anna. "My dear woman," she said in full throat, "I thank you for your consideration of my home; now we must all set out to remedy the circumstances that make you hesitant to join us at table. My daughters will accompany the ladies to the hot spring to enjoy the waters and wash clothes.

"The men-folk can take their turn thereafter and in the meantime repair to the stable to talk of whatever men talk of when not in the presence of the ladies. Mr. Portier will assist in getting your carts and belongings into the barn. His oldest son sleeps with the livestock and his mastiff dog. No man nor beast would be fool enough to do harm to your family's things."

Perhaps the family members had heard of the pink-eyed woman from Jacob's father. Perhaps they were all just too polite or too preoccupied with the excitement of guests to give obvious notice, but for whatever cause, there was never a reference to her appearance by word or deed. Anna resolved to do away with her veil and make her way into her new life without any self-consciousness. And so it was and so it would be.

The men at first were apprehensive when they heard the high pitched shrieks of Anna and Christina. But quickly their minds were put at rest as they realized the shouts were of pure joy.

The women laughed and sang as they felt the hot spring water wash the miles, the anxieties, and the dirt of the past days of travel from their weary bodies. After an hour, the men put up a howl to get the women to abandon the spring. "It's our turn!!"

By the time of supper, the travelers were clean and spirits were high. Clothes were fetched from the Kramer women's chifforobes to cover the modesty of the women and Maggie. Eva was simply wrapped in a tablecloth. The men were suited up by Mr. Portier and his sons.

Mrs. Kramer was now able to lead the happy procession into her home. The front door opened into a small anteroom with wall hooks for coats. Directly ahead, a flight of highly polished stairs led up to a wide balcony from which doors opened to three bedrooms and a cozy sitting room. This was Mrs. Kramer's and her daughters' area to engage in the ladylike tasks of needlepoint, reading aloud and neighborly gossip.

To the left of the main entranceway was a formal front parlor and to the right was Mr. Kramer's office that was dominated by a massive oak desk. Anna gaped at the row upon row of books balanced on the deep shelves that lined the far wall. Windows at the front and the sides of both rooms bathed the interiors in evening light.

A narrow hallway to the left of the stairwell led straight to the back dining room. Family meals were taken there at a long dark-wood table flanked on either side by a sturdy bench and anchored at the ends by two high-backed side-armed chairs for the master and mistress of the house. A pantry and storage area at the right back of the house completed the first floor.

Mr. Kramer returned from the docks before supper and joined the men in the front parlor for ale and lively conversation. He expressed his deep regrets to Jacob over the death of his father.

"Your father was a wise and courteous gentleman. I considered him a close friend. During all the many years he traded here in Wiesbaden, he was accorded all the respect due him. It was always a great pleasure to have him as a guest and I am now honored to share the hospitality of my family's home with his family and friends."

Meanwhile, the women busied themselves readying the dining room for the evening meal being prepared by the Kramer's cook in the detached two-story outbuilding behind the house.

The first floor of the kitchen was reserved for food preparation. The Portiers lived above on the second floor loft. Tonight, Portier men would join the male guests in the barn while the ladies would enjoy the warmth and comfort of the loft.

The good cheer of all assembled was magnified even further by the splendid supper meal of fresh breads with honey, pork meat and root vegetables. Wine was served liberally for the adults and milk for the children.

After dinner, they all repaired to the parlor where wine and music flowed. Mr. Kramer played the recorder competently while his daughters sang with varying degrees of proficiency.

Jacob joined in and played his recorder in concert with Mr. Kramer. The room was made warm by a crackling fire and the contented smiles all 'round.

A full meal, ample quantities of spirits, soft music and the gentle motion of candle-lit shadows on the walls all combined to produce an overwhelming need for sleep. The gathering dismissed and Anna led her contingent to the kitchen loft.

All their wet clean clothes were hung near the fireplace. The cook was assigned the task of maintaining a low fire throughout the night to dry them and to warm the guests sleeping above.

As she was dozing off, Anna mused to herself, "This must truly be what heaven will be like if I am blessed to see it when I'm called away."

This one day would be as close as she would get to that happy place for some time to come.

Chapter 8

Saturday, April 6

Mr. Kramer's family had been in the trading business for generations; through the hard work of his father and grandfather, the family had become quite wealthy. Their businesses included three sailing ships for river traffic, a large wharf for loading and unloading trade goods, a large storage warehouse, a tavern for thirsty travelers, and a two-story building which served as a store on the first floor and lodging for the storekeeper and his family on the second.

Goods arrived from as far south as Strasbourg and north from Amsterdam and Rotterdam. At Wiesbaden, these traders could elect to pay a wharf fee and unload their goods for sale.

However, if there were no river traders available for an immediate sale, they had four options: take whatever price Mr. Kramer himself offered for the goods, barter for dry goods at Kramer's store, rent storage space in Kramer's warehouse, or push on in search of buyers at another wharf. If a man chose to pay for storage, there would be an additional broker's commission charged to him when Mr. Kramer acted as his representative at a sale at some later date. At every turn, Mr. Kramer made a profit.

While all this financial dickering was in progress, the river men could eat and drink liberally at Mr. Kramer's establishment, the Pfeife Taverne. He kept the price of beer low; a drunk customer made his business negotiations much more profitable.

*****

Eva was left in the care of Mrs. Kramer and her daughters while everyone else went into town to explore. The men did most of their exploring at the wharf and tavern, talking with the sailors and inspecting their wares. Under the guidance of Mr. Kramer, they chose some food staples and small hand tools for purchase.

Under the protective eyes of Mr. Portier, the women and children explored the main streets of the city and wondered at it all. He was a loquacious and knowledgeable guide who entertained them with stories of city life and local history.

They were suitably impressed with the remains of the Heathens Wall, a relic of the Roman rule more than a thousand years ago, but completely overwhelmed by the beauty and majesty of the Church of St. Nicholas, built over five hundred years before.

They had seen the steeple of the church from Mr. Kramer's home but when they came down into the valley and entered the narrow winding streets of the city, they lost sight of it.

Their happy chatter was silenced as they rounded a corner in the town center and suddenly stood before the man-made mountain of stone that dwarfed the people coming and going through the towering front doors.

From the little knot of dumbstruck country folk was heard a whispered, "Großen Gott im Himmel."

Anna was the first to regain her senses and led a march into the sanctuary. Mr. Portier and Christina followed in her wake. Maggie and Hans did not. The smell of baking bread beckoned to them from a small alley to their right. When the adults were safely out of view, they joined hands and ran off to find the source of that wonderful aroma.

Anna donned the veil and hat she had brought to wear in the church. She and Christina spent several minutes at the altar in silent prayer before finding places on the few benches at the back of the sanctuary. They had just gotten seated when there was a commotion of shuffling feet behind them.

Looking back, they saw two men rushing through the congregation frantically but quietly sounding an alarm. Their message was met with mixed reactions. Some looked around with bemused interest, some simply went back to their own meditations, while others scurried for the side exits.

Anna and Christina, at first confused, quickly became frightened.

What is happening?" Anna asked Mr. Portier.

"The Elector's men are in the plaza. They are looking for those who are trying to flee the country. He is losing tax monies from them and in anger is sending his most vicious men out to search for those such as yourselves to send back to their villages or, if they refuse, to send them to prison!"

Mr. Portier's brief answer was fully comprehended. Now the women's emotions ran to utter panic.

"Oh my God! Oh my God! What should we do?"

Mr. Portier asked them to listen carefully and follow his instructions exactly and without question. They shook their heads in agreement.

"Those that tried to escape have been captured outside the church. By running, they have marked themselves as exactly what the Elector's Hell-hounds are seeking. You must remain in the church.

"Mrs. Schäfer, move over to another bench and do not pay any attention to Mrs. Seiler. When you are questioned, tell them that your husband is a trader from the countryside and is at the wharf selling his wares while you came to pray for your family's safe return to your village. Now go!"

Christina did not hesitate. She moved up three rows and took her place in the center of the bench. Anna remained seated and awaited her instructions.

"Mrs. Seiler, you remain here. Pay no attention to Mrs. Schäfer. When questioned, you are awaiting your son's return from the wharf where he has sold his carpenter's wares and purchased supplies for your return to your village. Keep your head down and look respectful. Tell them you agree with the Elector's distrust of those who are abandoning their homeland. Play to their egos and try to remain calm."

Anna suddenly looked around and became even more agitated at what she saw, or rather, what she did not see.

"Where are the children?" she demanded of the world at large.

Mr. Portier had no answer as he could not see them either.

"They must be outside!" Anna said as she rose to her feet and tried to push by Mr. Portier.

"Wait, Mrs. Seiler! You must not go outside! These men know me and will do me no harm. I will go out and find the children. You must stay here! You must not go outside!" he shouted directly into Anna's face.

He was becoming frightened as well; but he managed to get his emotions in check and after extracting a solemn vow that Anna would not leave her place, he left her and Christina to their own devices to begin his search for Maggie and Hans.

No sooner was he out the door than there arose a frenzy of motion and murmuring from the congregants. A massively built man was making a theatrical entrance through the main doors. His form, back-lit by the afternoon sun, was made more terrifying by his shouted commands.

"Remain seated," he shouted. "Do not run or you will be brought to justice and punished severely. If you are among those leaving the Elector's realm, it will go better for you to stand up and surrender. You will be treated kindly and helped in returning to your homes."

Not one soul moved. The vast volume of space within the sanctuary fell impossibly silent. There was no sound of breathing.

As he made his way forward up the side aisle, he banged the floor with a long wooden staff he carried in his right hand. Each strike on the stone floor with his hardwood pole produced a thunderous shock that brought further terror to the congregants.

Between each clasp of thunder, Anna could hear the beating of her heart, her rapid breaths and the surrendering moans of despair of those around her who knew they were truly among the hunted.

Anna and Christina held firm; they kept their heads down, their eyes averted and their voices silent.

One elderly woman screamed and bolted when touched by the horrible staff. She was immediately marked by the hunter and designated to his minions as one to catch. She was led screaming and struggling out of the church to an unknown fate.

The hunter continued up the side aisle with erect posture and martial step. He passed Anna without a glance. She let out her breath and relaxed momentarily, but her heart stopped when she saw that he had found his prey. His shoulders dropped, his head lowered and his step became the gliding toe walking of a hungry alert predator. His eyes were riveted on the raven black hair of Christina.

He slid into the bench behind her and gathered a handful of her hair to his face and sniffed at it noisily. Cristina shuddered but did not leave her seat. He leaned forward and breathed something into her right ear. She jerked her head aside but did not rise.

There would be no questions asked of her; the hunter had made his decision; the wolf was playing with the tiny terrified field mouse before the kill. His pack members now pacing and watching from the front of the church set up a howl of delight.

"That's enough! Anna screamed. "That's enough!" And against all instructions, she rose from her seat.

*****

Maggie and Hans made only two turns before they had completely lost their way. The search for the bakery was quickly forgotten; the search for a way back to the church took its place.

The directions given them by the townspeople did not help. The city was a warren of winding streets and alleys. Maggie was becoming frightened; Hans put on a brave exterior and

69

continued to lead. But he was leading them away from his goal, not towards it.

Mr. Portier was not far behind. The people who had given instructions to the children now pointed Mr. Portier in the direction they had indicated. They also told him that he was not the only one trying to find them. A stout man who was very drunk was claiming Maggie to be his daughter and was crying that he had lost her while at the tavern.

Mr. Portier picked up his pace.

The drunk was quicker. He caught up with Maggie and Hans as they sat in a small public square. Tired and hungry, they were seated on a bench near the square's fountain. The drunk had sobered up enough to formulate a plan.

He ducked into a bakery and bought two biscuits fresh from the oven. They were wrapped in paper and tied with a string. He left the bakery and made his way directly towards them.

"You look very tired," he said. "Do you live close by?"

"No," Maggie sang out. "We're lost."

Hans saw something in the man's face that triggered an alarm. He had not had this feeling before but at that moment a newborn instinct - an inner voice warned him of danger.

The voice was a gift - a gift he would hone to a fine edge in the months to come. It would serve him and his companions well as they traveled in the company of other strangers.

Hans quickly interrupted. "No! She's wrong. We are not lost. Father told us to wait here; he will be back any minute. Perhaps you saw him in the bakery. He's a very big man with a large dagger at his waist."

He could see in the man's face that he didn't believe him. The drunk offered Maggie one of the biscuits. She took it hungrily and tore open the present. Hans did not stop her but politely refused his own offering.

The man stared gape-mouthed at Maggie as she ate. He reached to touch her but Hans pushed his hand aside and move between the drunk and his target. The drunk's attention switched from Maggie to Hans and his face changed from lustful watching to aggressive hate. Hans stood his ground.

"Get out of my way, boy," growled the drunk.

"No sir," Hans answered. "My father will be here soon and he does not want strangers touching us. He told that to us many times. I don't want to make my father angry."

Then under his breath Hans added, "And neither should you."

Unfortunately, the drunk heard the last statement. His anger turned to rage and he struck Hans with the back of his hand driving him to the ground. Hans came up screaming and fighting. He bit the hand that had hit him. This enraged the drunk further; he hit Hans a solid blow to the forehead. The boy's knees buckled, his vision dimmed, and he fell in a heap on the cobblestone pavement where the drunk delivered a hard kick to his stomach. Hans groaned and rolled into a small ball.

The bystanders were kept at a distance by the man's fury and his repeated ranting, "These are my disobedient children who need a lesson in respect for their father. You keep to yourselves!"

71

They obeyed.

By this time, Maggie was screaming at full pitch. She screamed even louder as the drunk grabbed her wrist and pulled her towards him. He spat out, "You come with me and shut up or I'll kill your little friend over there." Maggie's scream turned to a low howl but quiet enough to protect Hans from further injury.

That was the scene which presented itself to Mr. Portier when he entered the square: Hans rolling around on the ground holding his stomach and crying in pain and Maggie struggling against a man twisting her wrist and pulling her viciously along towards some hell awaiting her in a nearby dark alley.

Mr. Portier was not Hans's father as advertised. But he was indeed a very big man with a large dagger at his waist. And now the roaring rage that filled the square, that vibrated the fountain, that shocked the very air was his alone. The drunk's rage melted into sobriety and abject terror.

For the remainder of his days, the drunk would wear a long raised red scar from the corner of his left eye to the angle of his jaw. It would forever remind him of the personal miracle he had experienced the day he had escaped Mr. Portier with his life.

*****

At the sound of "Enough!" the hunter leapt up and spun around to confront the voice that would dare to command his actions. The sun had dropped further in the evening sky so the figure coming towards him was a silhouette against the blinding light streaming through the church's massive doors. With his eyes squinting against the light, all he saw was a tall black figure bearing down on him at a rapid pace.

72

Instinctively, he brought his staff up ready to do battle. But the voice coming from the apparition before him was turning from command to concern.

"Do not touch her. You could be harmed by her disease," said Anna with an anxious but solicitous tone. The hunter stood still at this and showed no immediate intention of attack. "What do you mean, woman?" he demanded.

Anna shouted as she continued her advance, "She is my daughter and we have come to Wiesbaden to bathe in the hot springs and pray at this church for her cure from the disease that has or' taken her."

The hunter looked over his shoulder at Christina and slowly moved away from her towards the aisle. There to meet him, as she loomed out of the glare, was Anna. She kept her head down to avoid his eyes. The hunter interpreted her attitude as a show of deference and respect.

Anna continued in the same soft voice, "Everyone can see that you are doing your just duty for our esteemed Elector. But I doubt he would ask you to endanger your health or your very life over a misunderstanding. Please know that our family is in the city for two purposes; our men are doing business at the wharfs and the women are on a pilgrimage of prayer and penitence. You must see I would do whatever necessary to keep my dear daughter from becoming what I have become."

With that she raised her veil and the hunter saw her porcelain-white skin and piercing pink eyes, eyes that stared into his - the widening coal-black eyes of a hunter.

He took in a quick gasp of air and lurched backwards. His foot caught on his staff. His evil weapon of physical and emotional terror served now as an instrument of humiliation as he tripped over it and landed backwards on his rump. In confusion, he let out a monstrous roar.

Anna quickly advanced over to him appearing to offer him aid in getting to his feet. When the hunter looked up, Anna was looming over him. Her fiery pink eyes were filled with white-hot anger belying her soft words of concern and the frozen smile on her lips.

He made a grand show of courtesy in declining her help, made sure not to touch her extended hand and, regaining his footing, marched out the church trailed by his swarm of henchmen.

In the confusion that had attended the hunter's encounter with Anna, his troops had left the courtyard unattended to watch with secret pleasure the embarrassment of their hated and much-feared superior. Their lack of attention to their duties allowed all who had been detained to escape. The first captured, the elderly woman, was the first to flee. With skirts hiked up, she was last seen running with amazing agility from the plaza.

The children were returned to the church by Mr. Portier and met by Anna and Christina with a mixture of shouts of joy for their safety, murmurs of concern and fright over their bruises, and finally wailings of parental-like anger over their wanderings and the dangerous result. But in the end, as they drew the two children to their bosoms, they were capable only of loving tears of relief and joy.

The women and children did not linger in town; they returned immediately to the Kramer's home on the hill safely removed from the valley and the city it embraced. They vowed not to leave that secular sanctuary again until their transport was ready to receive them. The religious sanctuary they had visited that day would not beckon them back for Sunday services. They would worship together with the Kramers in their home with invited friends and neighbors.

The men returned to the house in good spirits. Their merriment was dampened by the demeanor of Anna and Christina and completely deadened when they heard the details of the dangerous encounters of the women and children.

The men's crescendo rage at the perpetrators combined with their sustained inebriation produced a scene of ranting and thrashing as Mr. Kramer, Mr. Portier, and three other men of the household staff physically restrained them.

Their plan of returning to the city to seek revenge was counted as foolhardy; they were finally convinced such a show of bravado would only serve to call attention to their loved ones and place them once again in mortal danger.

The late-night meal was a solemn occasion. Each person reckoned with his or her own interpretation of the day's events. They had come to the attention of evil; attention that was been uninvited, unwelcome and unwarranted.

Childlike innocence and adult complacency about the exciting possibilities of their upcoming travels, the complexities of their new lives, and their belief in the general goodness of their fellow men were replaced with a gnawing premonition of uncertainty and dread.

Chapter 9

Sunday, April 7

A few chosen friends joined the Kramers and their house-guests for Sunday worship at their home, Schönes Haus. The men gathered in the front parlor, the women down the hall in the ample dining room. The minister led the service from the hall outside the parlor in a voice loud enough to be heard by the women just a few feet away. The youngest children sat along the walls of the hallway, girls on one side and boys on the other in order of age.

In keeping with the events of the day before, he began with a reading from the Book of Psalms 27:1-3

> The Lord is my light and my salvation—
> whom shall I fear?
> The Lord is the stronghold of my life—
> of whom shall I be afraid?
>
> When evil men advance against me
> to devour my flesh,
> when my enemies and my foes attack me,
> they will stumble and fall.
>
> Though an army besiege me,
> my heart will not fear;
> though war break out against me,
> even then will I be confident.

His sermon continued the theme of the place of evil in the world and the testing of men's faith in its wake. He solemnly prayed for those in attendance and any friends and neighbors who had suffered the loss of loved ones during the punishing winter. He ended his discourse with a hopeful prayer that warmth would once again return to the fields, the hearths, and the hearts of all in attendance.

There was the reading and the long-memorized recital of the Twenty-Third Psalm; then followed the benediction.

The men filed out of the parlor, thanked the pastor for his inspirational guidance, shook his hand and made their way to the barn. Mr. Kramer held back in order to speak to the pastor in private.

He looked down and shuffled his feet slightly as he informed the minister, "My Dear Pastor, please accept my thanks and those of my family and guests for your timely words of wisdom and hope. The men are now adjourning to the barn for some business talk in regards to my house-guests. You are welcome to join us but I thought I might tell you that some of the men may have brought ale from their family's storage to share with their friends."

The minister peered into the nervous eyes of Mr. Kramer and then answered with a lecture on the medicinal qualities of ale during the long hours of winter darkness. The exaggerated length of the talk served to sooth the consciences of both men.

The pastor threw his arm over Mr. Kramer's shoulder and guided him out the front door, down the wide step and towards the barn beckoning them with loud male voices punctuated by bursts of laughter.

There was a sudden silence as the minister entered the barn. Hands froze in midair with mugs attached. Other mugs froze at the lips of startled celebrants. Good cheer resumed instantly when the minister accepted a mug from Mr. Kramer and raised it with a hearty, "God bless this fruit of His fields and all those who partake of it!"

The meeting was called to order by Mr. Kramer who, with a sweep of a hand, gestured towards Mr. Portier and announced, "First, for those who have not already heard, I call upon Mr. Portier to retell what yesterday befell my house-guests in the city."

Mr. Portier made a slight bow to Mr. Kramer and stepped up upon the wood-splitting stump. He cleared his throat noisily, waited for all eyes to look his way and then started with the adventure that had befallen the children.

He was appropriately humble about his part in the outcome but the men knew their speaker well; no man among them would ever doubt his courage or ferocity. They smiled knowingly at the description of the blood-running slash on the evil drunk's face and wondered what possible good the drunk had ever done in his short lifetime to warrant his mortal escape.

Mr. Portier paused for the men to look approvingly at each other and raise their mugs with a toast to his courageous actions and storytelling prowess.

Then followed the story of the women's encounter with the Elector's henchman in the church. The retelling of events leading up to the frightful meeting was listened to casually and courteously.

But all eyes riveted on Mr. Portier as he recited the particulars of Anna's furious assault on the beast that had been mocking, handling, threatening and torturing her friend, Mrs. Schäfer.

He retold Christina's account as best he could remember.

"Anna was magnificent! She was a violent summer thunderstorm with lightning flashing all around her as she bore down on the hunter from her place at the back of the church. That's the name we gave him, The Hunter. When Anna came at him, he tripped on his staff and fell on his backside with a loud thump and a dreadful howl."

The men were familiar with and despised this monstrous man and his pack of wolves. They had known him as Ulrich Stab but he would forever after be called der Jäger, the Hunter. They pictured the fall from his feet to his rump and the fall from his height of brutality to his depth of humiliation. Oh! To have seen the look on his face! There followed a long pause in the story for the roar of their laughter and a salute to Mrs. Seiler all around.

"A toast! A toast to Mrs. Seiler!"

Mr. Portier continued Christina's account. "Mrs. Seiler told him a tall tale that scared him into thinking she had a skin disease. She said she had given it to Mrs. Schäfer and that he, der Jäger, would catch it as well if he touched either of them again. But you all know that this was a lie; Mrs. Seiler was born with her beautiful white skin and hair and her bright pink eyes. It is not a condition that one can catch."

There was another pause in the narrative as Mr. Kramer held up a hand and echoed the truth of the nonthreatening nature of Anna's condition. He allowed the story to continue only after all expressions of doubt had cleared the listeners' faces.

Mr. Portier moved on, "Der Jäger and his men left the field of battle so fast they lost all their captured pilgrims. It was said they were outrun by an old woman with lifted skirts and a limp."

The resultant uproar over this image was even louder than the last. Men seated on the floor held their sides and tried to catch their breath while laughing. Backs were slapped and hats were flung into the air. What a sight! It had been a very long time since this pitch and volume of laughter had been heard in these parts. The noise could be heard even in the house.

The women in the dining room paused their duties, turned their heads in unison towards the sound, and when certain it was their men-folk sharing some manly merriment, they smiled to each other in shared contentment and happiness.

"I say to you without fear of contradiction that Mrs. Schäfer was a brave woman to keep her wits about her when menaced by that evil beast," proclaimed Mr. Portier.

The cry went up again, "A toast! A toast to Mrs. Schäfer!" Dry lips and throats were wetted several times.

Mr. Portier concluded, "And remember always this heroic tale of Mrs. Seiler and der Jäger and agree with me now and forever that she is a brave and impressive woman."

The cry echoed even louder than before, "A toast! A toast to Mrs. Seiler!"

And indeed, they all agreed that Mrs. Seiler was indeed a most impressive and formidable woman.

The married men might wish for her as a wife but only if she never had occasion to turn on them in anger.

The bachelors would want her as a vigilant mother, the she-wolf protecting them against the world; however, the thought of

80

marrying a woman of her 'capabilities' would have to be carefully considered.

The boys in attendance resolved in future to give her a wide berth and to behave in a more genteel fashion if thrown into her company.

Mr. Portier came down from his dais-stump to the enthusiastic applause of his audience. Mr. Kramer, stepping up to take his place, let the toasting come to its conclusion and then turned to the business at hand.

"I have brought you together to receive your valued opinion on the safest way for my guests to make their way downriver to the sea. They have purchased their supplies and hope to leave tomorrow. I ask now for any advice you might offer," he said.

A tall man with a full blond beard rose at the back of the stable.

"Sir," he called. "We have readied two of your ships for sailing. The larger of the two, the Strum, will be carrying a heavy cargo of freight and will ride low in the water. This will certainly invite the attention of the castle's men and they will try to raise their chains across the river to stop her.

"Her deep draft will make it impossible for her to ride over the chains. She will be forced to stop as the proprietors of the castles demand their fees. I fear that with the boat held immobile, there would be time for the Elector's men to board her and discover your friends.

"The smaller of the two, the Blitz, is carrying a light cargo of cloth, buttons, pins and such from Switzerland. Her draft is very shallow - shallow enough to slip over the chains in the middle of the river now that the water is running high. And besides, there is a good chance that the castles will not even attempt to stop such a small vessel riding so high in the water. It will appear to them that there is nothing of value aboard. This vessel will be less likely to be stopped and your friends less likely to be caught."

Mr. Kramer pointed at him and said, "Thank you, Johannes. Those are very important points you have made. Now is there anything else to be considered."

There was a brief scuffle in the back of the group as one man poked another into action.

"Speak up, Jorg. Speak up," was heard in a stage whisper loud enough for Mr. Kramer to hear.

"What's going on back there," Mr. Kramer demanded.

"Sir! Jorg has something to say to you concerning the voyage," spoke the unidentified voice.

"Step forward, Jorg. I wish to hear your ideas," encouraged Mr. Kramer in a soothing manner.

Poor frightened Jorg was pushed one man at a time to the front where he would, for the first time in his life, be recognized by his powerful employer and, for the first and last time, be made to speak to his face.

He stammered, "But they're good boys, really Sir, they really are. They wouldn't mean no harm." His fright grew with each word and he was now struck dumb.

Mr. Kramer, becoming impatient, called over the boy's head, "You in the back where I can't see you. You there, the one who pushed Jorg to the front. Come forward and give this boy a hand in his telling."

The added and explosive, "Now!" produced a sudden parting of the knot of men revealing to Mr. Kramer the source of his rising irritation; there stood, or rather leaned, a heavy-lidded man held up by the back wall of the stable.

"Oh, it's you, Wilmar. Come here."

Wilmar belched theatrically and stumbled to the front. The men chuckled quietly and closed ranks behind him.

"Sir, I apologize. I thought myself too drunk to address you but I see that Jorg is too shy to tell of our concern. I mean no disrespect to your guests or to you by mentioning in this company that it would not go unnoticed by the young men that are to be passengers on the Sturm that the young girl who accompanies her father and great aunt is.. is.. well.. is," he stopped and stared at his feet asking for their help in finding the right words.

His feet failed him. He stood mute.

The men around him and Mr. Kramer were beginning to understand his meaning.

"You are trying to say that the girl might get unwanted attention by the passengers of the Sturm and that attention might lead to harm to her or others in her party?" Mr. Kramer offered.

"Yes, Sir. That's exactly what I meant to say," answered the much relieved Wilmar.

"So gentlemen, what is the answer?" inquired Mr. Kramer of the whole assemblage.

Mr. Portier held up his hands for silence and asked if anyone knew the passenger complement of the Blitz.
Miraculously, Jorg came to life again and offered, "There are only three persons signed on as passengers, Your Highness."

Mr. Kramer looked quizzically at Jorg at the title of "Your Highness." He knew from the bright blushing on Jorg's face that the boy didn't need his correction. The men in that barn would tease him unmercifully instead.

"And who are these people on the Blitz?" he asked as he glared down the men scoffing at the boy's expense.

Wilmar came to the blushing boy's rescue again, "There is a man and his wife and their small son. They are Mennonites making their way to Amsterdam. There are many of their faith there who will help them prepare for their journey to America."

"Does that mean the Blitz will not be going directly to Rotterdam?" asked Jacob.

"That's correct, Mr. Seiler," answered Wilmar. "The family will be given shelter and provisions and stay in the city for several days. Then as the weather permits, they will sail to Brielle, the main port city outside Rotterdam, and from there to London."

Jacob turned to Hendrick and summed up what he had heard, "It would appear that even though it will lengthen our journey by some days, we should go with the smaller Blitz to lessen our chances of being discovered by the Elector's men on the shore or harried by the men passengers on the larger ship."

"I agree with you, Jacob, and I appreciate all the thoughtful attention that has been given towards the safety of my family and companions by all here in attendance," replied Hendrick.

The meeting was closed with another thoughtful benediction by the minister and a recitation of the traveler's Psalm 121:

> I lift my eyes to the hills - where does my help come from?
>
> My help comes from the Lord, the Maker of heaven and earth.
>
> He will not let your foot slip - he who watches over you will not slumber.
>
> Indeed, he who watches over Israel will neither slumber nor sleep.
>
> The Lord watches over you - the Lord is your shade at your right hand.
>
> The Sun will not harm you by day, nor the moon by night.
>
> The Lord will keep you from all harm - he will watch over your life.
>
> The Lord will watch over your coming and going both now and forevermore.

The die was cast. The small band of Palatine immigrants would start their journey to the sea on the chosen boat, the Blitz; they would cast off the following morning.

Chapter 10

Monday, April 8: Day One on the River

And so the plan was put in motion. They arose several hours before dawn in bitter cold. The sky was as dark as the deepest coal mine. There was a new moon overhead but its token light was shrouded by the low clouds sheeting cold rain and sleet onto the silent travelers. Conditions were dreadful but perfect for a secretive boarding of the Blitz; the Elector's men would not venture out on such a miserable morning as this.

All members of the Kramer family and their staff were up and dressed; the family gathered in the parlor to say their goodbyes and the staff in the barn awaited their turn to wish the travelers well. To each group, Jacob led his fellow pilgrims in a blessing, "May the Lord be with you and bless you abundantly for all the kindness you have shown to us." There were handshakes all around and the journey began.

Mr. Kramer had arranged for Mr. Portier to take them and their belongings to the wharf. A horse-drawn wagon accommodated them and a canvas covering kept them dry and relatively warm. It was a trip of several miles and the going was slow. Mr. Portier had two men walking at either side of the horse holding tight to her bridle. Though she had made this trip hundreds of times in the past, she had never done so in the pitch black with driving rain. She was skittish when she heard unusual night sounds or saw the occasional spark of lightning in the distance.

The men did their jobs well and there were no mishaps coming down the long and winding road from the Kramers to the valley. They passed through the north city gate, rolled silently past the Roman Heathen Wall and the City Hall, and exited the city on the south. Anna shuddered slightly when she saw the distant silhouette of the spire of St Nicholas Church. As they arrived at the Blitz, the sun had just began to paint a streak of gold along a slit in the clouds at the horizon.

In spite of the rain and cold, the spirits of all were high as they boarded the boat. Mr. Portier went to the bow and shook hands with the tall figure of a man dressed from head to foot in black.

His hat had a wide brim all around; it hung low enough in front to obscure his eyes. His coat had a high collar in the back; it hung loosely to his knees; trousers were tucked into his high, heavy work boots. He looked as sturdy and strong as the boat's mast on which he leaned.

After a brief conversation, Mr. Portier asked all the travelers to gather together at the bow where they got their first look at their new leader, the captain of the Blitz.

In a sotto voce announcement, Mr. Portier began, "Friends, may I present to you Captain Severin Hraban. He has been a boatman for Mr. Kramer for over 15 years. He has made this journey to Amsterdam many times without ever losing a boat (he paused for effect) or a passenger.

"As is true on all ships afloat, the captain is in total command and his word is law. At first, you may not fully understand his directions, but be certain, he knows how to get you to your destination safely. So listen to his every word and follow his commands instantly and exactly as they are given you. Do you all understand my meaning?"

Anna and Jacob at the back of their group and were startled to hear, "Yes, we understand" coming from behind them. They spun around to see three figures huddled together in the darkness.

"Ah yes," continued Mr. Portier, "I have other introductions to make. The couple behind you are Aksel and Beate Koerber and their son, Baldewin. You will have sufficient time to get to know one another after sailing. But for now, it is important to get all your belongings onto the ship so Captain Hraban can set sail before full dawn."

A few moments of indecision and milling about were brought to an abrupt halt by the sounding of a single word from the dark figure at the bow. In a voice as dark and deep as the river below the keel came the simple command,

"Now."

The effect was riveting and from that moment on, there would be no questioning of the Captain's authority nor the slightest hesitation in response to his every command. In consequence, the people and goods were stored below deck in record time.

Jacob, Aksel and Hendrick were assigned duties as ship's mates. None had training or experience in the handling of a boat but assured the Captain that they were willing and quick learners.

He answered with an infinitesimal nod of the head and pointed to the bow and stern lines. The men scurried and with some difficulty released the lines from the dock cleats. The Blitz slid forward in the current. So far, so good.

Mr. Portier gave great relief to the men's sailing anxieties by telling them that he was to stay with them until they reached Bingen. He was an old hand at helping to man a boat of this size and would quickly get them shipshape.

The children were amused by their elders' obvious discomfiture at having to go back to school and chanted laughingly with them as they repeated the names of the ship's parts and pieces. Each lesson was immediately followed by a final exam.

"Where's the bow? Where's the stern?" barked the Captain.

"There!" coached the children pointing in the right directions.

The children scored again with port and starboard, jib and mainsail, mast and boom. The naming of parts went well with young and old alike.

But when the handling of the sails was called for, the lessons quickly went beyond the naming of parts and became complex and challenging.

Mr. Portier answered the Captain's commands and got the sails set as he ordered. Luckily the wind was mild and the current moderate so there was time for him to do the work of setting the sails while instructing his new students.

The three men were true to their word and set themselves specific duties quickly and efficiently. Soon the Blitz was underway and responding to the work of the new crew.

With no further need for his sailing instructions, Mr. Portier turned his attention to the ladies and older children. He gathered them all at the bow - all but Eva. He asked Jacob to amuse Eva away from the women. He silently did so without discussion or questioning. The men were learning their lessons well. The women awaited their directions.

He began, "Men on deck will not raise any suspicions, but the sighting of this many women and children would be unusual for a working boat and raise the likelihood of the Elector's men boarding and searching you and your belongings. You might very well be turned back.

"So it will be important that not more than one woman at a time be above deck and the children should stay below during the daylight hours. They may come up on deck at night for fresh air but they must keep their voices down as sound travels far and loud over water."

He looked directly at Maggie, Hans and Baldewin and somberly proclaimed, "As of this moment, you are no longer children. Children have the luxury of breaking rules and acting foolishly. But the safety of yourselves and your families depends now on your acting as adults; you must do as you're told without question, complaint, or hesitation. You have seen and heard the men in your company doing their duty as adults and you must now follow their example. You are no longer children."

All three looked inwards as they took in his message and then in perfect unison, sat up straight, looked Mr. Portier in the eye and nodded their decision to join the community of adults. There might be some backsliding in the future but there would be none on this boat.

And finally, the unspoken question of Eva was answered.

"At the back, the stern, of this boat there is a hidden storage space. I will take each of you, one at a time, down there to see it. If the boat is boarded by men searching for treasure or pilgrims, the women and children will hide themselves in that space and remain completely quiet. You will not come out until you hear the Captain call out the phrase, 'The Lord is my Shepherd, I shall not want.'

"We cannot be certain that Eva would remain quiet with you in hiding. She might get excited and cry or laugh or simply talk loudly. For that reason, if you are boarded, she must remain above deck with her father and she must not know where you are hidden."

They all signaled their understanding and compliance with the plan.

He broke the silence and the serious mood by announcing, "Class dismissed." This familiar dismissal brought smiles and relaxed all tension. The women began to chat among themselves and the children broke off from the adults to begin the process of getting to know one another.

At the stern, the women began to plan their share of cooking and cleaning duties and at the bow, the men continued to divide their sailor's tasks. The farmers and merchants were quickly becoming a well managed ship's crew.

Mr. Portier caught the captain's attention and nodded his satisfaction with the passenger complement and the captain in turn nodded his approval.

The wind and the current gained strength as the morning progressed. The Blitz picked up speed towards her first planned berthing at Bingen.

After their overnight anchorage at Bingen, they would leave the verdant, flat rift valley and begin navigating the deep Rhine Gorge cutting through 80 miles of the Rhenish Slate Mountains.

During that passage they would encounter numerous castles and their toll takers. With the castle's men and the Elector's hunters, there hung the threat of discovery and capture.

There was eager anticipation among the company to see the famed large stone Mouse Tower, the Mäuseturm, on its small island at Bingen. Hatto II, the Archbishop of Mainz, restored the tower from a ruined condition in 968 AD and set in motion a series of events that would make the tower infamous throughout the ages.

Chapter 11

Monday, April 8: Day One (continued)

But now the journey was really underway. As the men and women settled into their routines, Mr. Portier and Captain Hraban guided the Blitz into the river's center current. Quickly, the ship's complement relaxed into the rhythm of the boat's rocking motion and the sound of the sails' humming harmony.

The hours passed uneventfully in pleasant conversation and relaxation. As agreed, the women and children spent their day below deck. There was plenty of room for all of them to sit or lounge. There was cool water to drink and a selection of breads and meats for the midday meal. Mr. Kramer had stocked the larder with a bountiful selection of food for all to share. At each meal, the company gave thanks for their food, their safety, and for the generosity of their benefactor. The women spoke laughingly of the hold as "Heaven's Waiting Room".

Their hiding space was at the back of the hold. It was situated under what appeared to be a solid pile of heavy stacked carpets. Under the first three layers of carpets was the top of the wooden box that served as their refuge. The front of the enclosure was behind a stack of sail cloth. The false entranceway into the space was hidden behind a sailor's chest pushed up against the port corner of sails.

After the midday meal, Eva was sent up to be with her father on deck while the women and other children choreographed their disappearing act under the carpets. Thankfully, there was a slit window on the stern wall which let in some light and fresh air, lessening their feelings of claustrophobia.

One of the men was required to move the chest back and forth so Aksel volunteered to thus open and close the entranceway. During the day, there would be adequate warning time of potential boarding parties so the men could roam the deck at will. But at night, a rowing party could slip up on the Blitz with little notice.

Aksel and Jacob determined to sleep at the entrance of the hold so if an alarm was sounded, Jacob could carry Eva up onto the deck and Aksel could man the sailor's chest to help the others into hiding.

With only a few practice rounds, the entire complement of women and children was able to disappear in less than a minute.

The day passed quickly. Well before sunset, the Blitz was set at anchor in the passageway between the shore at Bingen and a little island that gave shelter from the cold winds off the river. On the island, the infamous Mouse Tower glowered down on them.

All the Germans knew some variation of the legend about the Mouse Tower, but the Swiss family, the Koerbers, had never heard of it. So after the evening meal and repeated entreaties, everyone gathered together as Mr. Portier prepared to recite his version of the gruesome tale. Eva was put to bed early and spared the details of the frightful fate of Hatto the Second.

The night air was cold, the sky was clear, the moon was at its new phase and stars blazed overhead. On the forward deck, Mr. Portier sat upon an upturned barrel; his audience huddled in blankets at his feet. His pipe produced a pinpoint of light that he brandished with a flourish at appropriate intervals. A small oil lamp placed strategically at his feet gave a diabolic glow to his face.

94

The stage was set. And he began.

"Seven hundred and thirty-five years ago, in the Year of Our Lord, 974 AD, a terrible famine struck our land. Hatto II was the ruler and archbishop of this realm. He used that tower as a platform for his crossbowmen and demanded tribute from passing ships even as the keepers of castles do today. If the ships did not stop, he ordered his men to fire upon them and kill the crew.

"He also used the tower to store grain and during the famine he hoarded grain there and in his many barns. He set such a high price on the grain that many could not afford to pay. Hunger and starvation stalked the land.

"In time, the populace grew increasingly hostile and a movement was begun to storm the archbishop's barns and tower. Hatto caught wind of the threatening plan and devised one of his own. He told the leaders of the revolt that he had seen the error of his ways and would now make every effort to feed the hungry. There was great rejoicing in the land.

"Hatto told them to gather in his largest barn on the mainland of Bingen and await his coming for the distribution of food. Scores of hungry men, women and children followed those instructions and packed into the building."

Mr. Portier paused, relit his pipe, took several long draws, and continued.

95

"Hatto appeared at the barn and received an uproarious greeting of praise.

'Long live our blessed leader.
Long life to Archbishop Hatto.'

"Hatto waved to the assemblage, smiled broadly and then ordered his men to bar the barn door and set the building ablaze. All trapped inside were burned to death. As the shrieks came from within the barn, Hatto was heard to answer them with, 'Hear the mice squeal. Hear the mice squeak.'"

Again Mr. Portier paused. He tapped his pipe's ashes over the side and taking his time, refilled the bowl and lit up once again. His audience sat dumbstruck before him as they meditated on the horror and evil that had been dealt to their fellow peasants so long ago. The story resumed.

"Hatto hurried through the town to his castle on the shore. As he made his way along the streets, a white mouse came out of the shadows and began to follow him. He turned suddenly and stomped the mouse to death under his boot.

"Immediately two mice came out of an adjacent doorway to take its place. Hatto picked up his pace but the mice easily kept up. From every doorway and every alley, more mice joined the throng that scurried at Hatto's heels, their pink eyes ablaze.

"He was running in a panic as he crossed his castle's drawbridge. He shouted back to its two guards to beat back the mice as he fled to his quarters. But from behind him, he heard the screams of the guards as they were attacked and killed by the rodents.

"'Fire,' he cried. 'I need fire!' Soldiers came to his side with burning torches off the castle's passageways. Using the fire to ward off the mice, he and his men made their way to the beach across from his tower island.

"On reaching the shore, Hatto leapt into a tethered boat big enough for his full complement. But he tripped the man in front - blocking the way of the others and rowed away leaving his soldiers to the mercy of the mice once their torches had burned their last embers. He was laughing as he rowed, 'They cannot swim. They cannot reach the island!'

"Unfortunately for his men, neither could they.

"Hatto was partially right, but partially wrong. The mice could not swim. But nonetheless, the hundreds, no, more likely, the thousands of mice that now gathered at the water's edge scrambled over each other to get into the river.

"As they drowned, others came behind them until there was a raft of mouse bodies afloat. The raft increased in size with each new drowning and soon the raft reached the island's shore; death was transformed into a bridge. Across that bridge poured a pulsating mass of maddened rodents.

"With a full-throated scream identical in tone and volume to the screams that still hung in the air over the burned barn, the mice became a single organism full of rage and revenge. The walls of the tower turned white with the curtain of swarming bodies as they scaled the ramparts to reach their prey. Their piercing screams were joined by those of Hatto who first screamed in terror and then in agony as the mice ate him alive."

Mr. Portier lowered his pipe and moved the lamp aside with a foot. He was now in total darkness. There was complete silence on deck - belying the fact that there were nine people sitting before him trying once again to breathe.

He broke the silence, "It has gotten late and you must make an early start in the morning. So I bid you all a good night and wish you pleasant dreams."

With rueful smiles by some at Mr. Portier's good wishes, the group found their way to bed.

Chapter 12

Tuesday, April 9: Day Two on the River

The following morning, Mr. Portier announced that he would be sailing with them until midday. The captain had requested his help in navigating past the Bingen Hole, a treacherous narrow in the river that had claimed many a ship in its whirling current.

"I will be with you all for a few more hours and then you will be on your way without me."

Though the travelers were happy to hear that he would be with them for awhile longer, they were distressed to be reminded that they would never again meet with this wonderful man. His quiet heroism, gentle good grace, witty humor, and competency on land and under sail had filled their days with pleasure and confidence in their safety. He would be sorely missed.

The day brought a fair wind for sailing but the sky was gray and threatening rain. Sails were set and the Blitz left the shelter of Mouse Island and moved gracefully into the river's current.

With no difficulty, her captain and experienced first mate maneuvered her through the narrows, past the mouth of the Nahe River and back to the starboard shore below the town; they tied up to a small wharf.

The women had delayed the morning meal until after the danger of the Hole had passed. They were all below preparing food. All the men but Aksel were on deck. Eva had cried to be with her father and now sat on his lap at the bow sheltered under his great coat. Mr. Portier and Hendrick sat with him.

Anna donned her long black cape and carried a pot of hot porridge up onto the deck. She was ladling the steaming contents into Jacob's bowl when there came the sharp alarm.

The captain was at the wheel, holding it with his left hand. In his right, he held a long metal gaff. He had given four sharp blows; the warning to those below to go into hiding.

Aksel had just been coming up from below. But without glancing about to see the matter, he dove back down and disappeared into the hold. There was not a sound from those below, but those above deck knew that pandemonium was in progress under their feet.

Anna froze in her tracks. Her back was to the shore and with her hood up, she was sure that her face and gender could not yet have been determined. So ducking her head down she glided towards the stern but determined not to go below. If she had already been seen, she could not go down and then disappear. The ship would be torn apart to find her and, as a result, all would be discovered.

The three seated men looked towards the shore and saw nothing but they heard a menacing voice call out, "Permission to come aboard, Captain." The tone was one of command rather than request.

Captain Hraban, standing at the wheel had seen the two intruders approaching. He saw their determined gait and the telltale baton each carried. These truncheons were the weapons of choice for the castle bullies, the toll takers. They knew how to hit a man, or woman for that matter, in places that would inflict pain, bring a target to the ground, induce unconsciousness, or indeed, kill outright.

"Permission granted," replied the captain after an acceptable interval to allow more action below but not long enough to warrant suspicion above.

Over the gunnel appeared two faces. The older of the two was obviously the leader. His face was fire-red, pimpled and pockmarked. His eyes were black narrow coals. His mottled beard was straggly, sparse and tattered by his skin condition.

The other was that of a younger person of indeterminate gender whose waxy yellow hair hung limp and filthy on either side of the face.

The younger cupped hands and hoisted the leader onto the starboard gunnel and then followed with a feline's agility in a single bound.

On closer examination, the youngster's feminine face and voice were contradicted by a frontal fullness in the tight britches and stubble on the chin that signified the gender as male.

The body of the leader was as unpleasant as his face. He was short and squat with a marked limp due to a shortened right leg. Mr. Portier hoped it had been the result of some sailor's wrath and retaliation. His arms were massive and covered in dense coarse black hair. His hands were thick; the right one held his baton with a practiced ease.

There was a long silence as the toll men surveyed the men on deck.

Finally the leader demanded, "What is your cargo?"

"Carpets," was the Captain's curt reply.

The boy squeaked, "Where are the other passengers?"

The leader glared at him for interrupting the more important questions involving money. The boy shrank beneath the baleful stare.

The leader continued his line of thought, "What kind of carpets?"

"They are made of poor wool from Switzerland. They are of little value. My ship is going to Amsterdam to pick up an expensive load of metal goods but I could not find a valuable cargo to carry on this leg of the voyage," growled the captain.

The boy's question made another passage through the leader's dull mind and this time caught his attention.

"Are there other passengers on board?" he questioned.

"The Swiss merchant is below," came the answer.

The leader's concentration was broken once again by the sight of a ruffling of Jacob's great coat.

"What do you have there?"

A small voice responded, "Father, let me *out!*"

"Oh! Let's see. Let's see," whispered the leader as he made his way towards Jacob.

Eva's head peeked out from under Jacob's coat. She was giggling and her face was wreathed in a wide smile; that is, until she saw the grim and ugly face of the leader. At that moment, she let out a howl and began to cry. Jacob held her tightly and quietly comforted her. The leader moved back.

Eva and the leader regained their composure. He stood back away from her to avoid a renewed stanza of screams. But he had a question for her.

"Where is your mother, little one."

"In Heaven" she answered and pointed to the sky.

"And where are the other people on the boat?" he inquired.

Remembering the women's name for the hold, she answered truthfully, "In Heaven's Waiting Room".

She started to point towards the ship's stern but Jacob quickly and firmly reached under her arm and directed her pointing finger up into the sky.

"There are others on the boat," volunteered Eva.

The passengers were dumbstruck as Eva wriggled off Jacob's lap and headed towards the stern.

But as everyone watched with either horror or relish, she stopped before reaching the hatch, detoured to the port side, and proceeded to open a small sailor's chest. She looked inside and tittered, "Come out. Come out."

And they did. Three large white mice with fiery pink eyes. One scrambled to her right shoulder, one to her left and the other to the top of her head. They faced forward and set their focus on the leader's face - a face turning as white as the mice.

"Look, Father," she grinned to Jacob. "These are my new friends. They came from the island last night. I put them in this box and fed them some bread from supper. This morning, I looked in the box and there were more. They haven't told me that they will be my friends yet. But I'm sure they will."

She turned back to the box and scooped out another three mice. These three raced onto the starboard gunnels while the other three left Eva and took up their stations on the port-side gunnels. They lined up in rodent battle formation and stared unblinkingly at the increasingly agitated toll takers.

Then on some silent cue, all six dropped down onto the deck and scurried towards the boy. He escaped the ship with the same agility he had demonstrated on boarding it. The mice whirled about and returned to Eva where they gathered at her feet; once again they turned their full attention on the leader.

With all eyes on the mice, Anna took the opportunity to leave her statue-like attitude; with head bowed, she moved forward. At her approach, the mice raced up Eva's clothing and settled on outstretched arms, shoulders, and head.

Anna took up her new post. Standing directly behind Eva, she suddenly raised her chin and threw back her hood. The leader was now faced by a grinning girl festooned with six large white rodents and a tall black-clothed figure with white skin, white hair, and eyes as blazingly pink as those of the mice.

Captain Hraban added to the leader's rising panic by raising his gaff and shouting, "Now leave this ship at once! Remember this, and tell your ugly little friend, if you ever see him again, that these mice have acted as protectors of this child and her companions. No harm should ever come to any of them from your telling of this day's happenings.

"And never forget; the Tower mice will be vigilant."

The leader dropped his baton and turned to run. He slipped and fell in the puddle of yellow liquid and black excrement that had appeared at his feet. Moaning wildly, he regained his feet and fled over the gunnels to shore. Four of the mice leapt to shore and were seen loping along in his putrid wake.

Again there was total silence and astonishment. Anna brought them all around when she spoke soothingly to Eva. "Eva, put your little friends back in their box so they will stay warm. We will feed them again later."

Eva gently plucked the two remaining new friends off her shoulders and placed them carefully in the box. She closed the lid and calmly walked back to her father and took her place on his lap.

The captain regained his composure, opened the hatch and shouted out, "The Lord is my Shepherd, I shall not want."

At this signal, the hidden ones emerged and quickly learned of the incredible encounter of Eva, the toll takers and the mice. At first, they all spoke together in hushed tones of wonder. But with each retelling and the continuing addition of details, there was a rising fearfulness. Panic was only avoided by the intercession of Anna.

She sat down, took Eva in her lap, lovingly stroked the child's hair and began, "My friends, today we witnessed an extraordinary event. We saw this innocent child acting together with some of God's smallest creatures to deliver us from evil."

"So as we saw, a little child *did* lead them."

This reference released a bit of tension as the adults looked to one another and smiled.

Anna continued, "I truly believe that the Lord *is* my Shepherd. I believe that his will worked today through Eva and her 'new friends' to bring us all to safety. I cannot question the mysterious ways of my Lord and will accept the actions of this child and the mice as the work of his hands. So saying, I reject fear and say, 'Thank You', for God's Grace."

A tentative, "Amen" was instantly followed by a declarative, "Amen!"

Although Anna's congregation now agreed with this new interpretation of the day's happenings as divinely inspired, they decided that outsiders might not as willingly accept this explanation. They voted *openly* not to speak of it to outsiders; and then quietly and *inwardly*, each decided not to test his own faith by speaking of it again with these, his fellow witnesses.

Within the hour, as Mr. Portier left the Blitz for home, his last sight of the ship was of the adults waving and wishing him well and Eva crooning a soft tune into the open sailor's box.

*****

The rest of the day was uneventful with the exception of Eva's crying fit when she found that *all* her new friends had disappeared. The captain had seen the last two scurrying down the bow rope to shore soon after their companions had chased after the toll taker. He had bid them, "Adieu and God speed," loosed the rope and pushed off the bank. The Blitz was now under full sail.

Christina decided to take charge of calming Eva.

"Eva," she explained, "your friends have families of their own on the island. Their children would miss their midday meal if their parents did not return. Wouldn't it be so sad to think of all those little baby mice going hungry?"

"I suppose," sniffed Eva. "But will they come back to visit before tonight's meal? I have more bread to feed them."

"I don't think that will be possible, my dear. The boat is moving too fast for them to catch up to us. But I'm sure they will miss you," spoke Christina with confidence in this, the first successful test of her mothering skills.

Eva seemed in accord with this homely explanation until she noticed that the less she cried, the less attention she received. Looking around at the now disinterested adults, she set up another great howl. In short order, Christina determined that gentle hugs and a soft murmuring song succeeded where reason and story-telling had failed.

Peace returned to the Blitz.

They anchored that night offshore near the town of Lorelei and waited until dawn to navigate past the mountain of rock on the eastern bank of the same name. The rock soared more than 100 meters overhead as they safely negotiated the sharp turn at that narrowest section of the river between Switzerland and the ocean.

The further they sailed from the Palatinate and its Elector, Johann Wilhelm, the less they feared capture and return to their destitute villages. The toll takers of the castles they passed showed no interest in their small, high riding vessel. The wind remained steady; the humor of the passengers becalmed.

By this third day on the river, the women and children were allowed to come and go above decks even during daylight hours. The men had become old hands at setting the sails and the women had the housekeeping chores down to a well-choreographed ballet performed in the small space available to them.

The sun shone brightly the whole day hinting that warmth might once again return to their cold-weary world.

The scenery was breathtaking; the adults passed hours relaxing on deck staring up at the wonders above them. The deep gorge through which they were sailing ran more than 80 miles from Bingen to Koblenz. They gawked at the size and grandeur of the numerous ancient castles clinging to the precipitous peaks or crouched on the flat rims of the canyon. They were heartened to see that some vineyards on the steep slopes had survived the cold and might once again produce a harvest.

They anchored that night along a deserted shore and left the following morning before dawn in order to reach Neuwied that evening. The wind was fair and the water calm so they reached anchorage at Neuwied in the early afternoon.

The captain and Jacob went into the small town to get fresh bread and other provisions. The others stayed below, quiet and undetected.

There was a gleeful commotion when Jacob returned, the heavenly smell of fresh baked bread proceeding him down into the hold. "Shhhhh," he whispered to the giggling women. So they giggled even more - but more quietly - and began to break off pieces of the warm loaves for the hungry-eyed men and children. There were also some root vegetables and a small piece of fatty meat of uncertain origin; the combination would suffice to make a heavenly, aromatic, hearty stew!

The new moon was barely visible that night and the sky was clear; they all wrapped themselves in blankets and stayed on deck long into the night to wonder at the beauty and multitude of the stars.

The following morning, day five on the river, the weather turned against them with cold rain and sleet coming out of the north and head winds from the west slowing their pace. But the captain quickly taught his eager crew how to set the sails to tack and draw the boat ahead. It was a long day of hard work, but they made it to Bonn shortly after sundown.

They had sailed 90 miles into their journey with some 200 more to go.

Chapter 13

Saturday, April 13: Day Six on the River

Captain Hraban pronounced the weather too severe for safe travel; they would have to remain at anchor at Bonn for the day. Anna was secretly pleased at the pause in their travels.

Today was Christina's twentieth birthday. Everyone had wished her well at breakfast but no special plans had been anticipated. Anna was determined to plan a celebration and brought Jacob and Hendrick into her happy conspiracy.

The two men made excuses to go into town to buy some "special tool" they needed for tending the sails. Anna gave them their real marching orders; they were to bring back some bakery sweets and a decorative candle.

They kept their business-like faces on until they were off the boat and then, laughing and slapping each other on the back, they ran off to find just the right ingredients for a festive party.

It did not take long to learn that their search for cake or any other form of bakery confections would be in vain. The baker told them they would not find such sweets anywhere in town. It was impossible because the ingredients to make such delicacies were not available.

"All the honey, sugar or other sweeteners we had were eaten by our people early in the winter," reported the baker. "And I fear that most of the apiaries have been lost to the cold so our supply of local honey will not be replenished this coming summer."

This was distressing news. The sweet cake was to have been the highlight of Christina's celebration.

"What can I do, Jacob?" asked Hendrick. "How can I give Christina a proper birthday celebration without a sweet treat?"

The baker inquired about the nature of the celebration and his wife overheard the details. In response, the good woman pulled down a small jar from behind the serving counter. From it, she carefully spooned out a small portion of her meager supply of precious apple butter.

She broke off the end of a loaf of bread and hollowed out a place to hold the butter for its trip back to the boat. Her husband added to the gift by presenting Hendrick with a long fresh loaf of bread.

Hendrick could now cut his dear Christina a generous portion of this fresh bread and cover it with the creamy, sweet apple butter. It would be wonderful!

Smiling broadly, and after half a dozen repetitions of "Thank You", the two men made their way out of the shop.

Now all they needed was the candle.

But candles were not for sale at any price. None had been made since before Christmas time. Beeswax candles had disappeared along with the apiaries. All available fat, whether from fish, fowl or beast, had been eaten during the lean times.

For the hungry, fat meant nourishment, not light from tallow candles. Without new wax or fat supplies, the candles of the town were nearly spent and homes had been made dark during the long winter nights.

Again, a sweet woman came to Hendrick's rescue.

Although the proprietor of the shop no longer had candles to sell, he did deal in tobacco, pipes, and flints to fire up a taper to ignite a pipe.

Hendrick had a flint in his pocket - one of several he had brought with him on this journey. The tobacconist offered to barter with him for the flint and asked what shop items might interest him other than candles.

"I don't see a thing here that a beautiful young lady could use," laughed Hendrick. "You have many wonderful items for men-folk but unless my wife takes up pipe smoking, I don't think we can make a deal."

The shopkeeper's wife stepped forward and asked, "What is the color of your wife's hair?"

"It is raven black that shines in the sun," he beamed.

"Well now, I believe I have just the thing," she replied.

She stepped into a side room and came back with a hair ribbon. It was a warm golden color, as long as Hendrick's forearm and of a polished smooth cotton material. It was splendid.

"I have had this ribbon for some while but it doesn't match my coloring," the missus lied sweetly. "I believe from what you say about your wife's dark hair, that it would suit her nicely. Let us barter this ribbon for your flint."

For just a moment, Hendrick stood slack jawed and mute. She would trade that beautiful ribbon for his near-worthless piece of flint? He held the gracious woman's eyes with his own.

Jacob broke the spell, "Hendrick, I do believe that would be a fair exchange."

Hendrick regained his composure, cleared his throat noisily and turned to get a final approval from the husband.

"I believe we can make such a trade," he replied. "But wouldn't you agree that my wife strikes a very hard bargain?"

Once again, Hendrick looked confused. Then the shop keeper guffawed and heartily slapped Hendrick on the back. Everyone appreciated the joke; loud laughter followed and the mood lifted.

The lady wrapped the ribbon in a bit of white paper and tied it with a piece of yellow string. It was to be one of the most precious gifts Christina would ever receive.

With heartfelt thanks, Hendrick and Jacob left the shop and returned to the ship.

They climbed aboard wearing faces of disappointment at not having found the "special tool" they had sought. Christina led the party in trying to brighten their humor over this failure. To Anna, they gave a sly smiles and a hooded winks.

They gestured her forward and told her of their successes. Anna was overjoyed; there was now a reason and the means to bring some joy into the hearts of her beloved companions.

By dinnertime, the weather had agreed it was time for a joyous occasion and swept the clouds and rain away. The wind dropped to a gentle breeze; the stars shone brightly in the sky above and echoed their brilliance as sparkling reflections on the waters below.

The dinner was to be a hot, aromatic, one-course meal in a bowl as the much anticipated mystery-meat stew. The captain had a store of salt with which the ingredients were nicely flavored.

In better times, the fat would have been skimmed from the surface of the stew for other uses; but in these hungry times it would be stirred in and greedily consumed.

The river was running quiet and they were tightly moored so Maggie had no trouble keeping the small red-hot coals safely in the iron pan suspended by three chains from a sturdy tripod.

There was only the slightest swaying of the pot to give away the motion of the Blitz. Over the hot pan, the iron cooking pot hung by its own chain and swayed in unison with the coals and the ship. The meal was a rare treat; in rough waters, there was no fire allowed and only salted or dried meat was consumed.

Now the pungent aroma of cooking meat and fat filled the hold.

No sooner had the stew begun to bubble when Christina announced the cooking smells were making her "sickish".

Anna noted that Christina had lost some of her color and quickly excused her, suggesting she join the men and children on the bow deck while she, Beate and Maggie continued the cooking.

In short order, the cooking pot, wooden bowls and spoons were brought on deck to raucous applause and foot stomping. The bowls were filled with steaming wonder as hungry eyes watched and hungry mouths watered.

Everyone sat and held a bowl with gentleness and care. As they were hungry and a bit cold, they were tempted to gulp down this piping hot miracle of aroma and texture.

But it *must* be savored! Smell it! Taste a bite; take a small bite; take one small bite at a time. Go slowly. Eat slowly.

Hendrick was having trouble eating at all he was so anxious to give Christina her wonderful gifts. Anna watched with amusement as he repeatedly felt in his coat pocket to make sure the prettily wrapped ribbon was still there. It was. But he checked again. And again.

Christina's sweet delicacy of bread and apple butter was warming over the last embers of the cooking pan. She had regained her natural color; Anna was certain she would be able to enjoy her birthday treat.

And finally the time came! Anna called for quiet.

"My friends," she began. "We have reason to celebrate a great occasion today - the 20th birthday of our own sweet Christina!"

Applause! Applause!

"We all have been blessed with a comfortable evening and a delicious meal. Hendrick has been singularly blessed with his beautiful wife and best friend. So, Hendrick, stop fumbling in your coat pocket and get on with your presentation!"

The darkness hid Hendrick's blushing as he arose from his box seat and knelt at Christina's feet.

"You are my life and my happiness," he said. "Tonight I have only my love and this small present to offer you on this your birthday. But I pledge that from this day forward I will work with all my physical strength and moral courage to make a safe and comfortable life for us both in the New World."

115

She opened her gift with copious tears and further applause. Anna tied Christina's hair into a braid and all marveled at the beauty of the girl-woman's hair and her slender gold ribbon.

Christina demanded that her sweet treat be shared by all. And so it was; though each one received only a tiny bit on the end of a finger. It would be a night to remember for a lifetime.

The moon and sun had set by 8 o'clock and once again the sky blazed with starlight. Eva was put to bed early but the other children were allowed to stay up with the adults to enjoy the fresh air on deck.

Captain Hraban had graciously supplied a generous measure of beer for the party. While savoring his third stein of the night, he had become unusually sociable and determined to entertain his guests with story-telling.

"We have lost some time in our journey due to the bad weather so we should get an early start tomorrow," he announced. "But as the sun comes up very early now, you will have the chance to see what towers above you at this anchorage."

He took a long pause and a drink of beer. Then with one quick motion, he leaned forward directly into the face of Hans and growled, "the Drachenfels."

Hans was so startled, he fell over backwards from his box seat.

The audience laughed uproariously but only for a second as the harsh, bass voice of the captain shouted out, "Quiet!'

Now it was the adult's turn to be startled and the sharp intakes of breath were followed by complete silence.

The captain leaned back and continued.

"The Drachenfels, the Dragon's Rock, is the mountain right over your heads."

Everyone shot a look upwards but it was too dark to make out anything on the shore; they returned their attention to the story teller.

"Atop that jagged mountain sits the hulk of the castle of the same name built more than 500 years ago. And at that ancient time, there was a long poem, the *Nibelungenlied*, written by an unknown man. It tells of the adventures of a brave warrior by the name of Siegfried."

At the mention of a "brave warrior," both Hans and Baldewin sat up straight and leaned forward to catch Hraban's every word.

"There are many ways of telling of Siegfried's heroic deeds; but this is the way my father taught me. So I know it to be the only right and true telling.

"Siegfried was the son of King Siegmund and Queen Sieglind who lived in a mighty castle on the Rhine in the town of Xanten. Siegfried was known to be uncommonly handsome, intelligent, brave, and honorable.

"He was a warrior and a knight. He possessed a cloak that made him invisible and gave him the strength of many men and a sword that could cleave an anvil in half."

He drew out the word "invisible" into four distinct syllables, and savored the children's murmurs of wonder that such a thing was possible. He continued.

117

"And far behind us, on the Rhine in the town of Worms, there lived a beautiful princess named Kriemhild. She had three brothers, Gunther, Gernot, and Giselher who ruled the powerful realm of the Burgundians."

"In times past, she had had a horrifying dream of the savage death of her future husband. To spare this unknown man, this one worthy of her love and her hand in marriage, such a fearful fate, she swore she would never marry."

It was Maggie's turn to take notice. A story with a beautiful princess in distress held promise.

"The poem is full of stories of betrayal and revenge, life and death, great battles, journeys to faraway places, the wooing of the beautiful princess, and a golden treasure of immeasurable value. There are kings of many nations, dwarfs, fair maidens, knights in shining armor, magic war swords, and dragons! These are the tales that have been told by evening fires throughout the ages.

"So it is that the tales of Siegfried's many adventures are much too long to tell in one night. Therefore this night, I will only have time to tell you what happened to Siegfried at this *very place* so long ago."

He stood up, stretched his tall frame towards the unseen mountain looming over them, drank another portion of beer, sat down and began again. The others shifted about, found more comfortable positions and eagerly awaited the knight's tale.

"A long long time ago, there lived a dwarf by the name of Fafnir; he was the son of the king of the dwarfs, King Hreiomarr. The king's house within his solid-walled castle was made of glittering gold and flashing gems.

"Fafnir was small in stature but exceedingly strong. He was loved by and loyal to his father. He was also the guardian of all his father's wealth.

"There lived in the same land a greedy and devious dwarf named Andwari. He had stolen a great horde of gold and a magical ring from three Rhine maidens. He was forced to give up the gold and the ring to King Hreiomarr as compensation for the accidental killing of the King's son, Otur.

"Andwari was furious at the loss of his fortune and pronounced a terrible curse upon the treasure and its possessors. The curse fell onto Fafnir's father, the great King.

"And what a terrible curse it was. It drove the King's two remaining and loving sons, Fafnir and Regin, into lustful greed. They did the unthinkable; they *murdered* the King, their very own father, in his sleep!"

His audience took on the role of a Greek chorus and shouted out, "Oh *No!*"

"Oh *Yes!*" shouted the Captain. "It was patricide and regicide spliced together in one dwarf-king!"

"And they took possession of the gold and the ring. Little did they know that they were also now the possessors of Andwari's horrible curse. Then Fafnir turned against his brother, Regin, and stole the treasure for himself.

"He fled to this very place, to this mountain, and hid the gold in a deep cave. Here he changed himself into a dragon and lay down upon the hoarded wealth to keep it all for himself."

Once again, the congregants stole glances into the darkness above. The sky had darkened completely covered over by a blanket of fog. Had the dragon been perched on top of the main mast, they would not have been able to see him.

But they would have sniffed him out; the stench of a dragon was said to be so horrific it could be detected for miles. Thankfully, the atmosphere about them smelled clean and sweet.

The captain lowered his voice to a whisper for dramatic effect. The ploy was successful. Tension vibrated in his listeners and they gathered their blankets closer; the dampening night air grew colder. He continued.

"Fafnir's dragon-form was as long as this boat and three times as heavy. He was the blood-red color of the deepest sunset. His long tapered tail and broad back held a ridge of upright spines - each the length of my arm. He walked on all fours with legs driven by bulging massive muscles.

"Each foot was festooned with razor-sharp claws able to rend this ship to shreds with a single swipe. Thick-skinned wings sprouted from his shoulders; full spread out, they could reach from here to the far river bank.

"His long dog-snout was broad and flat - his nostrils wide. His breath was noxious foul and his eyes were as burning coals of fire. But real fire was what burst from his mouth when angered; and he was so easy and quick to anger."

In describing the dragon, the captain rose from his seat and gestured wildly. The warming alcohol pulsed quickly through his veins. He flung his arms wide to demonstrate the impossibly wide wingspan of the beast. He huffed and puffed when telling of breath foul and fiery. His slick long black coat swirled around him; his wide-brimmed hat fell lower and lower over his hooded eyes. The children made themselves smaller and smaller in their blankets; the adults laughed at his antics but did so nervously. It was a great show and continued thus.

"After his father's murder, Regin fled to the kingdom of King Siegfried. His consort, Queen Sieglind, considered the dwarf intelligent and wise and chose him to be her son's tutor. And she was right; Regin taught him languages, music, horsemanship, swordplay, and all the chivalric manners. He was trusted completely by the Queen and his young pupil, Prince Siegfried.

"When the Prince reached his full manhood, Regin told him of his own father's murder at the hands of his uncle, Fafnir. He failed, however, to mention that he had quite willingly helped Fafnir do the horrible deed. Sometime later, he casually remarked on Fafnir's theft of their father's brilliant collection of gems and gold. Regin asked Siegfried to help him retrieve the wealth, 'for the betterment of my father's people,' and Siegfried agreed.

"And so they came to Drachenfels to a cave that lurks above your head."

They couldn't help themselves; they once again looked up into the fog-filled air and saw - nothing.

"Siegfried watched Fafnir in his guise as a dragon. From across the river, he noted the pathway Fafnir took to the river to drink each morning. He also noted that the dragon was very much alert throughout the daylight hours but that he slept soundly at night. Or so he hoped.

"He waited for the next cloud-covered night with a new moon and under the cover of darkness, he dug a pit in the middle of the dragon's drinking pathway and covered it with small branches and leaves of a nearby linden tree.
"The following morning, the dragon pounded down the path and fell into the pit. Siegfried was lying at the bottom of the pit waiting to strike. With his father's sword in hand, he drove the weapon into the falling beast's heart as it fell. Great screams were heard round the kingdom as the dragon died.

"Siegfried had been told that if he bathed in the blood of the dragon, his own flesh would be his armor and no enemy's sword, knife or lance could pierce him. So he smeared the dragon-blood on every part of his body he could reach and rolled in it to cover his back. However, a small linden leaf had fallen onto his sweat-soaked back and stuck there; blood never touched that small piece of his skin."

He abruptly concluded., "So that's the story for tonight."

"No!" shouted Hans. "You can't stop now!"

"Oh yes I can, young man! Don't forget who you're speaking to," answered the angry, inebriated man.

"I'm very sorry sir. I meant no disrespect. But how am I to learn the outcome of Prince Siegfried's adventures?"

"I know these stories," came a voice from the back of the group.

It was Hendrick.

"My grandfather knew the whole saga through and through and delighted in telling his grandchildren the tales of magic, giants, dwarfs, dragons and other beasts. My mother was much against this as it was not thought proper to speak of such things in our religion. She was very strict and devout.

"But my father made it clear to us children that the tales were just that - stories made up to help instruct children in the best ways of man and also to teach them how to avoid man's wicked, greedy and lustful ways.

"He let Grandfather tell his stories but only in the out-of-doors or in the barn - never in the house - never in front of Mother.

"Eva is too young for these tales, but I will entertain the other children - and any of the adults who wish to hear these children's bedtime stories - when the time is right and chores are finished.

"Do you boys and you, Maggie, agree to my terms?"

"Yes!" they answered in unison. "We agree!"

So with one last furtive upwards glance into the still impenetrable darkness, the group dispersed to seek the possibility of dreamless sleep. Some were successful - some not.

Chapter 14

Sunday, April 14: Day Seven on the River

The captain was a man of his word; they were up very early the following morning. The air remained still, damp and cold. There had been no breeze or warmth to scatter the clouds still wrapped over Drachenfels peak. The children would never have a chance to see the dreaded mountaintop where the dragon had lived and been slain.

But their imaginations were quick and keen; they filled in the hidden scene with great and vivid detail. Their word-picture was at first painted with a broad brush but over the next several days, they added the finest details of color, contrast, light and shadows. Their combined efforts rendered in their minds an image of the Drachenfels which was much more ominous and dreadful than if they had seen the very mountain for themselves.

Anna and Christina set about making the morning porridge but once again, Christina felt "sickish" and rushed from the hold.

"I'll go with her," Beate volunteered.

"Thank you, Beate. I'll be up in a moment once Maggie has the coals under control," answered Anna.

When Anna reached the deck, she was greeted with the sight of Christina leaning over the rail, retching loudly. Beate stood next to her with her right arm around Christina's waist and her left hand supporting Christina's pale and sweating forehead.

Anna hurried below and returned with a cloth soaked in cold water. While Beate continued to support Christina both physically and emotionally, Anna softly wiped her face and neck while joining Beate's soothing patter of comforting words.

"Oh my, Christina. Have you been sickly like this for many mornings?" asked Anna.

Christina had recovered herself enough to be able to sit down on the deck and lean against the sidewall.

"It's been coming on for the past week but this has been the worst. It is so strange. I feel sickish in the morning but feel fine the rest of the day."

Anna and Beate exchanged knowing looks and broke into wide smiles. With gentle laughter and loving pats to Christina's face, they broke the happy news.

"You're with child, Christina! You're pregnant," they said in a sing-song duet.

Christina sat mute and confused. But a moment later, the words of her women friends hit their mark and she beamed with understanding and joy.

At that moment, Hendrick appeared from below-decks and saw his wife still pale and glistening with sweat seated on the deck.

"She's sick!" he yelled. "How can you all be laughing?"

"Come here, Hendrick," Anna said in a soft voice. "Christina has something to tell you."

Hendrick went to Christina and squatted down astraddle her outstretched legs.

Christina took both his hands in hers and with tears of love and joy streaming down her cheeks, she said, "Hendrick, you are going to be a father."

It was Hendrick's turn to lose all color and strength. He fell backwards so that he and the mother-to-be were both now seated on the deck facing one another. He started to sweat and Anna thought he might faint. She vigorously fanned his face with her long skirt as Beate wiped his brow with the same cloth they had used to revive Christina.

Hendrick quickly recovered his senses, leaped up, and while dancing a jig about the bow, began to shout, "I'm going to be a father! I'm going to be a father!"

The other men, hearing the commotion, came quickly from below and learning the particulars of Hendrick's shouting, shook his hand with bear grips and beat him on his back. Dust rose off him with each blow; he looked like a carpet on a line being beaten by a determined and powerful farm woman.

In spite of the pain being inflicted on him by his friends, he continued to holler his joyous message to the world, stomp around, and smile from ear to ear.

Then someone noticed that Christina was still sitting on the deck and called for help in getting her on her feet. Hendrick stopped in his tracks and ran to her aid.

"I'm sorry, Christina! Oh! I'm so sorry. Let me help you up."

Christina was overcome with laughter at the antics of her husband. There was no reproach at having been forgotten. Hendrick helped her to her feet and took her into his arms; they fell silent together.

126

Moments later, Anna motioned for everyone to go back down into the hold. They did so, leaving the loving couple to discuss this new miracle in their lives.

*****

Knowing the cause of Christina's stomach distress, Anna was now prepared to offer assistance. Each morning, she banished Christina from the hold to separate her from the smells of breakfast cooking. She then boiled up a pan of ginger tea made from pieces of pealed ginger root. Christina sat at the bow, wrapped comfortably in a blanket and the arms of her doting husband, sipping the warm brew until her stomach calmed for the day.

The ship's "crew" settled into a comfortable routine. Meals were nutritious and timely, sails were set and managed to the commands of the captain, and the children performed their duties well and held up the bargain of not acting their age. The boys helped with ship chores and Maggie helped in the hold.

After four more days on the river, they reached the small market town of Wesel. They anchored just beyond the mouth of the Lippe River. Wesel had once been a member of the Hanseatic League - one of the most powerful trade alliances in history.

At one time, Wesel had actually been one of the League's busiest cities. But as the League weakened in political power, Wesel declined in economic power. Finally in 1669, it lost its membership and became what it was today - a shadow of its former self.

But this history, sad as it might be, mattered little to these travelers. They sought neither political nor economic power; they wanted only bread, potatoes, and salt. Except for salt, their other needed provisions were found in abundance in the local market near the steps of the Willibrordi Cathedral.

They had now left the territory of Elector Johann Wilhelm behind. They no longer had to fear capture by his hunters so everyone took advantage of the stop and went ashore. It was wonderful to walk and stretch after being confined for so long.

Anna and Christina took courage and entered the cathedral. After their encounter with the Elector's men in Wiesbaden, they had promised not to enter a German cathedral again. But once the food essentials had been purchased and handed over to the men-folk to transport back to the ship, the women and children gathered in the sanctuary.

There they worshiped in peace and safety. They gave thanks for their safe journey and for the comfort and companionship of their new friends. The women joined hands and prayed for the health of their mother-to-be and the child she was nurturing in her womb.

With newly exercised bodies, a full larder, and renewed spirits, they pushed on to their next destination.

They arrived at Emmerich in the late morning of Saturday, April 20, their thirteenth day on the Rhine. They had completed just half the distance to Amsterdam.

They determined to stay there through Sunday. The women insisted that there had to be time to wash clothes and to take proper baths while the men planned to strike out to buy salt and replenish the soap supply the women now promised to deplete.

As a boy, Jacob had stopped in Emmerich while traveling with his father. He knew of the soap sellers in the area and seemed to remember there were different kinds of soap available. But he couldn't recall the details.

He had Aksel and Hendrick to join him to ask the captain's advice on soap purchasing. The captain gave them a short lesson and having become new "experts" in the trade, the three men struck out to barter and buy.

They found the shop selling soap on Steinstrasse near the Mennonite church. The time of winter soap was passed. Winter soap was made between Martinmas (November 11th) and Shrove Tuesday (six weeks before Easter). The mixture contained two parts hemp-oil and one part coleseed-oil.

But it was now the season for summer soap made with a formula of *one* part hemp-oil and *two* parts coleseed-oil.

The barrels holding soap for sale on the store floor were appropriately marked with an "S". They were also marked with both the coat of arms of Amsterdam where it was produced and the mark of the soap-maker himself. The proprietor of the store assured them that the soap was of the highest quality.

The captain, however, had told them not pay the full price for *any* batch of this year's summer soap and had schooled them in the particular reasons why.

Jacob spoke to the shopkeeper with an air of authority. "I see that these barrels of soap are from Amsterdam," he said pointing knowingly at the trademark.

"That is correct sir. In our shop, we sell only the highest quality of soap and Amsterdam is known to produce the best there is."

"Well sir.   Could it be that you are unaware of the severe shortage of hemp-oil and coleseed-oil brought on by this winter's harsh cold? As a result, are you also unaware that the Amsterdam soap-maker's guild has allowed its members to alter their quality standards by adding talc to this year's summer soap? My friends and I certainly do wish to purchase your soap, but we can offer you only two-thirds of the price you are asking for what we *all* know to be an inferior product."

The shopkeeper blustered angrily and marshaled all his selling prowess but, faced by the obvious expertise of the three gentlemen before him, he finally agreed to their price.

Success was theirs!

Salt buying was almost too easy; no bartering was involved. They were somewhat disappointed in the ease of the transaction. But they were not disappointed by the reception the women gave them when they returned triumphant from the successful hunt for the elusive soap. They were heroes!

The ship's supply had been decimated by the day's washing. Drying clothes were spread over the ground next to the boat and over every inch of the deck. The most personal women's articles were hung in the hold hidden from the stares of passers-by. Thanks to the men-folk, the soap supply was now fully replenished. They would be able to keep themselves clean for quite some time!

Chapter 15

Sunday, April 21: Day Fourteen on the River

Captain Hraban called for a day of rest. "We are over halfway there and making good time. I have business to attend to in town so I will be gone for the entire day. You are free to roam the town or go to church - whatever is your pleasure. But there must be a man with the ship at all times. Is that understood?"

Yes, it was perfectly understood. So Aksel, Hendrick and Jacob worked out a schedule so that one of them would guard the ship while the others went to town.

Aksel and his family were to leave first to get to their Mennonite service by 9 AM. The others, except for Jacob, would leave in time to join the congregation at the Lutheran church for services at 11:00 AM. Jacob volunteered to stay with the ship through the morning until Aksel's return at 1 PM.

They heartily congratulated themselves on their cooperative effort and started preparations. There was a great deal of joyful hustle and bustle as each group got ready for the day.

Anna was somewhat amazed by the appearance and demeanor of the usually dour Aksel. He hadn't been unfriendly towards her, just reserved. But now he was all smiles and chatter with his wife and son as they prepared to leave the ship for Sunday services.

She and Jacob sat at the bow and watched as Beate fussed over her two men, busily straightening their collars and smoothing their hair. Aksel had a blacksmith's broad shoulders and thick arms. His Sunday coat stretched tightly over his chest and appeared frayed at the bottom and worn at the sleeves. It was a very tight fit.

"Perhaps a hand-me-down from his father," thought Anna.

Aksel did his part in this get-ready choreography by repeatedly smoothing Beate's skirt, brushing off imaginary dander from her shoulders, and reassuring her over and over again that she looked "just fine" in her Sunday dress and that her beautiful auburn hair was arranged "just right".

Baldewin looked as uncomfortable as any tall, skinny twelve-year-old boy would who had been suffered into a Sunday suit. His mother had plastered his hair to his head with water or perhaps a little grease. He was all gangly arms and legs.

But, thought Anna, "He will make a handsome man some day."

"Just look at them," exclaimed Anna to Jacob. "Isn't Aksel a wonder! I've not heard that many words out of him at one time since we first met them in Wiesbaden!"

"He's a listener, not a talker," observed Jacob. "After his father died, he worked alone in the smithy. He has spoken a few times of his long hours with the heat of the forge and the noise of the anvil; it was not a place that invited conversation. And exhausted from work, he was unwilling to attend many community socials. He just got out of the habit of talking."

Anna replied, "I suppose Beate got used to his ways and became quiet herself. But now, I must say, she has really brightened up and become a real talker. Christina has taken a particular liking to her; they talk and laugh with each other all day long. Beate has been beaming with good cheer over

132

Christina's condition. You'd think she was the one who was going to have the baby!

"I don't know if Aksel told you, but he and Beate have been married only three years. His first wife was Baldewin's mother. She died of the pox during a second pregnancy. Aksel became sick too but survived with those scars on his face. Baldewin was away with his grandparents when the sickness came and was miraculously spared.

Anna concluded, "This is Beate's second marriage as well. Her first husband died in an accident within a month of their marriage and they had no children. I believe Beate is hopeful that she will be able to have a child with Aksel but is worried that so much time has passed."

Jacob replied, "No, Anna, he has never spoken to me of those sad particulars. But he has told me something about life in his home town.

"He comes from a Swiss mountain area where the majority of people are now Catholic. There is bad blood there between the Catholics and his Mennonite brethren; their grievances have been going on for generations. In fact, his grandfather was killed in a Catholic raid on his farm when Aksel was just a boy."

"Oh my! How horrible," exclaimed Anna.

"Indeed!" echoed Jacob. "And so it happened that though his church strongly opposes violence of any kind, it was forced upon men like Aksel in order to defend their farms, their shops and their families from the acts of violence brought down upon them."

"Wasn't there a safer, more tolerant area of Switzerland where Aksel could have moved his family?" asked Anna.

Jacob answered, "Well, his grandfather tried that. When his family became threatened, he moved to a district that had a Protestant leader. But when the long war ended in '48, a new leader was chosen by the winners; that leader was a Catholic who demanded that all those living under his rule convert to Catholicism. Many did.

"But his grandfather refused and ultimately paid for that decision with his life. Aksel's father then moved the family to a neighboring district that was independent; but that too changed to Catholic leadership a few years after the family was established. So this time around, Aksel has chosen to move his family, not to another district in his homeland, but to a whole new world. There he hopes to rid his family of all religious tyranny with its stress – and despair."

With hope in her voice, Anna replied, "Perhaps when they are among their own kind in America, they can find peace in their new household; and with God's blessing, Beate may yet bear a child."

"We can all hope for their happiness," answered Jacob.

"I will miss them all when we have to part in Amsterdam," said Anna. "And Hans and Baldewin have become such good friends; they will surely miss one another."

Jacob laughed, "I think Maggie will miss Baldewin too although I think she still has her cap set for Hans."

The dinner conversation that night was full of excitement and wonder. The night was warmer than usual and the full moon rose in the east as the sun painted brilliant colors in the west. All gathered on the bow to share the day's happenings.

"We heard him!" said Beate clapping her hands in joy. "We heard Hendrik van Voorst give such an inspirational sermon; so full of hope for our faith and for our people. Can you believe that? We heard him! We were in the same church with Pastor van Voorst!"

"Would you think much less of me if I confess I am unfamiliar with the gentleman you have named?" asked Anna. "I'm sure we would all share your joy more thoroughly if you would tell us more of him."

"Oh, Anna. I'm sorry," Beate answered. "Those of our faith in Switzerland know the history of this congregation and their respected pastor. I forget that you are not of our faith as you treat us with such kindness and respect!

"There has been a Mennonite congregation here in Emmerich for almost 200 years. Some thirty years ago, the mayor of this city granted the congregation the right to build a church. And that is where we worshiped this morning.

"Mr. Hendrick van Voorst has been the pastor there for many years. He is known throughout the Mennonite community for the way he bettered a Catholic priest sent here by the French King to force Catholicism on our faithful brethren."

Aksel broke in at this point, "Please remember that the French ruled this city only 35 years ago. This same priest had been sent to England by the French King to make a study of a Protestant community there called the Quakers. When he returned to France and told the King of his findings, the King forbade the Quakers to remain in France under penalty of *death*! So, as you can see, the appearance of this priest in Emmerich to examine the Mennonites was terrifying. Now, Beate, please go on."

Beate took up the tale, "The priest, whose name was Formantin, demanded a meeting with the pastor. The two met at the church where the priest questioned Pastor van Voorst on many topics related to the Scriptures and other matters of faith. It is said that he was so impressed with the pastor's religious knowledge and gentle unassuming nature that he highly praised the Mennonite to the King."

She concluded with, "So, for as long as the French held this place, the Mennonite faithful were free to worship in peace."

"How wonderful to meet such a man!" exclaimed Anna.

Jacob added, "What a worthy hero! We understand how you are so thrilled to have been in his company!"

"Yes! He is a hero!" proclaimed Jacob. "We will be able to hold this day's fulfillment of faith in our hearts all our lives. And we will be able to teach our brethren in the New World of the faith and courage of the good pastor of Emmerich, Hendrick van Voorst. It has been a wondrous day!"

"Anna, what did you and your family do today?" asked Aksel.

"Well, we went . . ." started Anna. But she was interrupted by an excited Baldewin.

"But Father, you didn't tell them about the birds!" he exclaimed.

Remembering the incident, Aksel offered, "Oh yes. There was some excitement as we walked up the slope from here to the town road. We passed the farmer's barnyard up there on the right and six white geese came running out of the barn to attack us. They were flapping their wings and screeching in a frightful fashion. I thought Beate was going to faint."

"It was very exciting!" added Baldewin. "But father was *really* brave! You should have seen him. He started flapping his arms and screaming louder than the birds. They became very scared and stopped in their tracks. Then they turned and ran as fast as they could back into the barn. It was great fun."

The audience appreciated the image of Aksel imitating and intimidating the geese and burst into laughter. When Aksel blushed, they laughed even louder.

"Well, it was very frightening," responded Beate, somewhat aggrieved. "And I did *not* faint! Anna, weren't you bothered by the same birds when you walked up the hill?"

Anna answered, "We saw the geese when we got to the barnyard but the children had gone ahead of us and were playing with them when we arrived. The birds were actually rubbing against Eva. They seemed very tame."

All eyes turned to Eva who was sitting on her father's lap smiling brightly.

Anna turned to Hans and Maggie sitting together quietly.

"Hans, did you have any trouble with the geese?" Anna asked.

"No." answered Hans quietly with downcast eyes.

"Maggie. Will you tell us about the geese?" asked Anna.

When silence persisted, Anna asked more insistently, "Maggie, I'm asking you a question! Did the geese run after you?"

Maggie looked directly at Anna and answered, "Yes. The geese came running out of the barn just as Mr. Koerber said."

She stopped speaking and looked down again.

Anna, now thoroughly aggravated, asked, "Maggie! What happened then?"

"Will you promise to believe us when we tell you what happened?" asked Maggie.

Somewhat confused, Anna answered, "Of course we will."

Maggie looked to Hans who nodded for her to tell.

"The geese came running at us making a terrible noise. They were so big and loud. We were very scared!

"I promise you, father, I was gripping Eva's hand as tight as I could but she got away from me and ran right to the birds. They stopped and became very quiet. We could hear Eva humming and making clicking noises. They folded their wings and made a circle. Eva walked up to them and they parted to let her get in the middle. When you arrived, they were rubbing against her and making humming and clicking sounds with her.

"Father, you saw her. You saw she was able to pet their heads and stroke their wings."

There was total silence. The adults sat thoughtfully, not speaking or looking at one another.

"See, Hans! I *told* you they wouldn't believe us!" yelled Maggie angrily.

"No, no, Maggie. It's alright," said Anna soothingly.

She walked over and put a hand on Hans' shoulder while she stroked Maggie's hair. "We do believe you, my dears. Eva has shown us before that she has a special way with animals and we love her for it. You must always feel free to tell us adults what you see and hear that might be worrying you. We will always listen with an open mind and heart."

Anna made tiny gathering gestures with her hands, raised her eyebrows and looked about for confirmation and support.

The other adults understood her meaning and hurried to utter words of encouragement: Yes! Of course! Certainly!

*****

The rest of the meeting was uneventful. Christina told of their peaceful church service and voiced disappointment that all the shops were closed for the Sabbath. Everyone listened politely but all her news seemed pedestrian in comparison to the other stories of the evening.

Jacob lifted the night's mood when he began to sing a familiar hymn. The other Lutherans joined in and the Mennonites listened with warm appreciation.

They were now only six miles from the Netherlands. Early the next morning they would leave their homeland forever; new cultures and new languages lay before them. These facts of life were discussed late into the night with wonder and dread.

Chapter 16

Monday, April 22: Day Fifteen on the River

It was still very cold at night but the men had decided to sleep up top. With everyone below decks, the group's body-heat made the hold uncomfortably hot by morning.

Early in the morning, Jacob was lying flat on his back at the bow wrapped in his warm woolen blanket and sleeping soundly. Over the sound of his own soft snoring, he heard a noise that made his eyes snap open. And what he saw was - nothing - nothing but a white glow in front of his eyes. It took a moment to come fully alert; but when he did, he realized he was enveloped by a cool wet fog.

Then he heard the awakening sound again. A man's voice calling out with volume and authority, "Make way! Make way!"

The captain heard the call as well, scrambled out of his bedroll, leapt to his feet and sounded the alarm. "There is a boat coming to starboard! Get overboard and release the bow and stern lines!" he commanded. "And be quick about it!" he shouted even louder.

Jacob, in charge of bow lines, was on his feet and making ready to jump over the starboard bulwark. Aksel, having been assigned the stern lines, slept at his station abaft the hatch. He too had bolted awake and was now on his feet trying to get his bearings in the dense blanket of fog.

"Make way! Make way!" called the phantom voice. He was closer by sound but still not seen.

140

"Now! shouted the unseen captain from somewhere at the stern. Over they leapt guided only by the memory of the ground beside the boat last seen the night before by the light of the full moon.

Aksel landed softly on both feet, as agile as a cat. He followed the stern line to the tie-off tree, loosed the knot, grabbed the rope and made it quickly back on board.

Jacob was not as fortunate. He landed on his right foot first and felt it go out from under him on a smooth wet rock. The rock that came up to meet his right forearm was not smooth. Its sharp edge tore into his skin; the force of the blow took his breath away.

"Make Way! Make Way!" came even closer.

Jacob heard and jumped to his feet, his pain suppressed. He loosed his rope and managed to hold it in his right hand while he used his left to pull himself back over the bulwark.

"Push off the bank!" was the next command. Each man grabbed a gaff and pushed against the bank; Jacob did so with his left arm only as his right hand had become numb and weak. The Blitz floated slowly out into the river.

"Make Way! Make Way!"

The captain materialized out of the mist, moved to the bulwark amidships and took a place between Aksel and Jacob hanging over the rail trying to catch their breath. They all saw the light at the same time - a small glowing ball of flame moving to and fro as it approached.

141

Then from the fog's white wall appeared the figure of a man swinging a lantern by his side. He moved with all deliberate speed as he approached, glided beside, and moved past the Blitz persistently calling his command, "Make Way! Make Way!"

The others appeared on deck. All eyes were now straining to see what might follow in the lantern-bearer's wake. All they saw was white and more white.

There was much rubbing of eyes and rapid blinking, intense staring and straining. But nothing to see.

"What's happening?" asked Hans as he came sleepily up on deck.

"Quiet!" said Aksel. "I think I hear something."

Everyone now stopped staring and strained to listen. Yes, there was a sound. A deep thumping rhythmical sound.

"Here they come," said the captain quietly.

And they came. Eight dark figures arrayed in a row, marching in step, their footfalls muffled by the water-choked air.

They tramped past the Blitz, bound together both by a dark thick rope draped across their shoulders and the intense effort they were using to carry it forward. Even as the last man moved beyond the stern, the rope still hung behind them floating gracefully on the thick air.

The men disappeared into the fog but the rope continued to glide by. Then with a soft bump at the bow, the barge appeared. A lone figure stood at the beam, gaff in hand, gently pushing the

Blitz aside. The barge and the man slipped silently by without a word, a gesture or a sound - and were gone.

"Set the jib!" ordered the captain. And once set, he steered the Blitz back to the embankment. Aksel and Hendrick went overboard and tied off the bow and stern lines. Anna took Jacob aside to tend to his injury.

Aksel became very agitated and angry. He marched up to the captain and demanded, "Why are those men pulling a barge in this fog? They have caused the injury to our friend!"

A sharp look from the captain caused Aksel to back away.

"Take a minute to listen to what I have to say before judging *those men* harshly," began the captain. Hendrick and Hans stole closer to listen.

The Captain's tone was hard as he explained, "Those men may have been pulling that barge for several days without stopping. There are probably two or three other men on board right now taking a rest. Those 10 or more men will rotate a few hours on and a few hours of rest.

"Since leaving Wiesbaden, it has been easy for us. We have been sailing with the current and have had the wind in our sails. That barge being pulled by *those men* is heavy laden and is going against the current and into a headwind.

"The river is running fast now as it swells with snow-melt in Switzerland. If they stop for any reason, it can take twice their number to get the boat moving again against such a current. If they are between towns, they would not find the extra hands to do so. They *must* keep going; stopping is not an option.

"I know the man who was at the bow. He is the barge master and carries cargo from Amsterdam to Wesel and back. They probably started this leg of their journey 18 miles downriver at Arnhem and they can't stop until they reach Wesel 25 miles upriver from here.

"They are courageous men who know the pain of hard work but do what is called for to put food on the table for their families."

There was silence as the captain stared at Aksel, awaiting his reply.

Aksel stood mute for a moment, then managed to say, "Thank you, Captain, for shaming me with your respect for the bargemen. I deserved your scorn. I sincerely apologize for my bad behavior."

No emotion crossed the captain's face. He simply turned away and called over his shoulder, "The fog is lifting. You two get the lines off! We set sail for the Netherlands."

The current was indeed running fast and the wind was at their backs; within an hour they had passed Schenkenschanz. A few short miles beyond, the Rhine waters found it necessary to make a choice - turn north to find the Atlantic Ocean at Amsterdam or continue a southerly course to join the sea at Rotterdam.

The Blitz and her crew swung to the north; here the waters divided and became waters calmed. The captain had warned them that their pace would slow at this point and that any headwinds would slow them even further, perhaps even to a halt. But the wind held steady at their backs so they were able to make the 17 miles from Emmerich to Arnhem in a single day.

From their anchorage, they could see the bustling activity on the piers. The towers of St. Eusebius' Church, the Groothoofdspoort and the Doorwerth Castle loomed high above the warren of buildings below.

Anna and Jacob spent the evening together quietly looking over the cityscape. They were positioned contentedly side-by-side seated on upturned barrels. Lanterns lit the riverbank and lamps flicked through the windows of homes and shops. As full darkness approached, people were still busy pulling carts, walking briskly through the streets or standing in groups discussing the day's events; all were going about their daily lives.

Anna mused, "Even if we ended our journey here and lived in this city for the rest of our lives, I don't believe I would ever get over my wonderment at the beauty and grandeur of these massive churches and fortresses. I have read about them, I have heard stories of them from travelers, but my imagination never painted a picture to match what I see now before me. It is a wonderment!"

"Yes," answered Jacob. "And we may see even more beautiful sights in Amsterdam and London. But when we leave England, we will be going into the wilderness of our new country. We will never see the likes of this life again. Do you think we will regret our decision?"

"No, I don't believe so," Anna answered. "We are leaving our families, friends, churches, comfortable homes and modern towns and cities. For that I am sad. But remember also that we are leaving behind the starvation of this past winter, the unending pillaging of war, and a tyrannical leader burying us under crushing taxes."

Anna swiveled around to face Jacob. She leaned forward, took both his hands in hers and said, "Dear Jacob, I certainly do not know what hardships we may face in the wilderness of America but I do know that we are all strong in mind, in body and in our faith in God. We will prevail."

Jacob squeezed her hands, gave her a sweet smile and echoed, "Yes, my dear aunt, we *will* prevail."

Anna turned back to face the shore. The two pilgrims sat in silence as the sun set before them.

Chapter 17

April 23 & 24: Days Sixteen and Seventeen on the River

Soon after they awoke, Anna prepared to clean Jacob's wound.

"I don't like the looks of your arm," said Anna. "It is not healing well."

Jacob examined the wound and agreed.

Anna added, "I've used up all of my marigold poultice. So until I can get a new supply, let's wash it with the goldenrod tea twice a day rather than just in the morning. I have enough flowers to last for a week and by then we should be in Amsterdam. We can find a some merchant there to replenish my supply."

Anna had treated many a farmer's wound in her home village. She had learned to clean the wound immediately with soap and water to get out the dirt. She knew this step was mandatory if the cut contained any manure. She had tried different soaps and waters and found that rainwater and spring water worked well but water straight from the cow-pasture creek did not. In fact, that water seemed to make things worse. The type of soap didn't seem to matter at all so she used whatever she had at hand.

Her mother had taught her to treat wounds with a poultice of marigold flowers. Anna always used the poultice but expanded the flower's use by boiling water and adding its petals to make a medicinal tea. When she used the *tea* and soap to scrub the wound, there was seldom any pus to treat and there was quicker healing. Then she found that if she boiled a linen cloth with the tea and used it to wash the wound and make a poultice, her results improved further. And finally, if she washed her hands in a cooled tea before tending to the wound, the healing sped along even faster. She was so successful with this technique that her neighbors came to her immediately for any bleeding wound and put up with the stinging pain of soapy scrubbing.

She never tried boiled water and soap alone for wound cleansing. What possible benefit could boiled water have over just pure spring water? It had to be the effects of the marigold flowers. Even though she was unaware of the reason for its effectiveness, boiled water tea and soap promoted healing; and so she used it.

*****

Soon after breakfast, they pushed off from Arnhem. The current held slow and steady, the sun yielded up increasing warmth, and the skies stretched from horizon to horizon sharp-blue and clear. The winds were fair but fell off periodically; for short periods the Blitz was completely becalmed by brisk headwinds.

"We're in irons again!" was the captain's mild curse whenever the Blitz came to a halt.

In spite of the starts and stops, they were able to make the twelve miles to Rhenen by early evening. Spirits remained high.

At the anchorage at Rhenen, Anna and Jacob once again spent time together at the bow tending to his wound and sharing their amazement at the scope of the city before them.

"That is the church tower I will remember among all others," offered Anna. "How can it be that mere men were able to imagine and then build such a thing?"

Jacob had no trouble spotting the object of Anna's awe. Though they could not see the church's main sanctuary, which was obscured by the intervening shops and pier warehouses, the three tiered tower stood out clearly against the sky.

"That's St. Cunera Church," said the captain.

Anna startled at his voice. He was right behind her but she had not heard him coming.

"He moves like a cat," she thought. "Even those big boots of his make no noise when he walks the deck."

The captain seemed not to notice the reaction to his sudden appearance and continued, "At the beginning, it was Catholic. But it's been Protestant for a very long time. They just kept the Saint's name as she was a local woman. They think she was murdered and buried on a hill o'er the town."

"Oh my, said Anna. "Did that happen recently?"

"Not really" answered the captain with the hint of a smile. "I would judge it about fourteen hundred years ago."

Anna gave him a sharp look. Was he making fun of her? No. He was not mocking her. He wore a warm smile on his face and a sparkle of kindness in his eyes. Anna opened her own broad smile and they laughed together.

"He has a nice laugh and a pleasant face when he smiles," thought Anna. "Why have we not seen this side of him before? But then, we know nothing of his life and what hardships may have been laid upon his shoulders. It's always best not to judge."

The captain had come to join them in the evening wound care.

The day after Jacob's injury, the captain had asked Anna for permission to observe her wound treatment. Jacob had told him of her many successes with injured farmers in their home village.

"We river men have accidents too," he said. "The laborers look to me for guidance in many matters including their injuries. I would like to learn from you how to better manage their wounds. May I observe your methods or help you in some fashion?"

"Most certainly," Anna had answered. "You may do both. I would ask your permission to boil water twice a day over the cooking pan below if you would not consider that too dangerous on your ship."

"That will be possible if the ship is anchored or is riding quietly," replied the captain. "I will tell you if it is too rough. I look forward to learning from you."

So for the rest of the journey, whenever he was not engaged in managing the ship, he came to observe and then to participate in Jacob's care.

Anna was pleasantly surprised at the captain's approach to his new learning challenge. His spade-sized hands were thick and calloused but were facile and tender as he handled Jacob's bandages. His concentration was absolute when watching Anna's demonstrations. He was never too proud to admit his ignorance of Anna's knowledge and was quick to ask good questions.

He was an apt pupil and quickly retained her answers. They made a good team. Jacob's arm was healing at a steady rate.

The following day, their 17th day on the river, they reached Wijk bij Duurstede. Once again they had sailed twelve miles downriver. The anchoring chores were completed and the dinner was prepared. There was a light rain falling, so everyone was below decks for the meal. The captain was seated on the chest that had served to block the entrance to the hiding space under the carpets.

At the completion of the meal, the captain stood, and went up to check the weather and found that it had stopped raining.

He called down into the hold, "Mr. Koerber and Mr. Schäfer, would you please bring the sailor's chest up on deck." The men struggled but managed to do so. The others followed and gathered around the captain and the chest at the stern.

"When we left Wiesbaden, Mr. Kramer entrusted this chest to me and asked that I open it when we were close to our destination. I do not know what it holds but he said there would be a note in the chest to explain his intentions. So as we are now just two days from Amsterdam, I will ask Mr. Schäfer to open the chest."

Hendrick stepped forward hesitantly and stared at the chest as though it might snap open and bite him. Everyone had gathered around the chest; the excitement grew.

Christina shook his arm and commanded, "Hendrick! Open it!"

He did as his wife asked and found an envelope on top of the other contents. He made to hand it to the captain who gave a dismissive hand gesture and pointed to Jacob who took the envelope, opened it and read the enclosed letter.

    "My Dear Pilgrim Friends,

"I speak for my entire family when I tell you what a pleasure it was to have you in our home as you began your journey to your new land. We so admire your courage, good humor, optimism, and your faith in each other and our almighty God.

"Our family took counsel together and determined we should offer you some small tribute of our esteem. Hopefully our offerings will make your days easier and more enjoyable as you begin your new lives.

"And we do confess, that in some selfish way, we estimate that by using these gifts you will give some thought to us, your constant but distant friends.

"Our hopes and prayers will follow you all the days of our lives.
        Yours in Christ,
        Mr. and Mrs. Paulus Kramer and Daughters"

The eyes of the children never left the open chest while those of the adults held on Jacob's face as he read the letter.

Christina broke the silent spell. "What a lovely letter," she said. And as one, the adults' eyes darted back to the beckoning chest. What treasures lay within?

The captain took charge of the proceedings once again.

He asked, "Mrs. Seiler, will you please do the honors of distributing the contents of the chest? I suggest you hand out one item at a time and have it examined before giving out the next."

There was a murmur of assent to the plan so Anna stepped forward and reached for the first package. Each was wrapped in plain white paper.

The order of packing had obviously been well thought out; the children's gifts were on the top. No doubt it was Mrs. Kramer, who understanding the impatience of a child, had arranged the packages just so.

"This is for Hans," said Anna as she handed the boy a heavy long box. Hans held the box in the crook of his arms and just stared at it. He had never before received a wrapped present. It was a moment to be savored and remembered.

But Maggie would have none of that. "Open it, Hans! Open it!" she begged.

Hans obeyed and tore off the covering paper. Inside was an envelope addressed to him. On it was a message asking him to read the enclosed note aloud to the assemblage. Standing straight and tall, he did so.

"My Dear Hans,

"Your guardian, Mrs. Seiler, told us of the bravery and strength of spirit you have shown during your recent times of trouble. She said that in the short time she has known you that you have grown from a boy to a man. She speaks of you with great pride.

"So we decided not to give you boy's toys but rather a man's tools. The hatchet was chosen for its sturdy handle, its excellent balance and for the shape of the head that matches the birthmark on your neck."

There was a pause as everyone shifted slightly to get a better look at Hans' neck. It was true; the hatchet head and the mark were identical.

"The second blade is an adze head. You will use it to shape logs with which to build your new home. You will first have to make a handle to fit the blade head. We look to Mr. Seiler to help you fashion such a handle and to teach you how to use both of these frontier tools.

"You will find the bark spud and the drawknife to be of great use as well. You will be of great help to Mrs. Seiler and will be highly valued by your new neighbors as you use these tools to make a new life in the American wilderness."

Hans held up the tools for inspection. There was a exuberant round of applause. Jacob clapped him on the back.

Anna dabbed her eyes.

"And the next," announced Anna, "is for Maggie." She handed over the small box to the girl.

Maggie was momentarily dismayed by the small size and light weight of her package. But she lost no time tearing off the paper. Again there was a note and instructions for reading.

"Dear Maggie,

"We were told that you are a very bright young woman with great skills in needlework. The gifts enclosed should suit those needs. In time, you will of course have to replace the thread but materials for that will be available to you in your new home.

154

"The second piece of your gift was also chosen out of selfishness on our family's part. We have supplied you with two excellent writing pens, some powder with which to make ink, and some sheets of paper to begin your correspondence. We would like to designate you as the official historian of your family, friends and community. There will be many stories to tell in the months and years to come.

"We are in great hopes that you will take the time to send us word that you all are well. We know such communications take many months to make the long journey but it is possible with some effort to get such news. We look forward to hearing glad tidings from you."

Christina and Anna helped Maggie examine the pins, needles, thread, and buttons in the sewing kit and remarked with pride the choice of Maggie as their party's historian.

The men continued to closely examine Hans's gifts showing only polite interest in the tools of women's work.

Anna dabbed her eyes.

Eva received two dolls; one in the likeness of a dog and the other, a cat. They were made of discarded men's socks with buttons for eyes and nose.

As Eva squealed with delight, Anna remarked, "Those dolls will still be on her bed when she has children of her own."

Laughter and applause of agreement followed.

Anna turned her attention back to the chest. There she saw only four more packages and a single envelope. If the wrapped packages were for Christina, Hendrick, Jacob and herself, there was no present for the last child in the group, Baldewin.

She glanced over at the boy and saw the excitement in his eyes.

Aksel saw the confusion in Anna's face.

"Don't be concerned, Anna," he said. "We never met Mr. Kramer; he would have no reason to offer Baldewin a gift."

The captain broke in, "Wait! There is an envelope addressed to Mr. Koerber in the chest. Have him open that."

Aksel received the note, opened it carefully and read:

"To Mr. Aksel Koerber,

"Captain Hraban has informed us that you, your wife and son have made a perilous journey from your home in Switzerland to join our fellow countrymen on their pilgrimage to America.

"The captain has recommended you as a man of honor and has spoken heartily of your family's bravery. So with his recommendation, our family would be honored to share our good fortune with your family."

Aksel's mouth dropped open in amazement as he took out paper bills from the envelope. But he then looked confused as he did not recognize them as money.

"It is Dutch money," explained the Captain. "I made the exchange with Mr. Kramer so you would have money to spend in Amsterdam. It will go far in helping you with your travel needs."

Aksel stood stunned and mute. Beate openly wept with joy.

Anna dabbed her eyes.

The last four gifts were distributed. The notes from Mr. Kramer to the men were brief and practical.

Jacob amazed the group with a lively tune on his new voice flute. It was made of boxwood and was highly polished. The enclosed note explained that the recorder had been made in the shop of the famous Denner family of Nuremberg. This was truly a gift of immeasurable thoughtfulness. Jacob would keep his father's old and battered recorder as a silent memento of the much beloved man but would praise him aloud with this new extraordinary musical instrument.

Hendrick's parcel contained a boot maker's kit, called in the trade, St. Hugh's Bones. In the kit was a group of tools called bones and sticks to be used to slicken, smooth and compress leather: a stitching stick, a petty boy, a mounter, a shoulder stick, and a baker's brake. The two awls fit comfortably in his hand: a long one with a curved blade and a short one with a straight blade. Each had a handle of smooth boxwood, the color of Jacob's recorder.

These tools would allow Hendrick to become a successful businessman and artisan in his new life.

Finally came the women and Christina took her turn.

"My Dear Christina,

"Mrs. Kramer and my daughters were much taken by your love of books. They said they could hardly get you out of the library for meals.

"Enclosed you will find 3 books. The first is a mathematics book in German.

"The second is an adventure book by Phillipus Baldaeus with the long title of 'A True and Exact Description of the Most Celebrated East-India coasts of Malabar and Coromandel and also of the Isle of Ceylon'; written in Dutch, it has been translated into German.

"The third book, 'A Collection of Curious Travels & Voyages' is also an adventure book but it is in English, a language you will need to learn as you will be living among the English in America.

"With your love of books and learning, we are certain that you will take the role of teacher to the youth of your new community. Good reading and good health!"

Christina stood shocked and still staring at the treasures in her hands. "Oh my! Oh my! Oh my!" rolled out over and over.

She suddenly turned to leave the group. Time was wasting. She must begin her studies.

Hendrick grabbed her and stopped her flight with a stage whisper in her ear, "Wait! Anna is going to open her package!"

Anna opened her envelope and scanned it silently. She refolded the paper and carefully slipped it into a skirt pocket. It was not to be read aloud. No one questioned the decision.

Anna unwrapped her gift, closed the chest top, and placed three objects onto its surface.

All three were made of glass. There were two pairs of spectacles. The glass in both were tinged a very light brown. None of the travelers, including Anna, had ever seen such a thing before. She stood holding them in obvious bemusement.

The captain, having been apprised of their use, approached Anna. He gently took the glasses, placed the nose-piece squarely on the bridge of her nose and wrapped the attached loops of string over her ears to hold them firmly to her face.

The harsh glare of the sun that always hurt her eyes suddenly disappeared. The world took on a soft yellow cast but was clear in outline. She beamed with delight at the sight. And then, her delight was magnified. Christina walked up to her, stared into her face and exclaimed, "Anna! Your eyes are *brown*! Come look! They're *brown*!"

The two women hurried to a pan of water sitting on the deck awaiting the day's laundry. Anna leaned over and stared at her reflection. Her eyes *were* brown!

No longer would she have to wear a thick veil over her face when among strangers. She would be able to mingle with fellow pilgrims in Amsterdam and London without suffering their stares and taunts.

She went back to the chest and picked up the second pair. The captain explained that Mr. Kramer had wanted her to have a spare pair in case of breakage. He told her that the glass was from a stained glass window in a small Catholic church that had been destroyed in the recent war.

Anna answered, "Though it is from a Catholic sanctuary, I feel twice blessed at having the glass to shield my tired eyes and at having it come from a house of worship."

159

The third object was a block of clear glass. It had a flat bottom and a rounded top that fit comfortably in her palm. The captain borrowed the mathematics book from Christina and had everyone gather around. He instructed Anna to hold the glass above the writing with the flat end facing the page.

She flinched with astonishment as the words jumped up out of the page to meet her eyes. For the first time in her life, she could read without strain. Another blessing in glass was brought to her by Mr. and Mrs. Kramer. They both had seen her struggling to read a book in the library.

Everyone now had gifts for a new life: the building tools for a man, the supplies for a budding historian and seamstress, the miracle of music, the instruments for a boot-maker's life's work, books to read and teach from, and pieces of glass to make reading possible and society kind.

Mr. Kramer and his family would be remembered in all their prayers each for a lifetime.

Chapter 18

True to his word, the captain made it to Amsterdam in two days of easy sailing. It had been 27 days and nearly 300 miles since they had left their homes and former lives behind; they arrived in Amsterdam on the evening of Saturday, April 27, 1709.

They sailed through Ij Bay and into the mouth of the Amstel River where they tied up to the bank between the Blauwbrug, (the blue bridge), and the Kerkstraatbrug, (the Church Street Bridge). The pass-through width for boats of the Church Street Bridge was very narrow; the locals had nicknamed it the magere brug - the skinny bridge.

Anna and Jacob stood together on the deck and watched flickering lights come to life on the bridges. Men were using ladders to climb the lampposts to ignite the oil lamps. The light's soft glow was warm and welcoming but it was also practical; fewer people fell into the canals during the darkness of the winter's long nights.

"What a beautiful sight," marveled Anna.

"Yes, that's true," said Jacob. "And it must give many men a steady wage."

"You're right," answered the captain who, startling them as usual, had appeared silently out of nowhere. "There are hundreds of bridges that must be lit every night. And the lamp-lighters have been doing this for the past hundred years. They light the lamps each night and return each morning to snuff them out and refill the oil cans.

"It's a lifetime profession and their guild guarantees that they will make a decent wage. Many generations of the same family have put bread in their children's bellies on a lamplighter's pay." The captain continued, "It's too late for any of you to leave the ship tonight. I will go ahead and make arrangements for your departure in the morning." And so saying, he was gone.

They all gathered on deck to learn that they were to spend one more night on the Blitz.

"Does anyone know where we will be staying?" asked Hendrick.

Shrugs and wagging heads answered, "No."

Hendrick explained, "I asked him for details when we started this journey and he told me to wait until we arrived. The second time I asked, he just glared at me. I didn't ask a third."

They would have to patiently await the captain's return. In the meantime, they would pack up their belongings and be ready to leave the Blitz first thing in the morning.

It was after midday before the captain returned. He supervised the unloading of their gear from the deck onto their two carts. Jacob took his position in front pulling the larger wagon and Hendrick followed behind with Anna's smaller cart.

The going was easy on these paved streets compared to the rutted muddy trails of the German hills. Captain Hraban led the way, the women and children brought up the rear.

They struck out to the north along the banks of the Amstel, crossed the bridge over the Herengracht canal and turned to the east. In a quarter of a mile they reached Muiderstraat and turned left and quickly came upon a massive brick building as tall as five normal houses. A row of square windows ringed the upper level and below each one an arched window several stories in height stared down upon the street.

"What is this place?" asked Hendrick.

"It is the Esnoga, the Portuguese Synagogue," answered the captain. "It's the largest Jewish place of worship in the world."

The captain called a halt and told them to wait. He entered a side door to the synagogue closing it behind him. A few minutes later, he reappeared with two women and led them straight to Jacob.

"Grandmother and Mother, may I present Mr. Jacob Seiler," he said to the utter amazement of all. "Mr. Seiler, please greet my grandmother, Mrs. Severin Hraban and my mother, Mrs. Aharon Hraban.

Jacob recovered from his astonishment and with a slight bow of his head, gallantly greeted the two women, "It is my pleasure indeed to meet the family of our honored ship's captain."

Both women smiled at this appropriate acknowledgment of the importance of their son and grandson.

The captain explained, "My parents and grandparents have been respected members of this synagogue since it was founded. My grandfather Hraban was one of the master brick-masons who built the sanctuary in 1671.

"At the beginning of construction, my father was a young apprentice with the brick-masons and was put to work carrying mortar for the masons. In the fourth and final year of construction, he had advanced to journeymen and worked proudly shoulder to shoulder with my grandfather.

"My mother and grandmother have also served the community well; for the past thirty-five years they have helped to clean the sanctuary each week. We are all proud to be members of the Sephardic Jewish Community of Amsterdam."

The adults looked from one to another and said silently with their eyes, "Our captain is a Jew!"

The younger Mrs. Hraban stepped closer to Jacob and said, "My husband and I will be honored to have you and your lovely daughters as our house guests as you await your ship to Brielle. It will be wonderful to have children's voices in the house again!"

"But what of the rest of us?" asked Christina anxiously.

The captain answered, "There are two other German-speaking families not far from here who are eager to share their homes with you. Jacob, would you please leave the girls with my mother and continue on with us so you can learn your way back and forth?"

Maggie and Eva settled in easily; the rest of the travelers marched off again. They crossed the Amstel and made their way to the east bank of the Singel. Several more turns brought them to the small street of Begijnensteeg where two families were waiting to greet them: the Jansens, a Lutheran family, with whom Anna, Hans, Christina, and Hendrick would stay and the Van Brearleys, a Mennonite family, with whom the three Koerbers would stay.

The two Dutch families were close neighbors and best of friends. Each had a busy shop on the first floor of their building and living quarters above. For the short while the visitors would be with them, they determined to have the men-folk sleep in the shop and the ladies would occupy the upstairs.

Everyone was in wonderful spirits. The Dutch were anxious to hear of the travelers' adventures and the travelers were eager to learn more of life in this bustling modern city. They were all talking at once; conversation was generously mixed with excited laughter.

Then out of the shadows stepped the captain. A short cough and a raised hand brought the crowd to sudden silence and focused attention.

"Tomorrow my family will join others in our community for a day of festivities. According to our custom we have all observed thirty-three days of quiet living. But tomorrow will be a day of celebration, the day we call Lag LaOmer. During the daylight hours, there will be outdoor singing and dancing. Food and drink will be plentiful.

"By tradition, three year-old boys will get their first haircuts and older men will shave their beards.

Candles will be lit in the synagogue and at night there will be a huge bonfire - a *huge* bonfire!"

The captain's eyes lit up with all the brilliance of the conflagration he was envisioning.

And with ever increasing enthusiasm, he continued, "And my mother and father would like all of you to be our guests for the day!"

A shaft of light from the setting sun pierced the darkness of the narrow alleyway and found the earth had stopped. No sound vibrated, no motion stirred. Statues stood in frozen postures, mute in its yellow-red light.

Time passed; time stood still.

Eyes sank inward as minds groped with a picture of themselves mingling with a community of Jews on a Sunday morning at a synagogue.

The floodlight disappeared behind the rooftops and the silence was broken by the sound of youthful voices shouting, "Oh please, Father! There is to be a bonfire! Please may we go?"

Maggie and Baldewin were in clamorous concert imploring their fathers to agree to this wondrous invitation.

The captain saw and believed he understood his invited guests' hesitation. After all, he was a man of Amsterdam, the most progressive and tolerant city in Europe where Jews and Christians, both Catholic and Protestant, had lived and worked with each other in peace for hundreds of years.

Granted, there were some tensions between members of the two Jewish populations; his Sephardic brethren and the Ashkenazim lived separately and worshiped separately but there was never bloodshed. In fact, the two sects' synagogues were just across the bridge from one another and their congregations would mingle together tomorrow at the festivities.

No. It would not enter his head that the hesitation could be due to distrust, to fear, to hatreds taught in some Christian Churches against "the killers of Christ".

He could not suspect any such sentiments from these very people he had come to like and trust in their weeks together on the river. It simply had to be that they were worried about not having the time to go to their own places of worship on the morrow for their Sunday services.

And so he jumped in to assuage their concerns, "But I forgot," he said apologetically. "You will want to go to your own churches in the morning. That would be just fine. The real celebration won't get underway until after the noon hour when the food and drink will begin to be served. And the synagogue is so close to here that you would be able to come and go throughout the day. I'm certain you would all enjoy the music in the evening and I can tell from their pleadings that the children would love the bonfire. May I tell my parents that you will all be able to attend?"

Jacob broke the silence, "Captain Hraban, I and my family will be honored to accept the invitation of your parents to join them tomorrow in their home and place of worship. Anna smiled broadly and nodded in agreement. Maggie and Hans celebrated the decision. Baldewin joined them and turned expectantly to his parents. Beate, eyes riveted to the floor, said nothing.

Aksel shuffled his feet and mumbled, "We will see, Baldewin. We don't know how long services will be. It may not be possible. We will see." And to the group he added, "Please excuse us. It has been a long day and my wife is very tired."

Aksel took Beate's hand and motioned Baldewin to follow. They turned and walked quickly to the house of Cornelis and Antje Van Brearley and disappeared through the door.

The Van Brearleys watched them go but stayed to conference silently with the Jansens. They looked to one another, then true to their Amsterdam upbringing, shrugged a "why not?" and announced their intentions to join the party.

"Excellent!" echoed across the alleyway as the captain stamped his approval on the vote. "Jacob will know the way back and will come tomorrow to gather you all together. I look forward to seeing you then."

*****

That evening, the Koerbers remained absent from the others as the Schäfers and the Seilers gathered together in the Jansen's living quarters to discuss the day's events.

Cornelis began, "Josina and I have lived here all our lives and never seen the inside of either synagogue. During their services on Friday night, they light candles and the windows facing the street blaze with flickering light.

"There have to be hundreds of them! Hundreds and hundreds! It is quite beautiful. I surely hope we will be invited inside!"

Hans enthusiastically agreed and couldn't stop talking about the *huge* bonfire!

Both Hendrick and Christina seemed confused and bemused by the upcoming celebrations but were quickly caught up by the excitement of the Jansens; by evening's end, they were wishing away the hours until they could make their way to this new, foreign and exotic land tinged with a hint of danger and fear.

They were about to enter the company of Jews - *hundreds* of Jews; a people they had never met before and had been warned of by their religion since childhood.

Yes! Amsterdam *was* splendid!

Anna sat quietly to one side, slipping in and out of an awareness of the surrounding excitement. A smile passed to her from across the room was instinctively returned; a nod was mirrored back to the sender.

But Anna was in a world outside this room, this street, this city, this country. She was at home silently communing with that one person with whom she shared all thoughts that defined her.
The thoughts of a bright woman with a dark side: those of a woman filled with warmth but capable of arctic cold: of a devout woman who trusted her God but at the time of her husband's murder doubted His existence. A complete woman, a complicated woman, and at present, a very confused woman.

"Peter, what is wrong with me?" she asked.

"For all my life, I have been the outsider, the object of fear.

"As a child, I was taunted and pummeled by the village children. As adults, they no longer attacked me with words or deeds. Instead, they shunned me; they turned inward and became silent. Their painful words were only spoken among themselves; secret words that bred potential danger.

"And then you entered my life. The boy who had watched me from afar - who had never hit or taunted. That shy little boy who never chased the frightened little girl - who now as a strong and confident man lovingly chased a shunned woman; and I was that woman who lovingly and gratefully allowed capture.

"But Peter! I have become them! How can this be?

169

"For the past weeks, I have been under the protection of another strong and confident man. A man I knew to be held in the highest esteem by our benefactor, Mr. Kramer. A brave man. A man hiding warmth behind a stern face. A man with a hunger for learning. A strict but fair-minded man. A man with all the qualities you would have admired had you known him.

"And I admired him. I trusted him with my life and those of the children.

"No, no no! That is not *right*! I *do* admire him. I *do* trust him. I still *do*.

"But, Peter, when he introduced his mother - his *mother*, for God's sake - and I knew he was a Jew, something awful happened inside me. I was frightened. I was repelled!

"How could I, the person feared and shunned for being different in color of skin and eyes, fear and shun this good man for nothing more than his having a different way of worshiping God?

"Where did I learn such a thing? To fear a man for being a Jew? There have been no Jews in my life.

"Well, yes, the pastor read from the Book of John this past Good Friday and all others before:

'Here is your king,' Pilate said to the Jews.

But they shouted, 'Take him away! Take him away!

Crucify him!'

"Peter, remember the time you became enraged at those local boys taunting the Jewish family in the market? That poor young couple with two small children just passing through our town trying to escape some horrible troubles to the north?

"You led the boys by their ears to their fathers for punishment then brought the family home for safety and a meal. I must confess, I was nervous at their appearance in dress and hair. But then, the children were frightened at seeing my eyes.

"It is so complicated, this feeling of fear when confronted with people different from myself. All I can do now is follow your example. I cannot bring the captain and his family to our home for a meal but I can bring them home into my heart.

"Hans and I will join the others and make a joyful noise unto the Lord at the local Jewish Synagogue on this Sunday afternoon!

"I know you will find that worth a smile.

"Oh, my dear Peter, I miss you every day, with every breath I take. I was such a better person when you hovered over me."

Chapter 19

Sunday was a long and exhausting day both physically and emotionally.

Jacob returned early from the Hraban household with Maggie and Eva. Questioning glances by Anna were met with Jacob's, "I'll tell you *later*."

Cornelis and Antje Van Brearley, with the Koerbers in tow, stopped by the Jansen house to say that they were off to services at Kerk bij 't Lam just a short walk up the Singel.

"Will we be seeing you later this afternoon?" asked Anna trying to determine Aksel's decision concerning the synagogue visit.

"My family is of the opinion that we should attend. I will pray on the matter at services this morning and give you my answer early enough for you all to make your plans," Aksel promised with an awkward smile.

Beate gave a shy glance to Anna; Baldewin sent a hopeful look to Hans. Aksel took a moment to readjust his serious face and then led them away.

The Lutherans had even a shorter distance to walk to reach their house of worship. The Oude Lutherse Kerk was just off the Spui, facing the Singel, and less than a two minute walk. The Jansens gathered their flock and led the way.

In single file, they skirted along the edge of the Spui against the north wall of an imposingly massive brick building. When they turned the corner they found the west side of that building to be the front of the church.

"We're here," announced Cornelis.

"It doesn't look much like a church," whispered Anna to Jacob. Jacob said not a word, answering only by more firmly gripping her elbow and shepherding her towards the door.

All doubts left Anna's mind as she entered the sanctuary. The tall street windows at her back lit the interior with a glowing pulsating light.

She looked back and saw that the rays streaming through the glass were reflecting the movement of the water in the Singel. She also saw the pipes of an organ reaching to the roof.

Her heart leapt into her throat and threatened to stop when those pipes rang out the first chords of her favorite hymn, "All Praise to God, Who Reigns Above."

They slid into a pew and joined the singing. Voices rang out in Dutch and German to the all-familiar tune.

> All praise to God, who reigns above,
> The God of all creation,
> The God of wonders, power, and love,
> The God of our salvation!
>
> With healing balm my soul He fills,
> The God who every sorrow stills,
> To God all praise and glory!

The organist played heartily from behind and voices rained down upon them from the balconies on either side.

For the remainder of the hour, Anna understood some parts of the service, some responsorial readings, which were similar in

Dutch and German. She knew when to stand and sit and managed to hum the tunes of two other hymns. There were words in the sermon so similar to German that she could catch their meaning but the message as a whole eluded her.

So her mind was wandering when she was startled as Jacob jumped to his feet. Looking around, she saw that about 50 other people were standing. Those who remained seated were craning their necks to get a look at those on their feet; and then they started applauding!

The Jansens were seated and looking at Anna with wide smiles; they also were applauding with gusto.

"What's happening?" asked Anna.

"Shhhhh," answered Jacob.

The pastor looked down from his elevated pulpit and said something containing the word, "Welcome."

A young man ascended the stairs of the pastor's elevated pulpit and translated into German, "The pastor wishes to welcome you all to our church. Our congregation wishes you Godspeed on your long and arduous journey to America.

"He wishes to let you know that there will be a prayer said at each service in your behalf for the next year; he hopes that you will have found safety and peace in your new homes and churches by that time."

The young man descended the stairs and the pastor invited the congregants to rise. Then in his firm bass voice he led them in the Twenty-third Psalm. This universal hymn of blessing resounded in Dutch and German. Anna couldn't help it - she began to cry and could recite no further than, "The Lord is my Shepherd, I shall not want."

The pipe organ bid them goodbye with the recessional hymn, "Now, the Hour of Worship O'er".

> Now, the hour of worship o'er,
> Teaching, hearing, praying, singing,
> Let us gladly God adore,
>
> For His Word our praises bringing;
> For the rich repast He gave us
> Bless the Lord, who deigned to save us.

On the street, they were greeted warmly by the Dutch; their fellow German exiles eagerly introduced themselves and sought to exchange tales of their Rhine travels.

An hour of conversation passed quickly but they had to excuse themselves to get ready for their synagogue visit. All agreed that they would be able to resume their talks when they arrived in London.

"We will find you there," Jacob promised one particular family, the Dygerts.

"After all, how many more of us can there be than what joined us at church this morning?" wondered Anna aloud.

When they made it back to the Jansens', Baldewin was on the front stoop with Hans and both were laughing and gesturing wildly. There was no question that Aksel had decided to let his son see the *huge* bonfire. Upstairs, Beate was helping Josina prepare the midday meal. They were talking with great

175

animation and Beate was bright and cheerful. For certain, she was going to the synagogue as well.

"It's a good thing," thought Anna. "Thank you, Aksel."

The Hrabans had invited the Jansens and the Van Brearleys to come as well. The women were beside themselves with anticipation. Questions flew back and forth with no possible chance of answers. All was speculation at what they would find when visiting this new and exotic world. They chattered and laughed. Hands flew in food preparation and in feigned exasperation over their fellows' lack of helpful particulars.

The men calmly stood back and watched in wonderment and confusion.

"Women are different," observed Jacob. The other males hummed and nodded their agreement.

*****

At dinner, Jacob disappointed them with his lack of any details concerning his overnight stay with the Hrabans.

All he would say was, "They were very busy planning and preparing for today's festivities. The girls went to bed early. I asked if I could help but they excused me from all labors so I went to bed as well."

Not to be deterred, Christina asked, "What is their house like?"

"Like any other house, I suppose," answered Jacob to the consternation of the women. "You will all just have to wait until we visit this afternoon. They have suggested we be there at five o'clock."

For the occasion, the women unpacked their freshest clothes and scrubbed the children thoroughly. The men polished their boots to a brilliant shine. All in all, they turned out clean and smartly dressed. Anna inspected her brood with obvious satisfaction.

At five o'clock sharp, Jacob led them all up to the door of the Hraban household. His knock was answered by the captain's elderly grandmother.

"Please come in, my friends. Welcome to our home," she offered.

The men stepped aside and the women cautiously entered the hallway. Mrs. Hraban motioned them to the left into a large well-lit parlor.

"Please have a seat and make yourselves comfortable," she said as she disappeared down the hallway.

Overstuffed sky-blue chairs and a long couch with curved arm rests at either end allowed plentiful seating for the women and girls. The men and boys stood. They waited.

After a minute or two had passed, shifting eyes became swiveling heads as the ladies took courage to search the room for any exotic objects. Their gaze fell upon a tall, stately intricately carved cabinet on the wall opposite the windows.

They rose as one to peer behind its glass front and found a gracefully sculptured silver chalice nestled next to a tall blue glass decanter, a long silver stick with the shape of a hand at its end, two matched candlesticks and a nine-branched silver candelabrum. The silver of all the pieces was highly polished and stunning.

The men just stared ahead, shifted from one foot to the other and held the room's silence close to their chests.

Once again, came a surprising entrance by Captain Hraban.

"Good afternoon," he shouted.

His greeting was as electrifying as a thunderbolt. But by now, his sudden appearances had become a legend with the travelers and they found their own startled reactions to be humorous; all tension was broken by their own soft laughter.
"Good afternoon, Captain," echoed the chorus.

"My family is honored by your visit. We all hope you will enjoy the festivities of the evening. But before we begin the celebrations, we ask you to join us in the synagogue for prayers."

At that moment, the captain's mother, Esther, entered the room on the arm of a tall man of imposing stature. He was wearing a fringed shawl over his shoulders that fell to his knees. A tiny black cap was near invisible against his raven-black hair.

He spoke. "Good afternoon ladies and gentlemen. I am Rabbi Aharon Hraban, your captain's father. My family welcomes you to our home and to our community."

Jacob managed to recover his power of speech.

"Rabbi Hraban, we thank you and your family for your hospitality. It is very kind of you to include us."

"It is good that you all could come," the Rabbi continued, looking approvingly at the number of his Christian neighbors

178

who filled his parlor. "We invite you now to join us in prayer before the festivities."

"So, ladies, please follow Mrs. Hraban and, you gentlemen, follow my son." So saying he turned and left the room, leaving in his wake the stunned gathering once again struck into silence.

"Come, ladies!" commanded Esther with a laugh. "Follow me." As one, they shot to their feet and sailed in the wake of their captain's mother. They entered the sanctuary through the door for women, climbed stairs to the lower of the two balconies, and were directed to seats in the front row.

Anna sat between Christina and Beate. Each was holding - no - crushing one of her hands in a death-grip. However, Anna was feeling no pain. She was in rapture at the scene before her. The synagogue was breathtakingly beautiful.

No words would come. Only a repeated exclamation filled her mind, "Mein Gott in Himmel! Mein Gott in Himmel!"

It was the candles - the hundreds and hundreds of white flickering candles: candles that stood erect from elegant brass chandeliers suspended from the soaring ceiling and candles shimmering in candelabras that covered all available flat surfaces.

The huge open space of the sanctuary was ablaze with light.

Anna looked from side to side into the faces of her companions where she saw in their eyes the reflected dancing light of the candles and her own expression of awe. Still no words would come.

The entrance of the men onto the floor below drew her attention. The men had followed the captain as instructed and at the main entrance had been fitted out with their own black skull caps.

As they were led to their seating, they looked down to discover they were walking on soft sand; when the captain abruptly stopped they ran up against each other in mild confusion.

They recovered their bearings as the captain turned and motioned for them to enter a line of benches arranged in a long row that reached from a raised dais at the back of the synagogue to a cross aisle at the front. They were in the back of four such rows that faced across the center aisle to an identical rank of benches.

The lights caught Jacob's eyes as quickly as they had captured Anna's. Just as quickly, his gaze fell in wonder at the beauty of the wood throughout the sanctuary. His seat, on the end of a bench, had an armrest. The wood was dark and highly polished.

The tree's life shone out from the interior and the surface reflected the light of the chandeliers above. He ran his hand over the wood; another man's learned craft had created this surface free of even the slightest imperfection. Lights were beautiful but this workmanship was awe-inspiring.

Anna took a deep breath, her first in several minutes, and looked about for other marvels. She found them in the four massive stone columns supporting the roof. There were six smaller pillars holding up the women's balcony facing her from which women's eyes smiled back at her, their faces softened by the candlelight. And like Jacob, she began to marvel at the beauty of the woodwork.

Just as Christina and Beate were beginning to loosen their death grip on Anna's hands, from somewhere below, out of their sight, came the swelling tones of a full and longing male voice. His song welled up to fill the building's every inch of space.

Anna understood not a word of this new tongue but there was no doubt in her mind that their meaning was a joyful prayer sent up to his God. His tone, so pure in pitch and meaning, bristled the hairs on her arms and brought tears to her eyes. And Christina and Beate again crushed her hands. The song ended on a long plaintive note.

After a full minute of silence, a man began to speak.

Mrs. Hraban, sitting right behind Anna, leaned forward and whispered into Anna's ear, "He is telling the congregation that you, your family and your friends are attending prayers with us. He is explaining your long journey and asking all worshiping here tonight to keep you in their prayers as you continue your travels. He asks them also to join the song leader, the cantor, in a song in your honor."

The singer's voice rose again. But this time, his words were echoed by the whole congregation.

> "Mizmor ledhavidh Adonay ro`iy lo' 'echsar
> bin'othdeshe' yarbiytseniy `al-mey menuchoth
> yenahaeniy"

Mrs. Hraban began her translation,

> "The Lord is my shepherd; I shall not want.
> He makes me lie down in green pastures."

This time, Anna was just able to keep her composure. She was able to sing out from her heart the responsorial hymn. The other Christian women quickly understood what was happening and joined her in song - some in German and others in Dutch.

The Christian men below heard her clear strong voice, saw the ecstasy in her face, and answered the cantor's call with their own male chorus. Hearts, minds and souls of all persuasions reached up to praise their God.

The evening's entertainment after the service was delightful; there was singing and dancing by young and old alike. Anna loved the food and tried a little bit, or as Mrs. Hraban laughed, "a bisl" of everything.

She learned new names for foods such as tabbouleh, couscous, hummus, matzah, cholent, tsimmes, blintz, and spices like saffron, cinnamon and rosewater. And the bonfire lived up to the expectations of the boys. And that included all the boys - even those over the age of twenty!

This splendid night would give the participants stories to tell and retell all the rest of their days.

Chapter 20

Monday, April 29

Anna left for the market at first light. The Jansens had been totally confused by Anna's shopping list. They were unfamiliar with the names of any of the plants, leaves, or roots she sought. In the end, they had suggested the vegetable market as the most likely place to find her items and directed her back towards the Amstel River.

She wrapped herself in her cloak and set off. It was cold, overcast and damp, but thankfully not raining. The street lamps had already been extinguished so it was very dark in the smaller streets shadowed by tall buildings; her tinted glasses made it even darker.

The streets were already bustling with people bringing their wares to market. She walked past the Lutheran Church and turned south along the Singel. She wandered for almost an hour, passing markets for fish, for cheese and butter, peat, straw, flowers, and even one for pieces of wood. She finally came upon the vegetable market but was thoroughly frustrated to find no medicinal leaves or roots for sale.

She tried to ask for further directions but her dialect was not understood by passers-by. She was becoming frightened that she would not be able to properly treat Jacob's wound.

She tried one more time to make herself understood, but the pleasant man to whom she spoke just shook his head and muttered a Dutch word that sounded like the German, "sorry." She replied with a weak smile and a German, "thank you" and turned sharply to move on.

As she did so, she bumped heavily into a little girl - knocking her to the ground. Anna reached down to help the poor thing to her feet and found herself looking into the beautiful face of an elderly woman, not a child at all.

Completely flustered, Anna still managed to give aid. So quickly the ruffled woman was standing before her. Anna towered over her; she could look straight down and see the top of the woman's stark-white headdress.

"I am so sorry, Madam," Anna said as she helped the lady rearrange her garments. "I am so *sorry!*"

"I don't seem to be hurt," the lady replied. "Only my pride may have been injured with my skirts up over my head," she added with a gentle laugh.

It took Anna a moment to realize that she had actually understood what the lady had said.

"You speak German!" Anna gasped.

"Yes, I know," came the reply with an even longer laugh. "I have seen that you are having trouble making yourself understood here in the market. May I be of some assistance?"

"Oh yes, dear lady, that would be so kind of you. I am in dire need of a medicinal plant. I have wandered about for some time now but I haven't found anything of a medicinal nature being offered for sale."

"In Amsterdam they do not sell such items in a general market. You have to go to the apotheker, the pharmacist, to get them. There is one close by and he speaks both Dutch and German; I can take you there if you wish."

"I would be so grateful if you would. Otherwise I might wander these streets into all hours of the night."

"My dear woman, you do not want to be found walking the streets at night alone. Some might get the wrong impression of your intentions even if you were *not* escorted with flute music and drum rolls as required by law for women of that profession."

Anna noted the quick wink and shy smile. After a moment's pause, she took the lady's meaning. A blush rose in her cheeks and very quietly she murmured, "Oh dear!"

Her new friend's laugh rose again at her blushing. It was an infectious laugh that demanded participation. The two women now found themselves facing one another, holding hands; their laughter causing those around them to smile in response. It was a wonderful meeting.

They walked side by side on the cobbled street introducing themselves as they went. Anna Seiler met Agatha Arents.

Anna had to take short mincing steps so as to not outpace her diminutive companion.

"If it is not too personal, may I inquire what it is you are searching for?" asked Agatha.

Anna answered quickly, "No. No. I can certainly tell you the reason for my search. I need to make a poultice of marigold flowers. My nephew, Jacob, cut his arm and it was festering. The poultice has drawn out the pus and hurried his healing. But I have now used all my marigold supply. I only require two more days of treatment for Jacob, but I will need a full supply to take with me to America."

"Do such things really work?"

"Oh yes. I have used the marigold treatment many times at home with good success."

Agatha became quiet. She cast down her eyes and withdrew into her own thoughts. They walked in silence for several minutes before stopping at the house with the sign, "Apotheker," over the lintel.

Agatha knocked at the door and it was opened by a young girl.

Agatha asked in Dutch, "Young lady, is the pharmacist available for consultation? And is it true he speaks German?"

"My father does indeed speak *perfect* German. And can also make himself understood in English. He is a very learned man," said his daughter with obvious pride.

And the part about being learned was in fact true. In 1638 the leaders of the city had allowed the pharmacists to form their own guild. Until that year, pharmacists and physicians had been members of the hawkers' guild so they were very low in the societal ranks.

After the pharmacists formed their own guild, their members demanded a certain level of knowledge for those seeking entry into their society.

Before a prospective pharmacist could start his practice, the board of the guild examined him on his knowledge of Latin, herbs and the production of powders and ointments. If he passed these exams he had to pay a substantial fee to the guild for admittance.

As with all the other guilds, the requirements for educational standards and the payment of significant fees limited the numbers entering the field of endeavor; this had the desired effect of limiting competition for the active members.

The girl continued, "My father is just now finishing his morning meal. It should be only a few minutes before he can speak with you. I will tell him you are here and wish his professional help. Please take a seat at the table and wait."

As instructed, they took seats on the upturned logs next to the sidewalk table and waited. At first, they commented approvingly on the maturity and poise of the young girl.

But then Agatha offered these contrary observations and conclusions, "Folk in the city often talk of their concerns that the youth of today are not living up to the standards of their elders. It is true that not all are falling away from proper behavior but there are many that have very bad manners. They're loud in public. They're thoughtless in their manner of dress. They show disrespect to their elders and the authorities in word and deed. It is a shame that so many of our youth are going in such an unfortunate direction."

Anna opened her mouth to comment but Agatha was thoroughly caught up in her topic and pushed ahead.

"I once visited in the home of a successful merchant and saw his children interrupt the conversation of the adults at the dinner table and gobble up dainties without asking permission of their parents. And they failed to rise when the guest of honor was introduced in the parlor. Imagine! Whatever will become of our society if the young do not adhere to proper behavior and etiquette?"

187

Anna again started to respond. She wished to reassure Agatha that the behavior of the youth of the countryside seemed to be in good order. But she was dramatically interrupted by an elderly, tall, thin man with full beard who exploded out of the Apotheker shop with the bellowed greeting, "Now my good ladies, what can I do for you?"

Anna thought, "Thank goodness, he speaks German!"

To the pharmacist, she snapped, "Good gracious, sir, you near startled us to death!"

"What?" he barked.

"I said that you almost frightened us to death," Anna repeated.

"You'll have to speak up, dear lady. I am somewhat deaf."

No - that was not entirely true. He was not "somewhat deaf", he was near deaf as a stone.

Not only did they have to yell for him to hear *them*, he found it necessary to shout at full volume in order to hear *himself*. It was all quite painful to the ears.

Putting her surprise and pain aside, Anna forged ahead with her request.

"Sir!" she shouted at him. "I have a nephew who has a festering *wound*. I have come to you for a poultice of marigold flowers to help his healing."

"I have never heard of a Mary Gold," he yelled. "Does she practice herbal medicine in your home town?"

"Marigold! The flower! Marigold - not Mary Gold," she shouted back.

"Oh! The flower! Why didn't you say so?" he asked somewhat annoyed.

"I don't have any," he pronounced throwing his hands up in resignation.

"Oh my! Oh my! What am I to do for his wound?" anguished Anna.

"Who has a wound?" he asked.

"My *nephew*!"

"Your nephew has a wound?"

"Yes! My nephew has a festering wound!"

"Well! Why didn't you say so in the first place?"

Anna, now thoroughly outdone, screamed, "I did tell you so! And now you tell me you have no marigold available."

"You don't have to shout at me, madam. I'm not totally deaf, you know."

"I'm sorry sir. It's just that I'm so worried about my nephew, *Jacob*," she responded in a slightly less shrill voice but with firm emphasis on her loved one's name.

"Jacob? Who's Jacob?"

"My *nephew*. The man with the festering wound!"

"Well! Why don't you ask me for the proper medicine for such a trouble?"

"I asked you for the marigold and you told me you had none!"

"Well, yes, I did say I have no marigold! But I did *not* say I have no *treatment* for such a wound. An ointment of yarrow works wonders in these circumstances! And I do have yarrow," he said with a deafeningly loud open-handed smack on the table surface.

"Yikes!" they exclaimed. They stumbled backwards but quickly recovered their balance and composure.

Anna grabbed Agatha's arm and said excitedly, "I have used the yarrow ointment in the past and know it to be as effective as the marigold. I am *so* pleased!"

The old man turned his attention to Agatha and slipped into Dutch. "It is a long process and one that only a true professional can accomplish."

"What did he say?" asked Anna.

Agatha translated and then loudly reminded the man to speak German.

"Wasn't I speaking German?" he inquired in German.

"You are now," answered Anna. "Please continue."

"I will have a supply of the yarrow ointment fully prepared on the morrow. My special concoction has been stewing for the required two weeks. It was then I mixed the fat of a large and healthy Amsterdam pig with the yarrow leaves and cooked the brew over a low fire."

"Tomorrow I will melt the fat again and strain out the flower parts. It will be the perfect medicine for your needs."

A self-satisfied smile burst onto his face revealing a row of uneven teeth flecked with areas of decay.

"He could use some of my help with my tooth-pulling tool," thought Anna.

Anna, now much relieved, shook the old man's hand vigorously and promised to return in the morning. But then she thought to ask, "How much money will I need for the purchase?"

"You will have enough ointment for ten days for a schelling," he answered.

Turning to Agatha, Anna asked, "Is that a lot of money?"

"It is about 6 pfenigge," Agatha answered.

"Oh! That is fine! Only six pfenigge!" Anna proclaimed.

"Who's Fennig?" he asked to the backs of the two ladies leaving his shop and laughing as they fled.

*****

As they strolled beside the Singel Canal, Agatha exclaimed, "My! That was exciting! Would you mind sitting for a few minutes to let me catch my breath?"

"I would not mind a bit. Let's rest here in this lovely warm sunshine," agreed Anna.

They settled themselves comfortably on a bench facing the canal and took up conversation.

Tentatively, Agatha began, "You are obviously a newcomer to Amsterdam and your dialect makes me think you come from the south of Germany. Are you one of the Palatines trying to make your way to America?"

"Yes, Agatha. You are quite right. I'm traveling with my nephew and his two girls, a young boy I have accepted as my ward, and a wonderful young couple who joined us on the way."

"Where are you staying here in Amsterdam?" Agatha asked.

"We are presently staying in the home of Cornelis Jansen. He and his wife and young son live over a small shop on a street called Begijnensteeg. Do you know the area?"

"Why yes! They live very close to my own home. We will walk there together."

"Do you know the Jansens?" Anna asked.

"Yes indeed. They are my neighbors. Cornelis is known to be a dedicated family man and a hard worker. He has made a great success of his leather shop. And his lovely wife, Josina, helps out with many of my community's charitable projects through her church and Cornelis' guild.

Anna smiled widely and declared, "Ahhh. So you're a Lutheran also."

"No, dear Anna, I'm a Roman Catholic."

"Oh … Oh," stammered Anna.

192

Agatha saw Anna's confusion and took her hand.

"It's quite alright, Anna," she said reassuringly. "People of all faiths are welcome and safe here."

Anna looked at Agatha with fresh eyes. She now saw the little woman's clothing with new clarity: the full-length cloak with long open sleeves and the pure-white linen headdress.

"Are you a nun?" Anna asked.

"Oh no, Anna, I'm a Beguine."

A moment of thoughtful time passed. Then Anna, rapidly nodding her head in the affirmative, murmured, "Oh yes. I should have known."

But she hadn't known; and in truth, even now she had not the slightest idea what a Beguine might be.

*****

They reached the Jansens' shop where Agatha bid Anna goodbye. She turned and started across a small flat bridge over the narrow waterway, the Begijnensloot. She hesitated, looked back at Anna and for a moment seemed to be considering the answer to some yet unfocused question. Appearing still undecided, she turned and disappeared through a heavy arched gate into the walled area beyond.

Anna hurried up the stairs of the Jansens' shop to find Josina.

"Josina, what is a Beguine?"

"Oh. So you've met some of our neighbors?"

"Yes. I have spent the morning with the most delightful little woman, Agatha Arents."

"I know her. She is a lovely lady. She and her fellow Beguines help out on many of the charitable projects of Cornelis' guild."

"But, Josina, I ask again, what *is* a Beguine?"

Josina answered, "I've never been inside their walled community grounds nor spoken at length with any of their members. They are a bit secretive and keep to themselves when not out and about doing their charitable kindnesses. So I only know what I've learned from the head teacher at the orphanage where they help out almost every day.

"First and foremost, you must know that they are all Roman Catholics."

"Yes, Josina, Agatha told me so. I asked her if she was a nun as she seemed to be attired in a nun's habit. She laughed at the suggestion and told me, 'No'."

"Indeed. That's true. None of them are nuns. In fact, several are widows and have grown children.

"They call their living area within the walls, the Begijnhof and themselves a cloister. I'm not sure how that is different from a convent, but I am certain they are not nuns."

"How many live inside there?" asked Anna.

"Believe or not, I'm told there are over 40 lovely homes within those walls. It's hard to tell from outside and, as I said before, I've never been inside. From across the Singel, you can see the

194

top of a church steeple. From the size of it, the church must be very large."

"So if you say there are more than 40 houses in there, then there must be at least 40 to 50 women. Wouldn't you say?" asked Anna.

"Not all of them come out into the community regularly so it's hard to say. But I would think that would be a good estimate," agreed Josina.

"How long have they been there?"

"The Begijnhof has been there all my life and I'm told by that orphanage teacher that some of the buildings and the wall have been there for over 300 years.

"Do you see many Catholics pass by here going to the church inside?"

"No, strangely enough, the church is Protestant. Lutheran in fact. There is a story that the Beguines have their own hidden Roman Catholic church somewhere in the compound. Catholics are not allowed to have their services in public but are not forbidden to continue the sacraments of their faith. They only have to do so in private.

"If there is a hidden church in one of those houses, I would really love to see it!" exclaimed Josina.

"It's all very strange," mused Anna. "Perhaps Agatha will tell me more when I see her tomorrow. But I will not pry. A woman's religious beliefs are her own and should not be made the topic of idle conversation."

Chapter 21

Tuesday, April 30

The following morning, Agatha came back across the little bridge and met Anna at the Jansen shop. Mrs. Jansen offered coffee but the two were anxious to be on their way and asked forgiveness for rushing off.

"We want to get to the pharmacist's shop as soon as he opens," explained Anna.

"Well! That's alright for now, but you both must stop on your way back to join me for coffee and a sweet treat," answered Josina.

"We promise," they sang over their shoulders as they rushed out the door.

They turned to the left and briskly walked the short distance to Kalverstraat. Two quick right turns brought them past the waters of the Spui. And from there, it was but a few strides to the curve on Spuistraat taking them down the hill to the Singel Canal. On their left was the monumental Old Lutheran Church and on the right, the canal.

Anna, less flustered and anxious than on the previous day, was able to take in the remarkable sights and sounds of the city's morning activities. Small boats being poled along the canal were laden with commerce to be delivered to the houses and shops along the canal banks. Children were hurrying off to school. A man, preceded by a small boy loudly beating a drum, was shouting at passersby with a bellowing voice.

"Why is he yelling at those people?" asked Anna.

196

"He's a stentor," explained Agatha. "He shouts out the news of the day and announces any local events we might find of interest. We give him a small sum for his efforts. He just reported that another dike at Hardinxveld broke last month and the polder of Alblasserwaard was totally flooded. Several people were killed. Those poor souls have been flooded out so many times."

"Could such a thing happen here?" asked Anna nervously. "I don't know how to swim, you know."

Agatha chuckled, "Oh no, no, my dear! This canal and others like it throughout the city keep the water controlled and off the land. You are safe here. You will not be swimming on our walk!"

Anna laughed nervously in response.

The first canal bridge they reached was particularly high and steep. Two men were grimly engaged in their attempt to move a lumbering pushcart across it. The first was behind straining with all his might to push the heavy load. The second was in front pulling on a rope attached to the cart's handle. He held his end of the rope, not with his huge bare hands, but with a large and dangerous looking hook. He was grunting and groaning as he pulled with all his strength to get the load up the steep grade.

At the top, the men turned the cart and with both holding the hook started the cart down other side. Halfway to the bottom, the cart gained speed dragging the men by their heels. A third man ran to their aid and together they regained control of the load before it could escape their grasp and crash into another cart at the bottom.

"I can see that it would take two or three men to safely move such a load over that high bridge. But what happens if only one man owns the cart?" inquired Anna.

"Only one man owns that cart and its load," answered Agatha.

"The other man, the one with the hook, is a business man on his own. He's called a kargadoor. He stations himself at this bridge everyday and charges a penny to men needing his help to get a heavy load safely across. There are many men like him working at other bridges around the city. It is an honorable profession."

"All work that helps others is honorable work," observed Anna.

"So it is," echoed Agatha.

On they walked and Agatha once again asked Anna about the effectiveness of her wound treatment.

Anna wondered at Agatha's repeated interest in the matter and asked, "Is there some particular reason you are curious about the treatment?"

"Anna, I don't wish to burden you with my troubles," she answered.

"Agatha, your concerns cannot be a burden to me. What is the matter?"

"Thank you, Anna, for your generous spirit. In truth, I am quite anxious to know if your treatment would be of help for my dear friend, Beatrice Presler. She burned the back of her hand quite badly some two weeks ago and it is not getting any better in spite of the doctor's care.

"Beatrice agreed to the doctor's recommendation for bloodletting so he sent for the barber who came to the house on three separate occasions. This past time, so much blood was taken that Beatrice had a near swoon. We were all alarmed at her condition but the doctor said that swooning was a good sign; it meant that the treatment was working. But from all appearances, it is not working. The hand is not healing."

"What is this bloodletting and why on earth would a barber be called in to care for a burn?" asked Anna in amazement.

"That's the way it has always been. The doctors do certain treatments and barbers do others - including bloodletting and pulling teeth. The barber has her sit in a chair with her arm resting on a table. He ties a cloth tightly around her upper arm and has her grip a wood stick tightly in her hand. When a vein stands out below the tied cloth, he pierces it with a sharp, pointed piece of metal. The blood is released and flows into a bowl. There was a frightful amount of blood this third time."

Anna, her eyes glazing over, was herself beginning to turn pale at this recital of medical practice.

Agatha saw her discomfiture and quickly drew her attention elsewhere. "Do you see that striped pole across the canal - the white one with the red and blue stripes?" she asked.

Anna nodded, "Yes," and refocused her eyes.

Agatha continued, "That's the sign for a barber. The pole is the stick the patient squeezes to lift the blood in the vein, the white in the color of the cloth wrapped around the arm to make the vein bulge, blue is for the vein itself, and the red is the color of the blood. The little bowl capping the top of the pole is where leeches are kept and the bowl at the bottom is for collecting the flowing blood."

Anna, now even more wide-eyed, cried, "Leeches!? Those loathsome lake-dwelling beasties that bite into your skin and writhe about sucking your blood? Those leeches?"

"Yes. Those are the ones," answered Agatha. "Since there has not been any progress in healing, the doctor is now suggesting to Beatrice that she allow him to place *leeches* directly on her wound. He says this will pull out the bad humors and release more blood. Beatrice is mightily afraid just at the thought of leeches - much less having them placed upon her body."

"Oh my goodness!" exclaimed Anna. "I can understand why! It seems poor Beatrice has suffered quite enough from both her injury *and* her medical care without adding leeches to her troubles!

"We had neither a doctor nor a barber anywhere near our small town. And now having heard of Beatrice's treatment, I believe I will always be grateful for their absence. We did very well on our own using treatments for both illness and injury that were given to us by our elders. And now, dear Agatha, I can assure you that we had very good results with ointments of yarrow and marigold in treating women's cooking burns."

"That is *very* encouraging, Anna. I will purchase a supply of the ointment myself. Would you be so kind as to visit my friend and give us instructions in its use?"

"I will be honored to be of assistance," answered Anna.

They entered the Muntplein town square and stopped in front of the Munttoren, the Mint Tower.

Anna exclaimed, "My gracious! *Everything* is so big in this city. Is this a church tower?"

Agatha found this very amusing. She had never looked at the tower with that question in mind.

"No. It is not part of a church. But many have worshiped over the contents of the tower in years past."

This confused Anna but she waited patiently for the answer to the riddle as Agatha gave her explanation.

"It was originally part of the Regulierspoort, one of the main gates of the old city wall. There was a big fire some hundred years ago that badly damaged the gate and the tower. Soon after, the tower was rebuilt and the clock faces and the bells were included. It remains unchanged from that time."

Almost on cue, the clock turned to eight and the carillon sang.

Anna exclaimed, "My eyes are sore from all the grand sights I've seen today and now my ears will be tender from listening to the glorious sounds of those splendid bells!

"But, Agatha, why would people worship a clock tower. Is that some other unusual religion?"

"Some might think so. But no, it is not a religion. Let me explain myself.

"In 1672, the year we describe as the 'disastrous year', the English and the French declared war on my country. The French occupied much of our land *except* for Amsterdam. It became impossible to safely move silver or gold from our city to the official mints in the occupied towns. So our government set up a mint here in this tower to continue producing coins.

"So when I said some people had worshiped what was in this tower, it was the *money* that was produced here."

Anna understood the riddle's answer and commented, "Well, as the Old Testament says, 'For the love of money is the root of all evil'. And I believe that to be true."

"Well said," agreed Agatha as they turned from the tower and hurried down an alleyway to their left. They were quickly in front of the pharmacist's home and apothecary shop.

This second encounter with the pharmacist was very tame in comparison to the day before. He brought out Anna's ordered ointment and greeted them graciously then turned the financial reckoning over to his young daughter. As Anna had suggested, Agatha rounded up the order by buying a small quantity of fresh yarrow root and her own supply of yarrow ointment to treat her friend, Beatrice.

The daughter took their money and disappeared into the shop to make change. On her return, she was thrilled and delighted when Anna asked her to complete a new and substantial order.

First, she ordered a full pound of ginger. Christina's morning sickness was now completely under control with morning ginger tea. Surely there would be other pregnant women needing her help in the wilderness.

And yes, she could supply Anna with a large bag of dandelion flowers and roots. The order was completed with a pound of yarrow root, and various quantities of horseradish, goldenrod, klamath weed, pellitory leaves, and dried thorn apple.

The girl handled the transaction flawlessly. She promised the order would be ready for pickup by the next morning.

Anna and Agatha were again impressed with her skills and deportment.

"A young woman of such competency should be encouraged and allowed to follow in her father's footsteps and become a pharmacist," Anna remarked.

"Perhaps someday in the future such opportunities will be available to a woman with intelligence and ambition, but, regrettably, that is not the case in our time and place," Agatha replied. "Sadly so."

"Yes. Sadly so," echoed Anna.

They turned and retraced their steps to Begijnensteeg. There were even more carts on the streets with men waving samples of their contents in an attempt to attract customers.

Agatha explained, "Those men with the small carts are peddlers. They are not members of the guilds and are a nuisance to them since neither their methods of selling nor the quality of their goods can be controlled. They usually sell only small items such as cloth, buttons, needles and pins, other small metal-ware, and simple jewelry. As long as they keep moving and do not harangue the public, they are generally left alone."

It was still early in the morning when they arrived at the Jansens' shop. Once more, they had to offer apologies to Josina for delaying her hospitality.

"We are going to visit a friend of Agatha who has need of some of this ointment for a burn on her hand," explained Anna. "I am going to show her how to apply the medicine and then we promise to return."

Josina didn't hesitate a second before asking, "Please Agatha, may I come also to learn about this treatment. My women friends often get burns while cooking. Men also are burned in their work when fire is required. It would be a great comfort to know there was something we could do to help the healing."

Anna and Josina looked to Agatha for her answer. There was a moment's hesitation and then came a hearty, "Yes, you certainly may join us, Josina. I will, of course, have to ask permission of my friend to have us all enter her home but I'm certain she will welcome the company."

"Wonderful!" exclaimed Josina. To Anna she whispered, "I've never been inside those walls. This is very exciting!"

So all three marched across the bridge and through the arched gate. Agatha continued walking briskly ahead but Josina and Anna stopped in their tracks and stared. Before them was a large garden courtyard enclosed by beautifully colored multistory homes. Elm trees provided shade for several comfortable-looking benches.

"Oh my," Anna whispered. "How wonderful!"

And then to their left, they noticed what had at first appeared to be a continuation of the walls of the compound. This wall had glass windows. It was a church! A magnificent, towering church with a steeple reaching to the sky.

Failing to hear the sound of their footsteps behind her, Agatha turned to see Josina and Anna with mouths agape staring up at the steeple. "Come on ladies, we have work to do," she insisted.

They obeyed and rapidly caught up. Agatha stepped off the path to avoid stepping on a long flat stone and her two followers did so as well.

Looking down at the stone, Josina whispered to Anna, "It has dates written on it! It looks like a gravestone right here in the middle of the walkway!"

They rounded the side wall of the church and immediately found themselves in front of its heavy wooden double doors. They stopped again and gawked straight up at the brick-faced tower over their heads.

"Ladies! Ladies! Please *follow* me!" exhorted Agatha again.

And they did—straight to the black-faced building across the walkway from the church entrance.

"Wait here while I go inside to announce our visit," said Agatha.

They did not mind waiting at all as it gave them time to take in many of the details of the buildings around the courtyard. There were over forty and no two were alike. Some were two stories high, others were three or four stories in height. The upper pediments were of various styles and shapes. Windows were thin, thick, tall, or short. Lintels were plain or decorative.

The house into which Agatha had entered was different from the rest. It was made of wood, not brick and was black in color. It was, in fact, one of the oldest houses in Amsterdam.

"This is all too much to take in," said Josina. "I will never be able to remember it all to describe to my husband. I am so glad I was able to come with you. But what of that grave?"

Agatha reappeared and motioned for them to enter the house.

"Beatrice is most anxious to meet you. Please come in."

They were shown into a small sitting room. Sitting in a tall-backed chair next to a wide front window was a woman of generous proportions. She was dressed in the same undyed cloth as Agatha. A multicolored woven woolen blanket lay across her lap; her right hand lay there on an open book. Her left arm rested on a side table with its injured hand propped upon a pillow.

Her white linen cap had side flaps that framed her face; a face shown by the slanting weak afternoon light as ghostly pale and drawn. In spite of her obvious illness, and evident discomfort, her posture was erect and steady.

She greeted them kindly, "Please make yourselves comfortable and excuse me for not rising. I am rather weak from my recent troubles."

Both visitors answered together, "Thank you," and impressed by the quiet dignity of their hostess, each gave an instinctive hint of a curtsy. Agatha saw and smiled discretely.

Josina's eyes wandered the beautifully appointed room. She gave a little start when she noticed the two young women up against the far wall. They stood motionless and mute as they watched the room's activities.

Anna's eyes remained fixed on the injured hand wrapped in a blood-stained bandage. She looked to Agatha for instruction.

"Beatrice," Agatha began, "Anna would like to examine your hand. May she?"

"Yes, my dear. Please come closer."

One of the young women abandoned her post and moved with surprising speed and grace to place a straight-backed chair at Beatrice's side. And just as quickly, she glided back to her companion's side to resume her place against the wall.

Anna nodded her thanks to the girl as she walked over to take the proffered seat. To Beatrice, she asked, "May I remove this bandage?"

Beatrice replied, "Agatha has told me that you may be able to assist me with this affliction. Please do whatever you need to in order to assess the problem. I hope you will be able to help."

"As do I, dear lady," Anna answered.

Anna began the task of unwinding the bandage but found that the dried caked blood had cemented the layers together.

"When was this bandage last changed?" asked Anna.

"One week ago," answered Beatrice.

"Oh my gracious," thought Anna. "That will never do. I'll need to soak this off to get to her skin."

"Agatha, could you please bring me a bowl of warm water. I will also need a clean towel and a flat blade. A small knife will do; fish knife would be the best."

Beatrice looked alarmed at the request for the knife but Anna was quick to reassure her that she would not touch her hand with the implement, only the bandage. Relieved, Beatrice motioned both girls into life. Agatha followed them out the room to find and retrieve the needed materials.

After soaking Beatrice's hand in the warm water, Anna was able to successfully use the flat blade of the fish knife to pry the layers of bandage off one at a time. It took time and patience so as not to hurt her.

When the last layer was removed, Anna was horrified to see what lay beneath. The wound was festering with a hard yellow crust covering the round area of the burn; fresh thick pus oozed from around the edges.

As Anna's work had progressed, Josina's attention had turned from the beauty of the room's furnishings to the increasingly unpleasant sight of Beatrice's unbandaging. As the last layer was removed and the fetid wound exposed, the air was filled with the stench of dried blood and fresh pus.

Josina's face became ghostly pale and she was about to swoon when Agatha caught her and ushered her out of the house into the clean fresh air of the courtyard where she helped her to a welcoming bench.

"It would probably be best for you to return home to ready your family's dinner," suggested Agatha.

Josina had been recovering her color with the fresh air, but at the mention of food, she paled again.

"Oh! Sorry, my dear," apologized Agatha. "Just go home and rest."

This instruction had the desired effect and Josina's color returned. She rose from her bench and made her way home.

Agatha returned to the house and was given further directions in the care of her friend.

Anna instructed, "Fill a pot with three cups of well water and add a thimbleful of your finely chopped yarrow root; then bring it to a vigorous boil to make a tea.

"Let the water cool and wash your hands with the tea and your favorite soap before touching the wound. And be sure to wash your hands that same way with a fresh cup of tea when you are finished."

Agatha didn't see the sense in this but had second thoughts when Anna asked, "Who wants to go to her supper table with that awful stuff on her hands?"

Everyone glanced back at Beatrice's wound. The obvious answer to that question made aftercare wash-up a reasonable activity.

The tea was brewed and Anna carefully washed her hands under the studied gaze of her apprentices.

She cleaned Beatrice's wound with a soft cloth bathed in the warm tea and a lathering of soap. She then applied a thin layer of the yarrow ointment over which she laid a clean linen rag impregnated with the ointment. The poultice was held in place by a clean handkerchief.

"Tomorrow make a new poultice with a clean rag and boil this one to be used the following day. Never use the same rag twice without boiling it in the tea. And never use the same tea twice."

Anna turned to Beatrice, "I will be leaving for London in a few days but I hope to see improvement before I have to go. I will come with Agatha in the morning to observe but I'm sure that your friends will give the best of care."

"Thank you for coming, Anna. You have been an enormous comfort," said Beatrice.

*****

Jacob had awakened that same morning before dawn to the aroma of baking bread coming up the stairwell. His bed was in the attic of the Hraban's home; the girls slept in a guestroom on the second floor.

Mrs. Hraban had supplied him with a pitcher of water and a ceramic bowl to use for washing and shaving. She had even arranged for his shirt to be washed; it hung clean and dry over the back of a chair. She exclaimed approvingly at his appearance when he entered her kitchen.

The girls were already there. They too were carefully washed and wearing clean clothes. Their hair was brushed and shining. Both girls commanded their father to admire their hair ribbons. He readily did their bidding. Everyone was in good spirits.

A breakfast of cold meats, warm bread and soft butter was served in the dining room. Rabbi Hraban sat at the head of the table and invited Jacob to take a place at the far end.

Under the watchful eye of their hostess, Maggie carefully carried utensils and platters from the kitchen to the dining area. Her face was a mask of serious purpose and concentration. She forked the meats onto the men's plates and passed the bread tray around the table.

At the end of each task, her full attention fell upon Mrs. Hraban. And each time, Mrs. Hraban's encouraging smiles, nods and

210

soft words transformed Maggie's face into one of delight at this wonderful woman's approval.

"How she misses her mother," thought Jacob. "She so loves the attention and blessing of this lovely lady."

After the meal, Rabbi Hraban excused himself. "I must get to work," he announced.

Jacob wondered what work a Rabbi did outside the synagogue but didn't ask for clarification.

Mrs. Hraban helped Maggie to clear the table and then asked Jacob to take a seat in the front parlor.

"Maggie has a surprise for you," she said.

He was standing in the parlor looking out the window when an apparition appeared at the hallway door. He almost spoke her name. But no, the person presenting the large tray was not his wife, but rather her striking image, their daughter, Maggie.

It took his breath away to realize how she had grown and matured in just the past few months. "She's lovely," he reminded himself. "She's truly lovely."

"Look father, I have prepared tea for you and Mrs. Hraban," Maggie said as she advanced into the room.

Mrs. Hraban followed behind her throwing an "isn't she wonderful?" smile over the girl's shoulder.

Jacob caught the silent question and answered it with his own smile and nod of agreement.

They took seats across from one another at a small round table. Maggie placed the tray there and proceeded to flawlessly serve the tea to her father and Mrs. Hraban. When cups were filled, and adult conversation was underway, Maggie turned her attention to the silver objects in the glass-fronted cabinet that had stolen the attention of the adult women the night before.

Unlike Anna and the other women, Maggie had no hesitation in asking Mrs. Hraban questions about their use. "Mrs. Hraban, what is the stick with the hand at the end?"

"Maggie," said Mrs. Hraban in an sharp tone. "Your elders are having a conversation. You do *not* interrupt."

Maggie visibly shrank before Jacob's eyes. Her eyes took on the fright of a small cornered creature as they searched the carpet for some hole in which to hide.

Mrs. Hraban softened her tone, "Maggie, I am delighted that you are interested in my family's treasured objects. I will be pleased to explain them to you after your father and I have finished our tea and he has left for his day's duties. But for now, please go to the kitchen and help with the morning's clean up."

Maggie began to breathe again and left the room.

Mrs. Hraban turned back to Jacob. "Maggie is such a lovely girl, Mr. Seiler. I am so sorry that she has lost her mother and that you have lost your wife. You have my deepest condolences."

"Thank you, Mrs. Hraban. You have been very kind. It is obvious that Maggie adores you."

212

"I have had several granddaughters of my own on whom to practice patience and discipline mixed liberally with love. It is easy when the child such as yours has a beautiful spirit."

She continued, "You know your captain, my son Severin, is unmarried?"

"No, madam, he never spoke to us of his private life."

"I'm not surprised. He probably thought the women in your party would scold him about getting married just as his mother does," she laughed. "I need more grandchildren! He needs to hurry up!"

"I'm sure you're right about the scolding. I can think of at least one of our party that would certainly have taken up the cry," he said, thinking of Anna. "So you have other children?" he asked courteously.

She beamed and replied, "I have two other sons and two daughters. All are married and have presented me with many gorgeous grandchildren.

"My boys are in business with their father. They are diamond merchants and do the cutting as well. It has been our family tradition here in Amsterdam since the our ancestors were forced out of Portugal.

"Our people, the Sephardic Jews, had a great migration just as your people are doing now. Two hundred years ago, during a time called the Great Inquisition, our ancestors, under the threat of death, fled Catholic Spain and sought refuge in Portugal.

"Only a few years later, the Catholic king of Portugal declared that all Jews in his realm must convert to Christianity. Some determined to stay in their new homeland and affirmed that they had indeed converted. But the Inquisition, suspicious they were still secretly practicing their faith, continued to investigate and harass them.

"The majority of Jews fled the country; thousands came to Amsterdam including my ancestors and those of my husband. Here, for over two centuries and many generations, our families have lived in peace with Christians.

"That is a *wonderful* thing," interjected Jacob.

"Yes, Jacob," said Mrs. Hraban, "but there is more to this story."

"In the Inquisition's early years, in both Spain and Portugal, there were some of the faithful who refused to convert or leave the country. They were interrogated, tortured and put to death - a slow and horrifying death - they were burned at the stake.

"Even some of those who had professed their conversions were judged to be lying and lost their lives to the flames. There have been no practicing Jews living in Spain or Portugal for the past two hundred years."

"Oh my God," whispered Jacob.

Mrs. Hraban leaned across the table and took both of Jacob's hands in hers. "No, Jacob, it was not *your* God nor *anyone's* God. It was the evil in the men who turned *away* from God.

We are so blessed to live in Amsterdam where people of goodwill and all religious faiths live in peace with one another and worship their God in their own way without fear. And

Jacob, my friend, it is my strong belief that we are, in faith, all praying to the same One."

*****

Later that morning, Jacob met Hendrick at the Jansens' shop to plan their day. They had talked about going to the docks to see what ships might be available for passage to Brielle within the next few days.

"Jacob, I wish you could have been with me last night! Had I known earlier what was to happen, I would have come to get you."

"So what happened?" asked Jacob.

"Cornelis and Karel took me and Aksel out with them on night patrol. It was wonderful!

"Cornelis and Karel met here about midnight. They and men from other guilds volunteer to patrol the streets at least one night a month. There are men who are paid a wage to be watchmen for the neighborhood but the guild-men's presence adds to the safety of the night.

"I went with Cornelis along the Singel towards the river and Aksel went with Karel up the Singel in the opposite direction.

"We met the paid watchman at his little hut at the river's edge. He was heating coffee over a peat stove getting warmed up for his patrol. He didn't wear a uniform but had the tools of his trade with him: a rattle, a sword, a lantern, and a weighted rope he could throw to save anybody who fell into a canal. The rattle he shakes before he announces the time.

215

"As far as the sword is concerned, Cornelis said that this watchman had never drawn his sword and thought the man would run for his life before doing so."

"Did you get to carry a sword," asked Jacob with hope and a tinge of envy in his voice.

"No, I didn't. But I did ask. Cornelis didn't have a sword either. He carried a thin club. He gave me one and showed me how to use it. You use it to poke a fellow in the gut. You don't swing it at him. I was hoping I could get to watch Cornelis use his. Or better yet, if I didn't get myself beaten up, that I might get to try it out myself.

"We walked for over an hour and nothing happened. We met a few men out in the night but they all had reason to be there when questioned by Cornelis. It was very cold, dark and damp and I was getting bored and miserable when I was suddenly frightened to death by a man charging out of an alleyway. He was pushing a cart yelling for us to get out of his way.

"And then it hit me."

"You were hit by the cart? Are you hurt?" asked Jacob anxiously."

"No, no. Not the cart, the stench. It was horrible!" exclaimed Hendrick. "The fellow was a night-soil man. His job is to go around town in the dead of night and collect all that day's shit and piss. He also cleans out cesspools, ash pits, and straw pits. How can his family stand to have him in the house?

"And Jacob, you won't believe this when I tell you! Cornelis told the fellow to leave the awful stuff in a pail hanging from the back of the cart at *his house*!"

216

"What? He wanted shit delivered to his house? You're right, I don't believe you!" exclaimed Jacob.

"No. I'm telling you the truth, Jacob. The fellow's apprentice has the job of searching the streets for dog shit. Can you imagine signing up for an apprenticeship as a shit collector? It turns out that Cornelis uses the stuff in tanning hides to make his leather goods. He actually *paid* the man to deliver dog shit. Imagine it!"

"I'll never again look at a piece of well-worked leather in the same way," admitted Jacob.

"We got back here before dawn. I was cold and tired so I went right to sleep down here in the shop. Cornelis and I sleep in the shop so the ladies can have their privacy upstairs.

"You should have heard Christina when she came down this morning and got a whiff of me. The smell of the night-soil cart was in my hair and on my skin. She hollered at me loud and long and practically scrubbed the hide right off me with hot water and lye soap. She gave me more excitement and Cornelis more entertainment than the whole night on patrol!"

"Well, you look very clean," laughed Jacob. "Do you still want to visit the docks today?"

"But first let me tell you that when I mentioned the possibility of a visit to the docks to Karel last night, he seemed concerned.

"He took me aside and told me,

'I don't want to alarm the ladies, but I feel obliged to give you a warning about life at the docks. There are ships there that bring goods to our city from all over the world. They

217

also bring sailors with strange languages and customs. But beware, these same men also bring sickness, disease and death. Do not get close to or touch any of them.'

"So he said we could go to the docks, but that we should not carry any money, we should not talk to the dock workers, and we should not go anywhere with any strangers, particularly if they invite us to come aboard their ship. He said there are men on the docks who kidnap men and boys to work the ships. I don't know, Jacob, it all sounds dangerous to me."

"But if that's true, Hendrick, how will we make arrangements for passage to Brielle if we can't go to the docks or even if we go there, we can't talk to anyone?" asked Jacob.

Hendrick answered, "I asked Karel the same question. He said not to worry. Over the past several years, the Mennonites here in Amsterdam have helped hundreds of their fellow religious get sailings to Brielle and on to London.

"From London, they sail to a land in America called Pennsylvania. There are several ships that sail regularly from Amsterdam with captains well known and trusted by the local church. He said he would arrange transport for us with one of those. I was much relieved to hear this."

"So am I," answered Jacob. "So do you still want to see the docks?"

"I told Karel so. He wasn't happy with that decision but said he would arrange for a guide so we wouldn't go astray. The man is one of the kargadoors - the men who help others get their carts over the high bridges. He should be here soon."

Soon became immediately. In response to a sudden drop in the light within the shop, Jacob and Hendrick turned to the door to find it blocked by the silhouette of the largest man either had ever seen.

"His name is Reus," announced Josina, "He says he's here to take Jacob and Hendrick to the docks."

"Well, that would be us," answered Jacob when he recovered his voice. "We should be safe in his company!"

When they got outside into the light, they saw a second reason besides his immense size to feel secure in this man's care. He was carrying the tool of his trade, a metal hook attached to a wooden handle, that he carried in his right hand with such familiarity and ease it seemed to be part of his body.

"No one will bother us with this fellow along," said Jacob admiringly.

The three men walked the Warmoesstraat to reach the city docks. The waterway was alive with ships and the men who worked them. They spent an hour sitting on a couple of barrels watching the choreographed business of loading and unloading passengers and freight.

They followed Karel's instructions and neither spoke to nor approached any of the sailors or stevedores. With Reus looming behind them, tree-trunk arms folded and hook in plain sight, no one came within two ship's oars length of them. The two men shared many a laugh at the looks on sailors' faces when they rounded a nearby corner and got their first look at Reus. It was great fun all the way round.

Anna and Josina were clearing the breakfast dishes when Christina returned from her husband-bathing duties. All three had a merry time laughing at Hendrick's night-soil outing.

Josina broke the laughter to announce, "Ladies, I have some guild business of my own to attend to today. Let me explain that while the members of the wealthy *merchant* guilds participate in charitable affairs of the city by donating large amounts of money, their wives do not have an active role.

"The men of the *trade* guilds give money according to their means but we wives do take an active role in the charitable works. We visit the homes of the well-to-do and collect old clothes, shoes and blankets to be distributed to the less fortunate.

"We use the donated money to buy food staples at the markets and collect what produce the traders wish to donate. And we are the ones who make sure that all these goods get to those in need and that all the donated money is spent wisely and is well accounted for.

"For instance, when a guild member dies, his guild makes sure he gets a decent burial and attends to the needs of his widow and children. But no matter whether the father was a guild member or not, all orphans are cared for by the guilds. Today being the last day of the month, it is time to visit the orphanage near here to distribute food and clothing. Would you care to join me?" asked Josina. "I promise you it will have nothing to with excrement."

"I would be honored to do so," Anna laughed.

"As would I," echoed Christina.

There were thirty guild women in the group by the time they reached the orphanage. Anna was surprised and relieved to find that the children appeared happy, well-fed and healthy. They were outdoors playing in a large sunlit courtyard.

There were small wooden toys carved by master craftsmen, and wire hoops fashioned by master metalworkers. Several energetic boys rolled them around the courtyard using long sticks. Other boys played tag, blind-man's bluff and hide and seek. The girls played hopscotch, skipped rope, or sat in groups, talking with great animation.

Josina introduced Anna and Christina to the head mistress, Mrs. Florence Tuteur, one of three women employed to watch over the well-being of the hundreds of orphans.

Mrs. Tuteur explained that she also was a German immigrant; she was brought by her parents to Amsterdam as a child and later, as a young woman, had married a French minister from another immigrant family. She welcomed them all to her orphanage.

Anna noticed three women dressed like Agatha. "Excuse me, Mrs. Tuteur, are those women Beguines?" Anna asked.

"Why yes, they are. One or more of them come each day to play with the youngest children and to help us with the lessons for the older ones. They also give aid to the sick and injured when needed. The women here today are widows - as am I. We have all had children of our own and love the opportunity of being around the babies and youngsters again. The Beguines are happy to be here; the children love them dearly."

"Do the children have school here?" asked Christina.

"Oh yes, they are given instruction," answered Mrs. Tuteur.

"This orphanage was formed fifty years ago by the Reformed Church and teachers were employed from the outset. Girls are taught to pray, to spell, to read, to knit and to sew. The boys are taught the principles of our Reformed Religion, to read and write and, to prepare them for life on the outside, they learn a useful trade."

"But aren't all the Beguines Catholics?" asked Anna. "How can they be teaching in a Protestant orphanage?"

"Oh, their religion doesn't matter to us, nor does ours matter to them. They're here for the children's sake and we love them for that. They don't teach any religion classes - only the reading, writing and counting ones. We are proud that so many of our pupils can write and do numbers when they leave the orphanage at age nineteen. It all works out just fine."

For the next hour, Anna looked over some cuts and bruises and offered first aid. Christina gravitated to a group of girls who were drawing in the dirt and started her own class in animal figures.

With Mrs. Tuteur, Josina went over the provisions list that specified what had been brought that day and the carefully documented ledger that kept the books for the money donations.

Everything was done in a businesslike manner. Everything was spot-on correct.

*****

That evening, Jacob picked up the girls at the home of Rabbi Hraban and brought them back to the Jansens' home for supper.

The table conversation was loud and lively as the men and women exchanged stories of their citywide adventures and discoveries.

The last three days had been filled with revelations and insights into religion, commerce, politics, seafaring, medicine, charity, sanitation, and the city's many examples of personal and community tolerance of its citizens' individual differences.

That night's narratives were painted with broad brush and primary colors. In future, there would be days, weeks, and months, spent on the open sea when these stories would be cherished and recited in the finest of detail and with all the colors that nature could supply. The elaboration of the particulars would become a source of entertainment and ultimately a reservoir of sanity.

Late that night, before bedtime, Maggie unpacked her pen and paper and began her career as the Palatine historian.

It seemed the perfect place and time to start.

Chapter 22

Wednesday, May 1

Anna was awakened early by the sound of a persistent rattle outside the front windows. She wrapped her blanket around her and went to look down onto the street below. There she saw a tall figure wearing a black coat that swept the rain-streaked street. The stranger's face was hidden under a wide-brimmed black hat adorned with a white ribbon. In the right hand was a rattle being shaken insistently.

From out the heavy door of the Begijnhof came a petite woman carrying a small white bundle wrapped with a knot at the top. She laid it carefully on the street and, keeping her eyes fixed on the caped figure, she backed her way through the doorway and disappeared into the walled compound.

The front door of a shop across the street opened with a startling bang and a woman stepped out with a similar parcel. Then from directly below her, Josina appeared holding an identical offering.

Suddenly, from behind the neighbor lady's skirt appeared a small boy. He rushed by his mother and into the street. His mother screamed his name and grabbed his arm; she pulled him back to her with such force that he cried out in pain and fright.

She shoved him back through the door and, regaining some composure, laid her package in the street. As with the Beguine, she backed into her home, her eyes never leaving the dark figure before her.

Josina had frozen still as she watched the drama played out by mother and child. With the exit of the boy from the stage, she recovered mobility and lofted her own bundle onto the street. The play concluded with Josina backing quickly into her own doorway and out of Anna's sight.

The stranger slowly and deliberately collected the three bundles and then, shaking the rattle loudly, walked off to the left, moving down the alleyway and out of sight.

Anna met Josina as she came up the stairs to the living quarters.

Anna's voice, filled with anxiety. questioned, "Josina. What is the matter? Who was that person? What was happening? You all appeared so frightened!"

Josina was startled at the sudden appearance of Anna. She gave out a little cry; her nerves were still on edge.

"Anna, I can't speak just yet," she whispered.

Anna stopped, stared at her friend anxiously, then took her arm and led her to a chair.

"Please sit here, Josina, and rest. I will fix you something warm to drink."

When the steaming cups were placed on the table, Anna sat across from Josina and waited in silence.

"Oh My!" began Josina. "They go through the city *every* Wednesday morning. You would think we would be used to it."

"Used to what!?" sputtered Anna.

"Thank you for the cider, Anna. I am feeling better and calmer.

Let me explain what you just saw. You are familiar with the disease called leprosy?"

Anna drew in a quick breath. "Yes," she whispered. "Was that a leper I saw in the street?"

"Yes," answered Josina. "Leprosy has been in the city for a very long time. Years ago, charities founded a leper house outside the city walls. They are allowed to come into the city each Wednesday to beg as long as they wear the ribboned-hat and the long black coat and shake a rattle to warn people of their presence.

"The people of the city are truly sorry for their plight and give generously to them as they make their rounds but all of us are sore afraid of catching the disease. Afraid for ourselves and for our children."

Anna thought to say words of comfort, or courage, or charitable praise, but cut them off before drawing the breath needed to speak them.

"Keep your platitudes to yourself," she thought. "You do not live this reality and have no right to tell Josina not to fear."

Instead, she reached over and took Josina's hand; they smiled at one another in silence and sipped their cider.

*****

Later that morning, as arranged, Agatha met Anna at the Begijnhof gate with Josina and Antje in tow. Josina was anxious to resume her lessons in spite of her earlier reactions to pus and gore. Antje wanted to join the class after hearing of Anna's successful care of Jacob's wound; she was also excited at seeing the interior of the Begijnhof.

They marched into the courtyard and up the path along the church wall. Once again, Agatha skipped over onto the grass to avoid the dated stone slab in the pathway. This time, Anna took courage and called out to Agatha.

"Agatha, what is under this stone? And why do you make certain not to tramp upon it?"

Agatha stopped, turned to Anna, and pondered her answer.

In an unexpectedly clipped voice, Agatha answered, "It's a long story, Anna, and one that will have to keep. Several of my friends are waiting for us at Beatrice's house. We shouldn't keep them waiting."

Anna murmured, "Sorry," and took up the walk again.

They found Beatrice in her usual chair but it had been moved from the window to the middle of the room. Behind the chair stood five women dressed in similar fashion to Agatha including the two young women seen on Anna's first visit. Anna also recognized two others from the orphanage the day before.

Their erect posture and serious bearing gave them the appearance of a monarch's attendants. Anna had no doubt that their loyalties and love for Beatrice would rival that of any queen's entourage.

Agatha stepped to the side of Beatrice's chair and began, "Anna, these are our friends and fellow Beguines. Many members of our community are independently wealthy while others find it necessary to periodically supplement their livelihoods by working for wages. But whether for pay or for charity, most members practice some sick-nursing from time to time.

227

"I have taken the liberty of teaching them what you have shown me so far about the care of wounds. They have come today to thank you for that knowledge and to watch you care for Beatrice's hand.

"They also wish to ask you questions concerning your other medical treatments - that is if you feel free to teach them."

"I would be honored to do so," answered Anna. "But first, let's see how Beatrice's hand is doing. How are you feeling Beatrice?"

"*Much* better. Thank you, Anna. I believe I have a bit more strength and the hand does not hurt nearly as much. And I must say, it smells a lot better as well," Beatrice said making a face at the thought of yesterday's wretched bandage stench.

With ceremonial pomp, the five Beguines moved with practiced precision to present Anna with her necessary supplies. Two of the women moved a small side table next to Beatrice's chair. Another spread a clean cloth over it for a third to lay out clean bandages and a bar of soap.

They had already produced a proper portion of boiled yarrow tea. A small wash basin made its appearance and warm tea was poured for Anna's hand washing. The fish knife was unwrapped from a clean white table napkin. All was ready for their expert's ministrations.

Anna so wanted to smile brightly at this demonstration of determined professionalism cum camaraderie, but held her face in a serious mask to match the mood of her assistants.

When the bandages were removed and the burn initially exposed, there was an audible intake of breath from everyone in the room.

Agatha spoke for all of them, "Anna, it is a miracle! The wound is clean and dry and there is no pus! Her hand is healing!"

"Amen!" shouted the onlookers.

"Amen is right," added Beatrice. "I thank you from the bottom of my heart for the improvement in my hand and body. I also thank God for bringing you to our community to teach us that which we can use to help our neighbors in future."

Anna had one of the Beguines clean and dress the wound under her supervision. She pronounced it a perfect job and noted with pleasure the smile that stole over the woman's face at the compliment.

The remainder of the morning was spent in lecture and discussion. Two of the Beguines took notes as Anna spoke on the medicinal benefits of various plants and how to prepare them for use. She also had warnings about the potential dangerous effects of some of those same plants if mishandled.

Anna had so much to teach! They noted her advice that:

There were other uses for yarrow root. It could help staunch bleeding and relieve the itching of a skin rash.

Dandelion tea could cure the body aches and pains associated with muscle pain and weakness and the bleeding and swelling of the gums that afflicted people during prolonged winter months. (*Scurvy*)

Horseradish could dampen the pain of swollen, aching joints of the hands and knees. (*Arthritis*)

Klammath weed could sooth anxious nerves and lighten heavy spirits. (*Anxiety-Depression*)
Tea made from the goldenrod could lessen the sudden excruciating pain and swelling of the great toe that could make even the strongest of men cry. (*Gout*)

The leaf of the pellitory plant could lessen that sudden pain in the head that brought on vomiting as well as agitation in bright light. (*Migraine Headache*)

She warned them about the dangers of dried thorn-apple but taught that a person inhaling the vapors from boiling the plant could open up the breathing passages and abolish sudden wheezing. (Asthma)

The dried root of monkshood could also be a deadly poison in large quantities but if used in small quantity could bring down a high fever, lessen pain, and help to calm the nerves. There was some uneasiness among her pupils as Anna was somewhat hazy on the exact size of a "small quantity". Trial and error seemed a bit fraught with danger.

And of course, there was the use of ginger tea for the morning sickness of early pregnancy.

Careful handwritten copies were made of the Beguines' class notes. These were distributed widely to the women of the neighborhood who, in turn, made other copies which they circulated at their churches.

Josina Jansen took her copy to her new friend, Mrs. Hraban, who in turn spread the word among the members of her synagogue.

Beatrice's hand would heal with a minimal scar in less than a week and Anna's name would become a household word among the women of the community.

Though she was to leave Amsterdam in a matter of days, her influence would stay in this Netherlands city for generations to come.

*****

In the early afternoon, Karel brought the news that there would be a ship ready to sail for Brielle on Friday's outgoing tide. He assured Jacob and Hendrick that the ship would be captained by a man trusted by the Mennonite community.

"There will be many Mennonite families aboard. Your families will be safe," he promised.

They learned that the Koerbers would not be leaving with them. Aksel had found some temporary need for his forge skills at the docks. The wages from that work, combined with the gift from Mr. Kramer, would be more than enough to pay his family's transport from London to America. Beate, beaming from ear to ear, received instructions on the use of ginger tea for her new morning affliction. Her prayers had been answered - there was to be another Koerber in her household.

So now with the certainty of the imminent separation to come, the Van Brearleys and the Jansens determined to have a farewell supper for their Palatine friends.

Agatha was invited and immediately offered to host the supper in the central courtyard of the Begijnhof.

The Beguines who had been in Anna's medical class begged to assist in the preparations. Their help was gratefully accepted but only on the condition that they join the supper party. Joyfully, they accepted.

Chapter 23

Thursday, May 2

Early Thursday morning, the women collected in the Begijnhof courtyard and excitedly planned the menu and divided the cooking duties. Agatha suggested that the women form teams of two to streamline the process. Her suggestion that each Catholic Beguine choose a Protestant woman to work with was met with shared delight. There was great laughter as the choices were made. It reminded them all of their childhood games in which sides were chosen.

Antje was the last chosen and received a round of applause and laughter as she stomped her feet in mock anger and whined, "I am always the last one chosen!" A few of the smaller women laughed along with the rest but remembered with some fellow feeling the hurt of being last picked.

Teams formed, they all rushed off to obtain ingredients and to begin their assigned chores.

By mid-afternoon, vegetables were chopped, cubes of fresh meat were browned, bread was kneaded, sweets were tempted from hiding in the backs of parlor cabinets, and the aroma of baking ginger snaps stole out of several kitchen windows into the courtyard below.

In the late afternoon, under the direction of the Beguines, Aksel, Hendrick and Cornelis gathered tables from several of their stately homes and placed them carefully in the center of the courtyard. Jacob's wound was entirely healed but under Anna's watchful eye, he was assigned the lighter task of carrying chairs to seat the increasing numbers of guests.

The men dug a small fire-pit in the center of the courtyard and a large metal pot was hung from a tripod over burning coals. The vegetables and browned meat were blended together with a liquid stock of water and wine to be cooked over a slow fire.

Liquid refreshments consisted of the wine not consumed by the stew, beer from the De Hooiberg brewery and a variety of fruit-flavored teas.

Anna asked Jacob to return to the synagogue to invite the Hrabans to join them. There was some consternation, when he returned escorting the wife of the Rabbi. Anna had told Agatha about her gracious reception by the members of the Portuguese Synagogue in general and this wonderful woman's family in particular. She introduced her two new friends to one another.

"Mrs. Hraban, may I present my friend, Mrs. Agatha Arents."

"How do you do, Mrs. Arents. It is my pleasure to meet such a good friend to Anna. She has told me wonderful things of you and your community," replied Mrs. Hraban.

"And I am so pleased to meet you, Mrs. Hraban. Welcome to the Begijnhof," replied Agatha.

"Thank you, Mrs. Arents. But please call me Esther," answered Mrs. Hraban.

"Gladly, Esther. And it will please me to have you call me Agatha. And now, I must introduce you to my sister Beguines."

So saying, she took Esther in hand and with Anna made the rounds of the participating Beguines' kitchens to introduce her to all the women preparing what was becoming an ecumenical feast.

234

Anna slyly added to the observed confusion at the introduction of a Rabbi's wife by announcing, "I'm so glad that Mrs. Hraban will be joining us for supper. But even more, you will be excited to learn that the Rabbi himself and his son, our riverboat captain, will also be joining us for the meal!"

Mrs. Hraban repeatedly broke the ensuing silence with, "Please call me Esther," as she was introduced to each of her new acquaintances.

The Rabbi and Captain Hraban arrived an hour later pulling a small hand cart. Under a clean white tablecloth was, much to Anna's delight, a large portion of hummus and tabbouleh.

The men gathered together, introduced themselves all the way round, seated themselves in a circle and took up conversation on manly subjects while standing guard over the bubbling stew pot.

Aksel started by giving a straightforward account of the guild's night patrols.

Rabbi Hraban spoke up forcefully, "The volunteer work of these men is much appreciated by the honest folk of the town and much maligned by the criminal element. Their presence adds much to the security of our streets at night."

"Are you a member of a guild?" Jacob asked.

Rabbi Hraban answered, "No, I am not. Jews have never been invited to join the established guilds of merchants or craftsmen. That is why we have taken our place in those areas of Amsterdam's commerce that have never been governed by guilds.

"For generations, we have entered the professions of medicine, finance, the clothing businesses and, as I and my sons have done, the diamond industry. Although my position as Rabbi is practically a full time job in itself, I do help out in the factory from time to time."

His answer was food for thought on several different levels but no further questions were raised concerning guilds. The subject changed to ships and boats.

Captain Hraban spoke admiringly of brigs, ketches, schooners, sloops, and barques. Two hours sitting at the docks watching men load and unload ships had not made Hendrick and Jacob experts in seamanship but they nodded affirmatively in what they hoped were all the right places; they made no comments nor asked any questions that would prove their complete ignorance of the subject.

When the topic turned to Cornelis' leather making and the night-soil fellow's home delivery of dog excrement, all the men understood that subject and saw much humor in the scenario. The more Cornelis tried to earnestly explain the craftsman's use of the product, the louder his audience laughed. He finally threw up his hands and good-naturedly gave the floor over to Mr. Van Brearley.

Karel sat back and turned the conversation to the more serious subject of obtaining necessary provisions for the ship-bound travelers. Pipes were lit and men leaned forward into the circle of attentive listeners.

*****

While the men rested around the fire, the women went about and continued their last minute supper preparations. The sun

236

had plunged behind Beatrice Presler's house; darkness was pouring into the courtyard.

Anna stepped into the circle of masculine conversation and spent several minutes listening to the men's chatter while stirring the bubbling stew. Satisfied that it would be done at the appointed suppertime, she put down the ladle, looked up from the fire and starred blindly into the night. Her eyes swept upwards to the last visage of that day's light, the sun-fired glow at the peak of the church steeple.

A moment later, her eyes were drawn downward to the front of the church by a sense of movement. Curious, she stepped out of the circle of men and the globe of the cooking firelight and saw out of the background darkness an even darker apparition; a wide undulating black formless cloud capped in white skimming over the ground moving in her direction.

Her eyes widened, the hair on her arms stood up, her jaw slackened and her heart began to pound. It was a primal response to the primordial form that continued its approach.

The cloud called her name, "Anna! Please join us."

The cloud continued to move forward, dissolved, and became a flock of black-clad women. Capes draped their slight frames from shoulder to ground. Their arms were folded across their chests; their hands hidden in flowing sleeves. At their present distance, Anna could not see faces. Only pure white caps broke the blackness between bodies and sky.

They walked with a sliding motion of the feet; they appeared to be floating above the ground. And they were continuing to glide directly towards her.

Suddenly, Anna could see her friend, Agatha, leading the flock and beckoning her to approach.

Still at a distance, Agatha called out, "Anna, do you know what the 'Alteration' was?"

Still somewhat shaken, Anna stood her ground and was silent.

Agatha walked directly up to her and the others separated to form a tight circle around the two women. Anna's anxiety was reborn. Her mind raced, "What are they doing? Why are they dressed this way? What do they want of me?"

Only when she remembered that close by her nephew and several other large protective males lingered was she able to find her voice.

"Agatha, what does all this mean?" she managed to blurt out.

"Anna, I asked you if you knew what the 'Alteration' was?"

"No, Agatha, I have no idea."

"Then join us and help to celebrate this day, May 2nd, as has been done for the past half century."

The circle broke and allowed Agatha to lead the women towards the north wall of the church. She led them straight to the stone slab in the pathway; the same slab Anna had stepped around each time Agatha had led her into the Begijnhof.

Agatha took Anna's hand and led her to the top of the slab; the other women arrayed themselves on either side. From around the corner of the church came two other women, each holding a lighted candle and took their places at either end of the stone.

The hands of all the other women were reclaimed from the depths of sleeves and clasped in prayer-like attitude at the waist. In each woman's hands was clutched a bouquet of pansies.

Agatha cleared her throat and began, "The day we call the Alteration took place 131 years ago in May of 1578. In a bloodless revolution, Amsterdam changed from a Catholic city into a Protestant one. The Catholic town council was expelled; the Protestants took over the reins of government. From then on, we Roman Catholics were forbidden to worship in public.

"Before the Alteration, this lovely 200 year-old church was the home of our Catholic faith. But afterward, it was closed by the Protestants and lay unused for almost 30 years. Then in 1607, the council gave the church to a group of English and Scottish Presbyterians; they renamed it the English Church."

A polite cough outside the line of Beguines announced the arrival of the men from the stew-fire and the women supper guests, Protestant and Jew. All had been drawn to the scene by the arriving candles.

Agatha acknowledged and welcomed them with a slight nod of the head.

She continued, "Though we Beguines do not have a formal leader, as time passes, one particular woman is usually looked to for counsel and decision-making. Sixty years ago, that woman was Cornelia Arents, my grandmother.

"It had always been the custom to bury our leaders in the church but when my grandmother was dying, she made it clear that she did not want to be buried in a Protestant church. On the other hand, her friends felt it would be an insult to bury her elsewhere.

"The discussion went back and forth and became more and more heated as her health declined. She finally told them, 'I would rather be buried in the gutter alongside it than in the English Church.'

"She died on April 30, 1654, and against her wishes was buried in a vault in the English Church. To everyone's consternation, her coffin was found in the gutter at this very place the following morning. Her coffin was replaced in the vault; on the next morning it once again appeared in the gutter.

"This time, her friends decided it best to comply with her wishes and her coffin was placed beneath this stone, in the north gutter of the church on May 2, 1654.

"Since that time, on the evening of May 2, our community gathers at her grave after nightfall to remember her devotion to her religion and to place her favorite pansies on her grave. Once again, we celebrate her life."

Agatha nodded and the women leaned over and placed the pansies on the slab. She led them in a brief prayer in Dutch and dismissed the assemblage.

Then she turned to Anna and with a beatific smile announced to one and all, "It's time to eat!"

Chapter 24

The dinner was a splendid success. The Gentile men had consumed enough beer before the meal to be willing to try anything presented on the table; they pronounced the hummus and tabbouleh strange looking but very tasty.

Maggie delighted the ladies by divulging the names and uses for some of the beautiful silver and glass articles they had seen in the antique breakfront in Mrs. Hraban's parlor. Mrs. Hraban apologized for not bringing the fragile glass objects to the dinner, but the ladies had burned their images into their memories so deeply that Maggie's introductory descriptions immediately called them to mind.

Her subsequent explanation of the use of the silver Kiddush cup they remembered seeing nestled next to the tall blue glass decanter was politely received. But when Maggie reached into her apron pocket and brought forth the long silver stick with the shape of a hand at its end, the women clapped in glee.

"This is called a Torah pointer," Maggie began. "The Torah is a book of Holy Scripture for the Jewish people," she recited as she looked to Mrs. Hraban for confirmation. A slight nod and warm eyes encouraged Maggie to continue.

She called out the names of the Torah books: Genesis, Exodus, Leviticus, Numbers, and Deuteronomy. The names struck a chord of familiarity and wonderment in the hearts of the Christian audience.

"We study those in our church also," marveled Beate. "They're in the Old Testament."

"We do too," echoed Agatha and Anna.

"But Maggie, what does that object have to do with the holy book?" Anna asked.

Flush with excitement at her new-found status as a teacher among adults, Maggie beamed and proceeded with her lesson.

"The Rabbi's Torah is very old."

"As am I," said the Rabbi. Laughter was followed by a warm-hearted apology. "Oh, sorry, Maggie, please go on."

Mildly flustered, Maggie regained her composure and graphically painted a mind's eye picture of the Rabbi reading the Torah holding the pointer and scrolling the small silver hand over the words of his revered and fragile book.

"So you see, using the silver hand avoids soiling the parchment with years and years of human touch."

Smiling broadly, Maggie took her seat to thunderous applause.

Show and tell was over - But not quite.

The Rabbi rose and stepped back to his handcart. He reached under a tarpaulin and brought out a nine-branched candelabrum. There was a gasp of wonder by the Christians and a gasp of surprise from Mrs. Hraban.

"Husband! You brought that out of the house?!"

"Don't worry, Esther, I will be certain that no harm comes to it. Remember that your large strong son and our friend Jacob will be accompanying us home. There is no fool in Amsterdam that would take on such a pair."

Anna reached over and patted Esther's hand reassuringly. Esther glanced at her and gave her the look that asked, 'what can you do with such a man?' They smiled in mutual recognition of the unspoken sentiment.

Following the Rabbi's account of the use and meaning of the candelabrum, Esther's beloved Menorah, both it and the Torah pointer were passed around the table for all to behold. Silver and eyes glowed in the light of the small warming bonfire.

The men resumed their places around the fire; the women cleared the table. The major work of cleaning up would wait until morning light.

Agatha asked the ladies to follow her to the front of the church. By now, all the visiting women were aware that the church was no longer a Catholic church but rather the English Church.

Agatha stood with her back to the doors of the church; the ladies were gathered together facing her.

She announced, "I have one more place to show you before you retire to your homes.

"You all know that although we Catholics are treated fairly by the peoples and government of Amsterdam, it has, for a long time, been unlawful for us to practice our faith in public."

There were murmurs of acknowledgment and glances of discomfort. Was this to be a lecture - a reproof of them as representatives of their faiths? Eyes narrowed and focused warily on Agatha's face. Postures straightened. Defenses rose. Agatha did not react to the change in the atmosphere before her.

She continued, "But we Beguines have cheerfully celebrated Mass each morning, each Sunday, each Holy Day since this building was denied us. We did so first in each other's homes and for the past thirty-eight years have done so in the Hidden Church."

Josina turned to stare at Anna. Earlier in the day, she had been afraid she might never see the Hidden Church. Now she was frightened that she might be about to. Anna took her hand and gently squeezed.

Agatha gave a soft laugh. "Don't worry," she said. "The Hidden Church has never really been hidden from anyone. In fact, the designer of the church, Father van der Mye, got approval of his building plans from the city council before construction.

"Everyone in the government and the populace knew we were building a church. According to law, it had only to be *hidden* from the street. Father combined two of the houses right behind you to build our church that we call the Church of Saints John and Ursula."

Her audience whirled around to stare at the house-fronts directly behind them. Two tall brick buildings, faced with large white windows stood side by side; the larger and wider of the two on the right. Each was four floors in height - even five if the windows at the top represented an attic and not a false front.

Stairs ran up the front of each to a common porch onto which two front doors opened at the level of the second floor. The two buildings had the appearance of two completely separate homes.

"Now, come with me," Agatha invited. She moved through the group and strode off towards the right-hand staircase. The group stood frozen until Anna commanded, "Let's go," and led the way.

As they stepped into a dark vestibule, they were invited to pass through a gauntlet of Beguine-clad women. As they did so, they were handed a short white candle. Two women at the end of the line held lighted tapers and lit the candle of each of their guests as they entered the church. Agatha's candlelit face hung in the darkness and led the way.

The room was at first pitch black. The visitors at the front of the line held their candles in one hand and ran the other lightly along a close wall to keep their balance. As the women continued to file in, the line of candlelight grew longer and filled the space with soft features and glowing colors.

The women could now make out that the sanctuary was as wide as the combined front parlors of the two adjoined houses; the room was also only parlor deep. They found themselves aligned along the long front wall of the faux-parlors; they could yet see but a short way towards the back of the room.

Then the Beguines of the welcoming gauntlet entered the room, each one carrying a lighted candle. Using their distinctive gliding manner of walk they made their way forward and lit scores of tapers on either side of the altar. The room was quickly filled with both shimmering light and awed exclamations of delight.

Agatha was heartily pleased with their response. And yes, dare she admit it, she felt pride in her place of worship. But even as she pondered Proverbs 16:18, "Pride goeth before destruction, and an haughty spirit before a fall," she was having difficulty extinguishing a tiny haughty smile.

Agatha quietly assured herself, "Yes indeed. Here, in our simple sanctuary, this small group of devout friends will continue to profess the tenets of our faith against all the odds of history past and sanctions present."

She promised in a whisper, "We *will* prevail."
After a half an hour of exploration of the historical wall paintings, the needlepoint kneeling pillows at the seats, the finely crafted woodwork of the pews, and the altar with its framing pillars, the women were called to return to the bonfire by the melodious sound of Jacob's recorder.

Not long after, the celebrants gave into fatigue. Eva and Maggie were buried beneath a pile of coats in the Rabbi's cart soundlessly sleeping, the embers of the fire were damping down and the sound of gentle snoring, both male and female, was coming from seats somewhat outside its circle of light.

Jacob stood and asked the Rabbi to say a good night prayer. Rabbi Hraban suggested they all join him in reciting together his favorite Psalm. And so they did; Jew, Catholic, Mennonite, and Lutheran sent the poetry of the 23rd Psalm soaring into the moonless night sky in Hebrew, Dutch and German.

Hearty men's handshakes and warm women's hugs finished the night's camaraderie.

Shortly thereafter, at hearth and home, all fell exhausted into sleep.

Chapter 25

May 3 – Last Day in Amsterdam

The day was filled with frenetic activity. With the combined efforts of all the previous night's celebrants, the Begijnhof courtyard was cleared of party furniture and detritus. All was put to rights before breakfast time.

The Hrabans bid the Beguines "Good Day" and the travelers "Safe Journey". Anna promised Agatha that she would make a last visit to Beatrice that evening. In turn, Agatha promised that all Anna's prized pupils would be there to wish her well.

Directly after breakfast, belongings were gathered outside the Jansens' shop and preparations for departure were begun. Anna's cart was broken down. The heavy wooden sides and back were to be left behind. The single axle and two wheels were to be brought with them.

"The wheels and axle are irreplaceable, but we can always fashion a new cart from local wood," declared Jacob. "We will try to get my intact cart on the ship. But if they make us leave the frame behind, Hendrick and I will put axles on our shoulders and hang the wheels between us. We may end up having to carry all our belongings on our backs."

With that in mind, everything was first divided according to need. Some heated discussions ensued between the men and the women as to what constituted an "essential" item.

The women convinced the men they would regret abandoning any cooking pots when they got cold and hungry in the American woods. Anna smiled broadly as all the pots were loaded onto the cart.

After the division by necessity, the portage was parceled out according to each person's ability to carry. Each bundle was wrapped separately and placed in Jacob's cart. The men would carry the "essentials" and the women, the "luxury items". Luxuries such as extra warm clothes.

Christina warranted she would crawl on hands and knees under her load before giving up her books. Maggie announced the same intent if asked to relinquish her writing materials.

Jacob assured them that unless a life or death decision arose involving those items, they would have them on arrival in America.

Only Eva was spared a weighted pack.

Jacob and Hendrick met with Karel to hear the final details of the sailing from Amsterdam to Brielle. Karel confirmed they were scheduled to sail the next morning on the outgoing tide.

Karel explained, "The ship is a barquentine that will comfortably carry you and the Mennonite families that will be with you. I don't believe you will have any trouble getting your cart on board."

He added, "Conditions along the river's bank between Brielle and Rotterdam are getting desperate. There are reports of over a thousand people camping out in the reed marshes that line the river in that area."

Jacob asked incredulously, "There are that many already there? Where did they come from?"

Karel answered, "They're pouring in from as far away as Switzerland to the south, Sachsen to the west, and Anhalt in the north. There are even some French immigrants from the Alsace trying to get to London. We have made plans for your group to take shelter with a Mennonite family on their farm away from the river a few miles east of Brielle. You will stay there until your passage to London has been secured.

"Have all your things together in the morning by six. We will walk to the docks to meet other travelers by seven. Can you be ready?"

"Most assuredly," replied Jacob and Hendrick together.

*****

And so they were. The Schäfers, and the Seilers with Hans in tow, left the Jansens' shop precisely at six. Jacob and Hendrick, hauling Jacob's overflowing cart, led the way. Hans walked beside the cart with Eva riding on his back. Anna, Maggie and Christina brought up the rear walking briskly to keep the men in sight through the darkness.

The sun was not yet over the rooftops and a thick fog off the nearby ocean added to the morning's gloom.

In short order a pouting, quietly sobbing Maggie slowed to a shuffling gait. Anna reached back to take her hand but Maggie angrily pulled away. Once again she was being forced to leave the safety of familiar surroundings and being wrenched from the attention and affection of a person she had come to adore - the motherly Mrs. Hraban.

She mumbled "This is not *fair*! *You* are not fair," both hoping Anna would notice her anger and yet fearing she might.

Anna did hear and understood the meaning of Maggie's distress. She managed to grasp and hold Maggie's hand and tried to

249

distract her with soothing words of their wonderful new life t
come. But her words fell on deaf ears.

Maggie stomped along at arm's length trying to pull away from
Anna's firm grip. She turned her angry eyes from Anna's face t
her father's laboring back.

"You're *both* so mean!" she fumed.

She turned to look behind - sure to see her Dutch friend
waving goodbye and mourning her departure. Instead she sav
an enormous form looming out of the fog. It came in ;
lumbering loping gait - arms pumping forcefully at its side. /
hook hung at the end of the arm reaching out to grab her.

Maggie screamed at the top of her lungs and rushed into Anna';
skirt. Anna gasped at Maggie's piercing wail and sudder
physical assault; she turned to see what had terrified the girl and
gasped at the approaching apparition.

Jacob reacted instantly to Maggie's scream. He dropped the
cart's handle, spun around and sprinted - crouching low - into
the blinding fog to attack whatever was threatening his child.

Hendrick and Christina joined the fray. Christina took up
position next to Anna to shield the whimpering Maggie.

Hendrick, who had hesitated for but two heart beats, was now in
hot pursuit of Jacob. Hans pushed Eva into Christina's skirt and
rushed to join the men.

The women's line of defense was quickly outflanked by the
bellowing masculine line of Jacob, Hendricks and Hans.

The figure was oblivious to this crescendo uproar and did not break stride.

The men's voices rose in ferocity as the looming danger bore down upon them. But their voices were cut short when they suddenly recognized their foe materializing out of the mist.

In both anger and relief, Jacob shouted, "Reus!! What are you doing here? You have scared us all to death!"

Reus, not understanding a word of German, took all the raucous noise as shouts of welcome. He laughed gleefully and gathered Jacob up in a crushing bear hug. The manly slap on Hendrick's back almost sent him to his knees.

Anna and Christina watched their men's manhandling with waxing confusion but waning fear.

"What's going on here?" demanded Anna.

Reus set Jacob down with a thump. When he had regained his breath, Jacob explained, "This is the man that Karel sent to guard Hendrick and me at the docks. His name is Reus."

"It appears he is very happy to see the two of you," laughed Christina.

Reus reached into a coat pocket, brought out a paper and handed it to Jacob.

"It's a note from Karel," Jacob announced. "He says he has become even more worried about the reports of the bad conditions at the Brielle port. He has sent Reus to travel and guard us until we are safely aboard our ship to England."

Jacob looked up from the letter, looked around and demanded, "Where's Eva?! Eva! he shouted in panic. Eva!"

And there she was - climbing out from under the cart on hands and knees. As usual, she was laughing. But her laugh cut short when she turned to look towards the sound of her father's voice and saw Reus.

Jacob saw the look of astonishment cross her face and started towards her reassuringly, "It's alright, Baby. It's alright. He won't hurt you."

Eva bounced to her feet, ran right past her worried father and fastened herself onto Reus's leg. With a roaring laugh, he swept her up, sat her on his hip and marched past Jacob to take his place at the head of the procession. He motioned them all to regroup and led them off to their waiting ship.

On reaching the wharf, Reus handed Eva off to Jacob and marched directly at the officer standing guard at the bottom of their ship's gangplank. The startled man retreated backwards with awkward steps as the giant bore down upon him.

Finally, trapped at the pier's edge he found himself at eye level with Reus' chest. Reus smiled kindly, took the officer by the elbow and escorted him back to the gangplank. He pointed out Jacob and handed the officer another of Karel's notes from deep inside his layered clothing.

The officer read the note, gave Jacob a smart military salute and motioned for all of them to come aboard. Rather than offering an objection to Jacob's cart, the officer offered the help of three able bodied seamen to wrestle it aboard and safely stash it at the stern. Reus took out a blanket from his knapsack and signaled he would be sleeping guard over their belongings.

252

The ship left port on the outgoing tide precisely on schedule. The sea was like glass and the air had warmed. The wind was fair for the entire journey and the ship sailed on the run with the sea current pushing them from the north.

The most excitement on the voyage came almost immediately when the travelers exclaimed in amazement at being out of sight of land. There was enough food and fresh water on board for several days and the weather permitted the serving of hot food.

Then to add even further to the comfort of the trip, the captain invited Jacob, Anna, Hendrick and Christina to join him at the captain's table the first night out. Reus watched over the children while the adults were treated to a delicious meal made all the more enjoyable by the captain's rudimentary but serviceable understanding of German.

They arrived in Brielle at mid-morning rested and refreshed. The ship was docked without incident and everyone made ready to go ashore. The captain stood at the head of the gangway as his passengers disembarked.

Jacob offered his hand. "Captain, we wish to thank you for all the courtesies you have extended us. You have been most kind." The captain smiled and firmly shook Jacob's hand.

Hendrick stepped forward and added, "Yes, Captain. We all thank you very much indeed. This was our first time on a ship at sea. We had been warned at home not to make this journey as the voyages would be hazardous and terrifying. We see now that that was a ruse meant to frighten us and keep us from leaving. We are relieved to see that the dangers of the sea have been vastly exaggerated."

The captain's smile faded as he studied Hendrick's face. "Is this man making a joke?" he wondered.

Concluding that was not the case, and deciding not to rob him of this naïve notion of his sea's potential for fury, he reignited his smile and warmly shook Hendrick's hand.

"It was my pleasure having you all aboard. I wish you continued fair weather and calm seas on your future voyages." He turned away to resume his duties.

*****

At the wharf the travelers were met with transportation to their promised safe haven. An elderly Dutchman awaited them with an open hay wagon pulled by the most magnificent horse any of them had ever seen. The gelding stood at least 15 hands at the withers and was coal black, young, healthy and strong.

Jacob and Hendrick stood with mouths gaping in amazement.

"That is the most beautiful animal I have ever seen," stuttered Hendrick.

Jacob just shook his head in agreement having yet to recapture his power of speech. The old man stood at the horse's head holding its reins and smiling broadly at the effect his prized animal was having on these strangers. German, he did not understand; open-mouthed admiration was a universal language.

But when the giant Reus bore down upon him with the women and children in tow, it was the turn of the Dutchmen to stand gaping in amazement. Reus walked directly to the horse's head and stroked it softly between the eyes. The horse, at first skittish of a man nearly his height, calmed and buried his head in Reus' chest.

254

Eva rushed to Reus' feet and cried out for attention. The horse spooked again and tried to rear. Reus took a firm hold on its bridle with one hand and with the other lifted Eva up to his chest; from this new height, she reached out to pat and pet the warm soft muzzle. The child cooed and the mountain-man whistled softly. The horse calmed, fluttered his lips on Rues' chest, and made the soft sputtering noises of equine contentment.

When men and beast had all regained their senses, the wagon was loaded down with women, children and their holdings. Jacob's cart was tied to the rear to follow along like an obedient foal. The Dutchmen took his place at the head of the parade and led the way. Reus had received permission to lead the horse; he walked along proudly holding its bridle with a soft touch.

The women perched themselves high on the driver's bench at the front of the wagon: the children were hoisted to their places at the wagons' back edge laughing, chattering and swinging their legs. Jacob and Hendrick walked, bringing up the rear.

At first, they were on a cobblestone street wide enough for three wagons to pass. It was flanked by brick two-story warehouses on either side. The warehouses gave way to long rows of handsome brick homes nestled side to side. Lace curtains hung from every window. It was a lovely harbor town.

As they passed the last homes at the edge of town, the cobblestone street fell into a deeply rutted wagon path and beyond lay a frightful scene. A muddy desolate marsh stretched out before them into the misty distance.

The wide terrain to their left was flat; that to their right sloped steeply down to the river's edge. The water in the grasses along the bank had captured the night soil of the campers above.

Rivulets of rainwater were meandering down the hill filled with excrement. Even with the wind at their backs, the travelers could smell the disgusting stench.

The wagon's pace slowed; they stared from side to side. What a moment before had been excited lighthearted conversation turned to disbelieving silence.

Hundreds of makeshift shelters had been constructed of whatever came to hand. The most fortunate had pieces of discarded wood and tarpaulins to serve as roofing and windbreak; the least fortunate were huddled under reed roofs, sitting on reed floors and shivering against the freezing north wind pouring through their reed walls.

This world had been drained of all color. Ghostlike figures shuffled about in slow motion in their gray-black rags. They moved silently in the cloying wet air; there were no sounds of civil conversation nor any moans or expletives to express the despair and anguish of their pathetic conditions. Small children sat together unnaturally still and quiet. Two men rolled in the mud struggling with each other over a filthy wrapped parcel. But even in their fighting fury, they were mute.

There were scores of people within hailing distance enveloped in the silence of dejection and hopeless resignation.

The marsh ahead appeared deserted except for three hunched figures moving in the shrouded distance. Heads down and unseeing, they seemed to be aimlessly wandering back and forth across the road. At first they showed no reaction to the sound of the approaching horse's hooves and wagon wheels.

Suddenly and simultaneously the three apparitions stopped shuffling and ever so slowly raised their heavy heads. Their eyes, at first dull and vacant, stared at the approaching wagon.

But a moment later, the eyes hardened and focused sharply as they saw before them the wagon-riders' healthy, clean, well-fed faces and mounded possessions.
The old Dutchman instantly became aware of their predatory transformation. Fear crossed his face as the two largest figures began a running lurch in his direction their arms raised with weapons aloft. Their intent seemed clear.

The Dutchman retreated to the back of the wagon. In contrast, Jacob and Hendrick advanced to the front and stood with Reus. The strangers were now not more than 20 paces ahead.

Reus was the first to understand the strangers' plight. Their starvation-weakened bodies were not capable of any highwayman fight. They were utterly exhausted and stood panting in the middle of the road. The third figure had crumbled at the side of the road too weak to even begin an assault.

Reus signaled for Jacob and Hendrick to take control of the horse. He went to the back of the wagon and opened the box containing the picnic basket that had been brought for the traveler's midday meal.

Taking the basket, he marched in the direction of the strangers. Seeing his size and strength, they despaired for their lives and collapsed where they stood. Reus walked up and knelled at their feet. He opened the basket and laid out the food. The two men let out strangled cries and dove for the bread. Reus caught their hands and motioned them to eat slowly so as not to become sick. They seemed to understand and took smaller bites.

Reus stood and went to the third man still lying beside the road. He picked him up as he would a small child and carried him towards the wagon. Reus held him in his arms and cradled his head.

Reus looked up and saw Anna hurrying towards him with a wine jug in hand. She insistently waved Reus aside, sat down in the mud and took the collapsed man's head in her lap.

She moistened a clean rag with wine and wiped his parched and bleeding lips. He weakly reached out the tip of his tongue and tasted the life-giving liquid. He gave out a haunting moan and fluttered his eyelids. Anna soaked the rag and pushed it into his mouth. He sucked at the golden moisture and opened his eyes to see her smiling down on him. A beautiful porcelain-white face was framed by a halo of swan-white hair.

"An angel," he thought. "I must be dead," he said and closed his eyes again.

On hearing his voice, the other two men looked up from their food and saw Anna cradling their limp companion. They dropped their food in mid-bite and crawled over to him. One began to rub his hands vigorously and the other took off his rotten boots and wet socks. He rubbed the blistered frozen feet and then, without flinching, stuck them under his shirt onto his warm belly.

Christina joined Anna with water and more rags. While Anna was getting him to drink, Christina took charge of cleaning his face and brushing the matted hair off his face. After several layers of mud had been removed, Christina saw his features and exclaimed, "Anna! He's only a boy!"

Anna stole a glance at the other men and whispered her lament to Christina, "Those poor souls look so miserable, so weak, so cold and sickly, and so *filthy*! They are *pitiful*! Oh! Christina, these are our own people. How have they come to this?"

Hendrick had been standing behind Christina trying to give her some shelter. Jacob and Rues joined him, hunkered down and huddled around the women and the boy to make a barrier against the cruel howling wind. Jacob opened his coat, sidled up to the man on his right and wrapped him up.

"Thank you sir," the shivering man said.

"My name is Jacob and you are welcome."

"My name is Johann Meyer. This is my baby brother, Peter," he said as he patted the boy's feet which were slowly gathering heat from his own stomach. He reached over and clapped the other man's shoulder. "And this is my big brother, Georg."

Hans came running from the wagon and squeezed through the wall of men to put a blanket over Anna's shoulders.

"No, Hans. Take the blanket back to the wagon and cover yourself and the girls."

"No, Mother," he refused. "Maggie is staying warm with Eva. I will stay here and help you."

"Mother? He called me mother!"

"Alright, Hans," she answered. Catching herself and seizing the moment, she repeated, "Alright, *son*, please get the rest of the food for Johann and Georg."

259

Reassured that their brother was in caring hands, Johann and Georg finished their meal. Peter responded to rewarming and additional wine with increasing mobility and speech. His brothers gathered him up, placed him on a blanket in the wagon and wrapped themselves around him for bodily warmth. They were to accompany the pilgrims to the safe house.

"We will be most thankful to sleep in a barn," Johann said with great sincerity, humility, and gratitude.

Rues took his place at the horse's head and they moved on.

Chapter 26

There was great consternation in the Yung household when the wagon first pulled up the front drive. Expecting two civilized families of four adults and three children, they were instead presented with a wagon full of harried, hungry and mud-caked travelers.

Matthias and Apolonia Yung stood hand in hand on the front stoop of their two-story field-stone home collecting their wits as they silently took in the scene before them.

Mr. Yung looked around confused as to whom he might extend his hospitality. He was relieved to see Jacob come from behind the wagon with Eva in his arms. Mr. Yung walked towards Jacob and extended his hand.

Jacob, with reflex courtesy, extended his hand but quickly withdrew. He rushed to explain, "Oh, pardon me, sir, I cannot accept your hand. I must apologize for being so horribly dirty. We have had a most unusual day."

"You may be assured, sir, no offense is taken," said Mr. Yung.

Hendrick then hove into view from behind the wagon with the three children in tow. The women, helped down from the wagon seat by Reus, joined them to form a tight knot of embarrassment at their unpardonably filthy condition.

Mrs. Yung was the first to break the excruciating silence. She took Anna's arm and spoke with warmth and understanding, "Come along, my dear lady. We must together make arrangements for getting these beautiful children clean and their clothes washed."

"Perhaps there might be a little soap left over for the adults as well?" asked Anna with a tone that acknowledged her hostess's sympathy and kindness.

"Certainly!" she laughed and led the muddy women and girls around the outside of the house to the warmth of a large detached kitchen. She stood aside at the door and invited Anna to lead the way.

The Yung's two long-serving cooks were busy at a chopping table. They had been told to prepare for honored guests at the evening meal; they were not prepared for the dirty disheveled group marching into their inner sanctum.

The older and stouter of the two drew in her breath and shouted, "Out!" at the top of her lungs.

She raised her butcher knife high overhead and lowered her eyes to safely scramble from behind her work station. She cleared the table's edge and looked up to engage her foe. But instead, she found herself staring directly into the furious countenance of her mistress.

"Gertrud!" whispered Mrs. Yung menacingly. "These are our welcome house guests. They are here to freshen up for supper. I am certain you will cheerfully help them with warmed water and soap and do all in your power to make their stay with my family as comfortable as possible."

"Yes'm," came the barely audible reply.

Mrs. Yung swung round, lightened her voice and gave out further directions.

Pointing out the obvious, she instructed, "And note too that their clothes will need washing. Please arrange to have them cleaned and folded by tomorrow noon. If you need more help, I will arrange for it with our neighbors."

She turned around and again faced Gertrud. "Are my instructions clear?" she asked quietly with just a hint of her initial anger.

"Yes'm," said Gertrud as she shifted her gaze from her mistress to stare at the woman with the pure white hair and strange brown eyeglasses.

"Freshen up, indeed," she mumbled under her breath. "She looks as though she has been wallowing in the mud with the swine."

*****

Hans had stayed behind. Gradually and imperceptibly, in his mind and those of the adults, his status within the group had changed. No longer was he told to "go with the children" but rather he was directed to "stay and help the men."

The men gradually fell into the habit of assigning him men's tasks according to their needs and his abilities. The work on the Rhine boat had increased not only his physical strength but his confidence as well. He took his new-found responsibilities as his due.

"Mr. Seiler, will you need other men to help you unload the wagon?" asked Mr. Yung.

"No sir, I believe we have enough help," he said motioning Reus to join them.

"Mr. Yung, may I present Reus, our group's heroic bodyguard," said Jacob.

"There is no need," said Mr. Yung, shaking Reus' hand. "I have had the pleasure of meeting Reus many times while visiting my cousin, Karel, in Amsterdam."

Reus chuckled and returned to the wagon.

"Your cousin is Karel Van Brearley?" asked Jacob.

"The very same," answered Mr. Yung.

Jacob cleared his throat nervously, shifted his weight back and forth, back and forth, then in rapid fire speech, he blurted out,

"Mr. Yung, there just is no simple way to tell you this - unexpected changes were made today in our numbers - we really had no choice in the matter - there was simply no way to walk away from the circumstances - I am truly sorry . . ."

"Mr. Seiler, just say what is on your mind," broke in Mr. Yung. I'm sure the problem, whatever it might be, will not strain the pleasure of your company."

Then Reus hove into sight from the back of the wagon, Peter in his arms. Jacob watched Mr. Yung's face and saw it fall. At that precise moment, Georg and Johann in their foul rags appeared from behind the wagon; Mr. Yung's expression turned from confusion to anger.

"What is this!? demanded Mr. Yung in a thunderous voice.

"Who are these men and what right had you to bring them to my home?" He turned as though to walk away.

"Please, sir. We intended no disrespect or discourtesy in bringing them with us. Please wait but a moment and let me tell you how this all came about."

Mr. Yung hesitated, turned, and faced Jacob as he called for an explanation. "Go on," he said.

Jacob hastened to explain the dilemma they had faced and the decision they had reached.

"These are three brothers from the Neuwied area. They are among the thousand or so refugees presently camping out in Brielle in the most abject conditions. And like so many others, they have been unable to get passage to England. No ships have left that port for over a month.

"They ran out of money four weeks ago. They were forced to sell their coats in order to buy food but that food soon ran out.

"For three weeks, they have been living on roots and whatever small game they could catch and kill - including rats - with their only weapons, a wooden club and a sickle.

"We came across the three of them weaving along the road, starving and freezing to death. They collapsed in the mud when they saw us. We fell down into the mud to offer them warmth, wine and comfort which accounts for the condition of all our clothing.

"Sir, we simply could not leave them there to die. We saw no other option but to bring them with us to your home and your mercy." Jacob conveniently omitted the details of the threesome's abortive hostilities.

Mr. Yung was still glaring at Georg and Johann but his voice was less harsh as he asked Jacob, "But how do you know they are not ruffians and thieves?"

"Sir, I have no way of knowing any of the details of their past lives. I can only tell you that in our presence, these men showed great compassion towards their young brother and courtesy towards us. I sensed no duplicity in their behavior and I will tell you that I did manage to examine their wrists. They hold no brands of past criminal behavior."

Desperate to curry favor, Georg and Johann immediately pulled up their sleeves, stepped forward and showed their arms to Mr. Yung. There were no brands.

"Very well," relented Mr. Yung. "They can stay in the barn and we will feed them. But Reus will stay in the barn as well and keep a good eye on them. They are not to enter my house or approach my wife or daughters. Is that fully understood by everyone?"

Georg and Johann broke into excited celebration. They hugged one another and gave loud thanks to God. When they broke apart, they turned their attention to Mr. Yung. They threw open their arms and appeared intent on hugging him as well.

The look on Mr. Yung's face stopped their advance. They regained their composure; then, with manly strides, they approached Mr. Yung, shook both his hands and once again uttered their thanks to God and to him as well.

Mr. Yung turned his attention to the limp form in Reus' arms.

"The boy should be brought into the house. We will make him a place in the pantry. He will be warmer there than in the barn. One of my man-servants will stay at his side through the night."

Jacob added, "My aunt, Mrs. Seiler, has a way with medicines and treatments for wounds. I'm sure she will be able to help."

"Alright then - let's get the boy inside and all the other men bedded down in the barn. I will have a servant bring you some hot bath water and arrange to have your clothes washed. The brothers will have to dress in blankets until their rags can dry. We'll see about getting them more serviceable clothing tomorrow."

*****

The farm of Matthias Yung was sizable and made even larger by the three adjacent properties of his two oldest sons and new son-in-law. But as in centuries past, the size of a farm made no difference in the sorts of the employment involved, only in the number of hands needed to accomplish the required tasks.

So as the day began, there was familiar work to be done. No job descriptions were posted, no instructions were needed. Both invited guests and those brought by surprise rose at the usual hour and found the jobs that needed to be done.

The older daughter and mother busied in the house making beds, emptying slop jars and filling washstand pitchers with hot water for bathing. Anna tended to the skin of Peter's cold-tortured feet.

The kitchen was abuzz with washing and cooking. Maggie and the younger cook chattered away while clearing the night's ashes from the walk-in sized fireplace. In the fashion of young girls, they giggled and shared their opinions of Hans' manly potential. Christina and Gertrud had found common ground; they shared sad smiles as they recounted memories of their ancestral Swiss homes. Hostilities washed away like the layers of mud from the visitor's clothes.

In the farmyard, Mrs. Yung's littlest daughter broadcast the meal to feed the chickens and collected the eggs to feed the farmhands their early morning meal.

Next to the barn, Georg sweated and swung a heavy ax to split the wood for kitchen cooking and home heating.

Inside the barn, Johann milked the cows. Field-cats got their share of milk in thanks for guarding stored grains from hungry mice and rats. Johann laughed as he squirted a stream of milk into the open mouth of a feral feline an arm's length away.

Rues pitched dry hay down from the loft to the animals below and then helped Johann turn the cows out to pasture.

Morning barn work was never done 'til the cow stalls were mucked and raked. Johann shoveled the stench into a wheelbarrow; Rues pushed the heavy load up a board ramp and emptied it at the top of the growing manure mountain.

The sun was up for an hour when work was called to a temporary halt by the heavy dinner bell ringing out the call to breakfast. Late morning chores, a midday meal, afternoon work, wash-up time, and supper would complete the timeless activities of a day on a family farm.

*****

After supper, Mr. Yung invited Jacob and Hendrick into the parlor for conversation and a drink of his special wine.

268

"This is made from our vineyard's grapes like any other wine but is treated somehow differently," explained Mr. Yung. "It's distilled to produce a higher alcohol content than regular wine. It's called brandy. What do you think of it?"

"Wonderful!" came the enthusiastic duet. "Wonderful!"

The three men took seats and talked for an hour of the hardships of the last thirty years of war in their home region of the Palatine. Mr. Yung's father had left the area forty years before when he saw the storm clouds of another war of European monarchs building along the shores of the Rhine.

"Your father was a wise man," concluded Jacob. "What he predicted unfortunately came to pass."

"Which brings us to your families' future plans and those of your foundlings," smiled Mr. Yung.

"Tomorrow evening, there will be a meeting of those men whose families are offering shelter and aid to those trying to make their way to the new America. I am inviting you both to attend with me. And I am considering taking Georg. He and his brothers have shown themselves to be eager and willing workers."

"We will be honored to attend," said Jacob. "And we will take responsibility for Georg's behavior at the gathering," added Hendrick with a grin.

*****

There were nine host-men in attendance at the home of Jay Getman. Each of their families had at least one pilgrim family on their farms at the present time. All of them had been hosting refugees for the past two months.

269

Jacob, Hendrick and Georg were introduced to the assemblage and told what had been done so far for the Palatines in their area. They learned that the Dutch people were acting both as individuals and through their governments to help those in need.

City families were sending food and spare clothing to these farm families to distribute to those in their care. Governments were responding both at the local level and from the nation's capital.

The Burgomaster of Rotterdam was sending Lutheran ministers to distribute money directly to the pilgrims. James Dayrolle, the British resident at the Hague, was working with the Dutch government to sustain the poor and arrange for their passage to London.

Mr. Getman walked to the front of the room and addressed his Palatine guests.

"We have been told that you were understandably horrified by the condition of your fellow countrymen in Brielle.

"Please know that the residents of Brielle have tried to give them help but have been overwhelmed by numbers.

"In early April, Mr. Dayrolle successfully applied to the English Queen Anne to send transport ships to Brielle to take Palatines to London. The Queen commanded that the ships carrying her troops to fight the French divert to the Netherlands on their return. The last ship left a month ago carrying some 850 refugees to England.

"Now it is my great pleasure to tell you that another ship arrived today and will be ready to set sail in few days to take you and some other 1200 tired souls in Brielle to the English capital."

"Oh, Thank God," shouted Jacob.

All the men rose to their feet cheering the excellent news.

Mr. Yung slipped over to Jacob. "Mr. Seiler, we have other business to discuss here but I know you are most anxious to carry this good news to your family. Please feel free to leave. These gentlemen will understand your need for departure"

And indeed they did. The farmers clapped backs, shook hands and shouted, "Hurrahs" as Jacob, Hendrick and Georg ran off into the darkness of the night and the brightness of their future lives.

*****

Three days later, on the morning of May 12, 1709, the Dutchman returned to the Yung's farm with his magnificent horse and sturdy wagon.

With Anna's attention, Peter's feet were healing quickly; though still in pain, he was able to walk to the wagon on his own.

The intervening days had allowed his brothers to regain strength from the nutritious and bountiful food supplied by the Yungs. They made short work of loading the wagon with all the families' belongings.

The women resumed their places high on the driver's seat, Eva and Maggie piled in the back with Peter, and Reus went to stroke the bridled horse's head.

Jacob, Hendrick, Georg and Johann stopped before the Yungs. The couple once again stood hand in hand while their guests' heartfelt words of gratitude spread over them.

Warm handshakes were exchanged, Reus clicked the horse into motion and the men fell in step behind the wagon. They were on their way to the next milestone of their journey to the New World.

Hans had fallen asleep in the hay loft up above the cow stalls and had failed to hear the commotion of departure.

One of the farm hands found him minutes after the wagon had left the house. The man poked him and shook him. He frantically motioned for Hans to get up and led him to the open loft door. From this height, Hans could see the wagon and his family far in the distance.

He scrambled down the haystack, into the cow barn and out the door.

"Wait! Wait!" he shouted. "I'm coming! Don't leave me!"

He ran.

Epilogue

The Low Countries sank ever deeper and deeper
    Under the weight of Palatine pilgrims.

Desperate thousands flooded to friendly Dutch ports
    Where the populace sought to feed them
    To clothe them - to shelter and comfort them
    While awaiting the English Queen's ships to arrive.

But many poor souls died of cold and disease
    As they awaited their fates in the marshes.

Then finally arrived the good Queen's relief
    To take them away to the safety of London.

The Schäfers, the Seilers, and the young orphaned Hans
    Are fictional characters wherever you find them.
    In England they will meet with historical figures
    Who will live in tent cities set up by the Queen
    And fed with compassion by good Englishmen.

The tale of their travails will continue in:

"Charity's Chains: The Palatine Journey, Part Two".
To be published in the summer of 2011

Made in the USA
Middletown, DE
24 November 2015